WHAT THE DEAD
LEAVE BEHIND

WHAT THE DEAD LEAVE BEHIND

David Housewright

MINOTAUR BOOKS

NEW YORK

WHAT THE DEAD LEAVE BEHIND. Copyright © 2017 by David Housewright. All rights reserved. Printed in the United States of America. For information, address St. Martin's Press, 175 Fifth Avenue, New York, N.Y. 10010.

www.minotaurbooks.com

Library of Congress Cataloging-in-Publication Data

Names: Housewright, David, 1955– author.
Title: What the dead leave behind / David Housewright.
Description: First edition. I New York : Minotaur Books, 2017. I Series: Twin
    Cities P.I. Mac Mckenzie novels; 14
Identifiers: LCCN 2017005603I ISBN 9781250094513 (hardcover) I ISBN
    9781250094520 (e-book)
Subjects: LCSH: McKenzie, Mac (Fictitious character)—Fiction. I Private
    investigators—Minnesota—Fiction. I Ex-police officers—Fiction. I
    Murder—Investigation—Fiction. I BISAC: FICTION / Mystery & Detective /
    Traditional British. I GSAFD: Mystery fiction.
Classification: LCC PS3558.O8668 W48 2017 I DDC 813/.54—dc23
LC record available at https://lccn.loc.gov/2017005603

Our books may be purchased in bulk for promotional, educational, or business use. Please contact your local bookseller or the Macmillan Corporate and Premium Sales Department at 1-800-221-7945, extension 5442, or by e-mail at Macmillan SpecialMarkets@macmillan.com.

First Edition: June 2017

10 9 8 7 6 5 4 3 2 1

FOR RENÉE.
IF I SAID IT ONCE,
I'VE SAID IT 17 TIMES.

ACKNOWLEDGMENTS

The author wishes to acknowledge his debt to Hannah Braaten, India Cooper, Tammi Fredrickson, Keith Kahla, James McDonald, Heidi Meyer of the Anoka County Central Communications, Sgt. Anita Muldoon of the St. Paul Police Dept. Homicide Unit (Ret.), David Peterson of the Bureau of Criminal Apprehension (Ret.), Alison J. Picard, and Renée Valois.

WHAT THE DEAD
LEAVE BEHIND

ONE

The way he paced recklessly in front of me, bouncing off furniture, tripping on the throw rug; the way he looked at me with unblinking eyes—I decided the kid was messed up. My only question: Was it a temporary condition possibly brought on by pharmaceuticals or permanent?

"It's been a year," he said. "A year. And no one's done anything."

I was sitting in a chair. He halted in front of me and waved his fist. The effort caused his body to sway uncertainly.

"Anything," he repeated.

"Malcolm," Erica said. She patted the cushion next to her. "Please."

He turned reluctantly and moved to the sofa. He didn't sit so much as collapse as if all the weight of the world was forcing him down. Erica took his hand in hers, and I noticed for the first time that his knuckles were scraped and a couple of drops of blood had dried in the creases between his fingers.

"It'll be all right," she told him.

"No it won't," he said.

Erica squeezed his hand, and he sighed. His eyes closed with the sigh, and she gazed at him with such affection that for a moment I felt anxious. What the hell was this kid to her, I wondered—besides being a good-looking boy who was in trouble that a strong woman like her might be able to help him with? I had known Erica since I had become involved with her mother—has it really been over six years now? I watched her evolve from an awkward, nerdy teen into a beautiful, smart-as-hell young woman who was a year away from earning both a bachelor of arts and a bachelor of science degree from Tulane University. I had never known her to look at anyone like she looked at Malcolm.

"McKenzie will help," she said.

You will? my inner voice asked.

"Won't you?" Erica said.

Yeah, probably.

"What do you need?" I asked. "Be specific."

Malcolm's eyes snapped open, and he practically leapt from the sofa. He was taller than I was but thin and pale, and I wondered—how could anyone going to school in New Orleans be pale? He began pacing again. I came *this*close to telling him to sit his ass back down, but resisted. I knew Erica wouldn't like it.

"You're a detective," he said. "Rickie said you're a detective."

Rickie?

"In a manner of speaking," I said.

"Well, are you or aren't you?"

"I don't have a license, if that's what you're asking."

"Then how can you help?" Malcolm's voice was suddenly high and out of control.

"I never said I could."

"Rickie told me . . ."

He made a noise in his throat that might have been a sob. He stopped pacing and gazed at his damaged hand as if seeing it for the first time.

"How did that happen?" I asked.

"What?"

"Your hand."

Malcolm hid it behind his back.

"None of your business," he told me.

"Okay."

I watched him. He watched me.

"What?" he asked again.

"Just waiting."

"For what?"

"For you to tell me the reason why you're here. While we wait, would you like something to drink? Coffee? Dr Pepper? We got milk."

"I'm twenty-one."

"You say that like you're old."

"Old enough to drink."

"Have you been drinking?"

"No. I—I guess I'm not making a very good impression, am I? Something my mother said earlier kind of threw me. Mr. McKenzie, I don't do drugs and I don't drink. Not a lot, anyway."

"Well, I'm going to have something. Erica?"

"Nothing for me, thank you," she said.

The high-rise condominium that Erica's mother and I shared in downtown Minneapolis was wide open. We didn't have rooms so much as areas—dining area, TV area, a music area where Nina's Steinway stood. The entire north wall was made of tinted floor-to-ceiling glass with a dramatic view of the Mississippi River. If that wasn't enough, there was a sliding glass door built into the wall that led to a balcony that I almost never use because I'm afraid of heights. The south wall featured floor-to-ceiling bookcases that turned at the east wall and followed it to a large brick fireplace. To the left of the fireplace was a door that led to a guest bedroom with its own full bath that Erica used whenever she was in town. Against the west wall, and elevated three steps above the living area, was the kitchen area. Beyond that was a master bedroom that also featured floor-to-ceiling windows.

I moved to the kitchen area. I found a Summit Pale Ale in the refrigerator, popped the cap, took a long pull from the bottle, and settled on a stool at the island. From there I was able to look down into the living area. Erica and Malcolm could see and speak to me, yet the distance between us was such that they were compelled to move forward, which was exactly what I wanted—anything to change the dynamic.

"I'm sorry," Malcolm said. "I just don't know how you can help me."

"Neither do I until you tell me what you need."

He turned as if he were contemplating a dash for the door. Erica grabbed his arm with both hands and gave it a shake.

"Talk to him," she said.

Malcolm lowered his head.

"I'm listening," I said.

The words were hard for him to speak.

"I need to know who killed my father," he said. "I need to know why."

The story came out in bits and pieces. It took a while for me to splice them together, to get the timeline correct.

What happened, Friday, December 13, last year—the final day for classes at Tulane University before the Christmas break—Malcolm couldn't wait to get home to New Brighton, Minnesota, a suburb of Minneapolis. He was surprised by how much he had missed snow and crisp, clean air. He walked out of his final class at 3:10 P.M., went to the dorm, finished packing, and left to meet his friends. Malcolm said he partied hearty—something that was not altogether difficult to do in New Orleans even when you're an underage sophomore. Eventually, he wandered over to PJ's Willow Café, grabbed a quick bite, took the shuttle to Louis Armstrong International Airport, caught the 5:55 A.M. flight, and, after a brief layover in Dallas, arrived bleary-eyed in Minneapolis at 11:20 Saturday morning. Only there was no one to meet him.

He called home. There was no answer. He called his father's cell phone. No answer. He called his mother's cell. She answered on the third ring. He tried to make a joke out of it. "Remember me?" he said. "Your one and only child?" That's when he learned that his father had gone missing. Apparently he had called Malcolm's mother Friday afternoon and told her that he needed to work late. He said he wanted to finish up a project that night so he could spend the entire weekend with his son without worrying about it. Except he never came home. She was in the process of making frantic phone calls to everyone her husband knew, to all the Twin Cities hospitals, when Malcolm's plane landed. Eventually they contacted the police.

Saturday passed and then Sunday. No sign of him. On Monday about 11:00 A.M. they received a phone call from the New Brighton Police Department. A man tentatively identified as Frank Harris had been found lying unconscious and covered with snow in a drainage ditch inside Long Lake Regional Park by a morning jogger. He was alive, but just barely.

Mother and son rushed to Unity Hospital. They were informed that Harris had been stabbed in the head. He never regained consciousness. He died on Christmas Eve.

Well, that sucks, I thought but didn't say.

"A year has passed," Malcolm said. "More than a year."

I don't know why, but I glanced at my watch to confirm the passage of time. It was 7:22 P.M. Monday, December 28.

One year and four days to be precise, my inner voice said.

"I still don't know what happened," Malcolm said. "No one knows. Or at least they haven't informed me."

"You said something happened tonight that messed you up."

"My mother told me . . ."

"Yes?"

"We were talking about my father, and she said . . ."

"Yes?"

"To get over it."

"Is that when you hurt your hand?"

He gazed at his damaged fingers again; flexed them.

"I hit something stupid," Malcolm said.

"Your mother?"

"No. A wall. God, McKenzie. I would never hit my mother. Not like . . ."

"Like what?"

"I would never hurt my mother."

"What exactly do you want me to do?"

Erica was staring directly into my eyes when she asked, "McKenzie, can you find out who killed Malcolm's father for us?" Making it clear that I would be doing the favor for her and not Malcolm. It was unfair. It would have been easy for me to tell the kid to take a hike, but Erica . . . There were maybe six people in the entire world that could claim a chunk of my heart, and she was one of them.

"I don't know what I can do that the cops can't," I said.

"Then what good are you?" Malcolm asked.

"You'd be surprised how often people ask that question."

Or maybe not.

"Mal, don't talk like that." Erica spoke calmly, almost soothingly, yet at the same time there was a metallic sound in her voice that demanded both attention and respect—swear to God, it reminded me of someone racking the pump of a shotgun. "McKenzie is my friend. We came here to ask for his help. Remember?"

"I'm sorry," Malcolm said. "I'm just—I'm just . . ." He hung his head. "I don't know what to do. I can't sleep. I can't study. My grades are shit. Every day . . ."

Erica draped an arm around his shoulders and drew him close. She said something to him, but I couldn't hear over my inner voice screaming.

This is the boyfriend? Are you kidding me?

"I'll look into it," I said aloud.

"Thank you," Erica said.

"McKenzie." Malcolm's head came up. His eyes were moist, his voice shaking. "I don't need anyone to go to jail. I don't even need to know who did it. I just want to know what happened."

"I'll be asking a lot of questions of a lot of people, including you," I said. "Not now, though. Tomorrow."

"Thank you. I'm sorry I was so rude. You're treating me better than I deserve."

"You've been through a lot, losing a father the way you did."

He nodded his head as if he agreed with me.

"Just out of curiosity, how is your mother taking all of this?" I said.

Malcolm snorted like it was a question asked in poor taste.

"I've never seen her happier," he said.

There was some hemming and hawing, and then they left. Erica said she would drive Malcolm home and return later. I didn't ask for an ETA, and she didn't volunteer one. Once they departed, I went to my PC. I found only one story; it appeared on the Web site of the *St. Paul Pioneer Press:*

NEW BRIGHTON MAN DIES AFTER ASSAULT;
LYING INJURED IN PARK FOR TWO NIGHTS

A New Brighton man recently assaulted and left badly injured in a city park for nearly two days has died. Preliminary autopsy reports conducted by the Ramsey County medical examiner's office indicate Frank Harris, 48, died on Christmas Eve of a penetrating wound to his brain, New Brighton police reported. His manner of death was "provisionally" ruled a homicide.

Harris was found unconscious shortly before 8 A.M. Monday, Dec. 16, in a drainage ditch in Long Lake Regional Park. His car was found in the lot near the park entrance.

A nearby resident was jogging through the park that morning and saw Harris in the ditch, lying still. Temperatures at the time hovered around the single digits above zero.

Evidence collected at the scene and other information uncovered through police investigations indicate that Harris drove to the park Dec. 13 between 5:45 and 10:20 P.M., got out of his vehicle, and entered the park, where he was violently attacked and abandoned.

Hospitalized and in critical condition in the days after he was found, Harris was not able to communicate with police about the circumstances of the assault.

Anyone with information about the case is asked to call Crime Stoppers of Minnesota at 800-222-8477. Callers can remain anonymous, and tips could lead to a cash reward.

The only part of the piece that I found informative was the bit about Crime Stoppers. My experience, cops rarely ask the public for assistance unless they have diddly squat.

I printed the document and was rereading it for the third time when Nina Truhler came through the door.

"Hey, you," she said.

We hugged and kissed like an old married couple even though we are neither old nor married.

"How was your day?" Nina asked.

"I met Erica's new boyfriend."

"Robin?"

"Who's Robin?"

"Who did you meet?"

"Malcolm Harris."

"What happened to Robin?"

"I didn't know there was a Robin."

"I told you. Engineering student goes to Notre Dame."

"Oh yeah, yeah, yeah. No, this one—he's from New Brighton, but he goes to Tulane; probably where they met."

"How do you know Malcolm is Erica's boyfriend? Did she say so?"

"She let him call her Rickie."

That's what people called Erica until her junior year of high school when she announced to one and all that it was a childish nickname and insisted that henceforth she would only answer to her given name. She even demanded that Nina change the sign above her jazz joint from RICKIE'S to ERICA'S. Nina told her that when she inherited the club, she could call it whatever she pleased.

"Sounds serious," Nina said.

"Oh, it gets better."

I gave Nina the hard copy of the *Pioneer Press* article. When she finished reading I said, "Malcolm's old man. They want me to find out who the killer is."

"They?"

"Erica asked for the favor."

"She did that so you wouldn't say no."

"That's my theory, too."

"You spoil that girl."

TWO

Tuesday morning with the gray sky promising snow, I sat at my computer and composed a list. When I finished, I attempted to contact the New Brighton Police Department only to discover that the city didn't have one. Instead, its Web site guided me to the Department of Public Safety. Tucked inside the bureaucracy were both a Police Division and a Fire Division, each supervised by a deputy director instead of a chief.

Under Police Division, I discovered a link to a page listing "cold case files." I clicked on it. There were three histories. The first involved a woman identified as Jane Doe, whose nude body was discovered, like Frank, in Long Lake Regional Park by two people strolling a walking path. Unlike Harris, she had been lying there for six weeks to three months before anyone noticed. The cops believed she had died of "homicide violence" yet didn't go into further detail.

That was thirteen years ago. Six years later, the body of Raymond Bosh, a seasonal employee working for the city's Department of Parks and Public Works, was found at Veterans Park. The brief description did not list how he died, only where—near the tool shed where he was loading a dry line marker with powdered chalk to line the baseball diamond—and when—between 3:00 and 3:30 P.M. on a Tuesday in July.

The final story belonged to Harris. It told me even less than the newspaper article had.

Beneath each description was a request for information, along with a phone number, e-mail address, and Facebook link. I called the number. A woman answered. She didn't know who was handling the Harris investigation, but she forwarded my call to one of the Police Division's three investigators.

"Detective Clark Downing," he said instead of "hello."

"Detective, my name's McKenzie. I'm calling regarding the Harris case."

"Yes." His voice sounded both surprised and hopeful.

"If you give me your e-mail address, I'd like to send you something."

"What?"

"A list—you'll see."

He recited his e-mail address; I sent him the document. Nearly ninety seconds passed with neither of us speaking before it arrived. I remembered when that used to be considered fast.

"What is this?" Downing asked.

"My references."

"I don't know the federal agents or the assistant U.S. attorney, but I met Commander Dunston, and I worked with Lieutenant Rask a couple of months ago."

"Give them a call. Ask them about me."

"Why?"

"So when I call back you'll know you're not talking to a complete moron."

I was going to give him an hour. Instead, Downing called me twenty minutes later.

"I'm not sure what to make of this," he said.

"What do you mean?"

"Bobby Dunston told me that you used to be a pretty good cop when you were with the St. Paul PD and that you've been very helpful to them in the past. Clayton, Lieutenant Rask, he said that you not only helped him solve a homicide a couple of years ago, you saved the Minneapolis Police Department considerable embarrassment, although he wouldn't give specifics."

"It left the restroom with its zipper down—what can I say?"

"They also said you could be a real smartass and that you like to play fast and loose with the rules."

"I'm sure they meant that in a good way."

"What's your interest in the Harris case?"

"His son, Malcolm—he came to me yesterday and asked me to look into it. He has a lot of unanswered questions. They're keeping him awake at night. In fact, I'd say he's displaying signs of PTSD."

"What do you think you can do about it?"

"I'm just hoping to give the kid a good night's sleep. He already said he didn't care if anyone went to prison. He just wants to know the truth."

"Sometimes knowing the truth . . . Never mind."

"Do you know the truth?"

"If I did someone would be in prison by now."

"I checked your division's Web site. The cold case page says, 'The NBDPS never forgets a victim of a violent crime.' But you and I both know that the Harris investigation was redlined a long time ago. Just like you did with Raymond Bosh."

"We didn't forget Bosh. I went back through the files just last summer."

"And?"

"He gambled. Did coke. The lead investigator—he's retired now—he believed Bosh was bludgeoned to death with an aluminum baseball bat by someone he owed money to."

"And?"

The detective's response was to sigh deeply.

"Clark, I get it even if the public doesn't," I said. "You have thirty cops in New Brighton; only three detectives. You simply don't have the personnel or the resources to keep the case active, to keep Harris's case active."

"So?"

"So how 'bout letting me take a look. If I find nothing, then you're out nothing. If I find something, maybe I can help you move it out of the cold case files."

"What do you want exactly?"

"Whatever you can give me."

"The case file isn't public record until it goes to court."

"I'm not the public."

"This is what Dunston and Rask were talking about, isn't it, about playing fast and loose with the rules?"

"I like to think of them more like guidelines."

Detective Downing agreed to meet me for lunch, but not in New Brighton. We settled on a chain restaurant near the Northtown shopping mall in Blaine. He arrived first and picked a booth facing the bar. He stood when I came in. His shield was attached to his belt; I think he liked that everyone could see it when he swept back the tails of his blazer. Pride of ownership, I decided. I was much the same way when I was with the cops.

We shook hands. I stuffed my winter coat against the wall of the booth and sat across from him. Downing slipped a thumb drive from his pocket. He slid it across the table toward me. I picked it up and put it into my own pocket without giving it much of a look.

"My case files," he said. "Incident reports, supplemental reports, autopsy—normally, I'd let you read them inside the office while under supervision; make sure you didn't take them home with you. That's usually how we do things, except . . . Anyone asks; you didn't get them from me."

"I understand."

"You don't talk to anyone in New Brighton, either. Not the ME. Certainly not the deputy director. If you have a question, you bring it to me and I'll get it answered."

"Whatever you say, but this isn't television, Detective. In real life, police and private investigators work the same cases all the time."

"*Licensed* PIs hired by the family or the family's attorney who carefully follow the regulations as laid out by the Private Detective Services Board. Not wealthy, bored ex-cops looking for something to do with their free time."

"Did Bobby Dunston tell you that?"

"No. I have my own sources; I reached out after I spoke to you on the phone. Tell me something—did you really quit the St. Paul PD to take a three-million-dollar reward on an embezzler you collared?"

Clearly he doesn't approve, my inner voice told me. *Well, get in line.*

"It seemed like a good idea at the time," I said.

"They say you were a good cop. They say . . ."

"If you must know, my father raised me alone after my mother died when I was just a child. I took the money to give him a cushy retirement; we were going to travel, see the world, shit like that. Only he died six months later. So, here we are."

"I meant no disrespect."

"A lot of cops think I sold my badge. I bet most of them would do the same thing if they had the opportunity."

Downing stared up and to his left wondering if he was one of them.

"Like I said," he told me. "No disrespect."

A waitress appeared. Three days after Christmas and she was still dressed like one of Santa's elves.

"Drink?" I asked.

"Not while I'm on duty," Downing said.

He ordered an iced tea; I had a Summit Ale. The waitress soon returned with our beverages and listed the daily specials, most with holiday names. We listened patiently before ordering sandwiches from the menu; I had a club, and Downing asked for a Philly cheesesteak. While waiting to be served, we decided that the Twins had a bright future but we weren't so sure about the Vikings. Actually, that's what I decided. Downing was into the Minnesota United Football Club, God help him. Turned out he played soccer when he was a kid. I played hockey. We eyed each other suspiciously until we were half finished with our meals.

"Who do you like?" I asked.

Downing knew exactly what I was asking.

"The wife," he said. "It's always the wife, isn't it?"

"Not always."

"Jayne Harris was in the emergency room five times in the previous two years with broken ribs, a broken wrist, broken nose. Apparently she was the most accident-prone woman in New Brighton."

"She never claimed she was abused?"

"Not in the hospital, and the docs and RNs asked a lot of questions; you know how they are. Apparently not to any of her friends or relatives, either. At least none would say."

"Her son?"

"As I recall, he became very agitated when I asked about it. Said I was full of shit."

"That sounds like him."

Downing gestured more or less at my pocket.

"When you read my notes, you'll learn that Jayne was alibied tight, too," he said. "The evening Harris was stabbed in the head, she was having potluck with seven other couples at the home of one of the couples. Fourteen witnesses. Exactly."

How convenient, I thought but didn't say.

"They were part of a group—called themselves the New Brighton Hotdish," Downing said. "Their kids all played park-and-rec baseball on the same team back in . . . I think it was six years ago. It would be seven now, I guess. In any case, they've been getting together the second Friday of the month ever since, alternating locations."

"Okay."

"What's more, Jayne could account for nearly every minute of her time from the moment that Harris left work until his body was discovered. We had forensic auditors go over their financial records; there were no expenditures large or small that couldn't be explained, that I could argue was a payoff to a hitter. We checked her cell and landline, texts, e-mails, Internet use, and talked to her neighbors—there was no suggestion of infidelity, that she had a boyfriend who might have done it for her."

"But you still like her?"

"A kitchen knife is a weapon of opportunity. Usually you get stabbed with a kitchen knife; it's in your own damn kitchen, am I right? The weapon close at hand."

"Are you sure about the knife?"

"The Ramsey County forensic pathologist, what he told me, the brain material holds the shape of the knife blade better than other parts of the body. He said it was a serrated blade consistent with a kitchen knife. Six inches."

What are you suggesting? my inner voice asked. *That Jayne Harris stabbed her husband in the head, dragged him to his car, drove the car to the park, dragged him out of the car, tossed his body into the ditch, and walked home? In subzero temperatures? Without noticing that he was still alive?*

My expression must have revealed my skepticism, because Downing dropped the remains of his sandwich on his plate and nudged it away.

"Yeah, I know," he said. "Seems unlikely. But Jayne is the only one who benefited from Frank's death."

"How did she benefit?"

"IRAs, 401(k)s, and company investment plans, totaling about $660,000. Insurance benefit from where he worked paid twice his salary, so that was another one ninety. Then there was a separate life insurance policy worth two-fifty. Just over a cool million, all told. Plus, they had a policy that paid off their mortgage if one of them died, so . . ."

"When was the life insurance policy put into effect?"

"They took out policies on each other a couple weeks before they were married."

"When was that?"

"Twenty-four years ago."

"Okay."

"Then there was the end to the spousal abuse."

"That she and her son claim didn't exist, that no one else claims existed."

"It was her, McKenzie. Maybe Jayne didn't stab him, but I know she had it done. I just . . . feel it."

I knew what he meant. Training and experience often reveal truths to police officers that physical evidence doesn't always corroborate. Back when I worked homicide with Anita Pollack, we could usually ID the killer ten minutes after we arrived on the scene. At least she could—she had been at it so long it was that obvious to her. Afterward, it was just a matter of connecting the dots. Except sometimes the dots wouldn't line up in a way that would make the case beyond all reasonable doubt. Which isn't to say that we ever had any doubt. Still . . .

"I don't think that's the answer Malcolm is looking for," I said.

"My boss and the assistant county attorney demanded more tangible proof, too."

"You said you couldn't prove Jayne was cheating. How 'bout Frank?"

"That's a different matter. We checked his cell, computer, work phone. There were a few things that made me go 'Hmm,' but no discernible patterns. He didn't call, text, or e-mail the same woman twenty times, for example. It's all in my notes. We do know that Harris called his wife at about five the evening he disappeared. She said that he said he was going to be late to the Hotdish because he was putting in some over-time. We have no proof that she was telling the truth. What we do have is video of him leaving his place of employment ten minutes later, climbing into his car in the company's parking lot and driving off."

"Did Harris drive directly to the park or make a stop along the way?"

"To pick someone up, you're thinking?"

I shrugged.

"No idea," Downing said.

"Why did he drive to the park?"

"*If* he drove to the park. Like I said, I'm not sure it went down that way. If he did, obviously, it was to meet someone."

"Yes, but why the Long Lake Regional Park? It was a little close to home, wasn't it, for a clandestine meeting?"

"A couple blocks from where he lived, yeah. My guess, he picked the location *because* it was close to home, a place he was familiar with."

"If *he* picked it."

"You're starting to understand my frustration."

"The article I read, it said he was stabbed between five forty-five and ten twenty," I said. "That's pretty specific."

"The five forty-five—we know exactly when he left the Szereto corporate offices and estimated the approximate amount of time it would have taken him to drive to the park providing the traffic wasn't unusually heavy, which it wasn't. The ten twenty—there we got lucky. The park had a posted curfew; no vehicles allowed in the lot after ten P.M. An officer making his rounds spotted Harris's car and wrote it up."

"Nearly four and a half hours. Damn, that's a long time."

"Yeah, it is."

"Where did Harris work, again?" I asked.

"The Szereto Corporation."

"Did he have any enemies over there?"

"Probably. Harris was the director of human resources. Everyone who was fired might have hated him. Everyone that made a complaint that wasn't addressed, I suppose they could be considered suspects, too. Only nobody stood out."

"What does the company do?"

"They make beauty products, shampoos, conditioners, what-not."

"That's a pretty competitive business, isn't it?"

"So I'm told."

"Could he have pilfered proprietary information and attempted to sell it to one of Szereto's competitors? Met his contact at the park, argued over price . . ."

"I have no evidence to suggest such a thing."

"Still . . ."

"Listen, McKenzie—it's possible I made a mistake by grabbing hold of the idea that Jayne killed her husband and not letting it go. Maybe I lost objectivity. Maybe I missed something. Don't do the same thing."

"I'll try not to."

"I promise I won't get angry if you solve the case. I will, but not at you."

"Okay."

"Something else. We don't get many violent crimes in New Brighton, much less a dead man in the snow. Not being able to solve it . . . What I mean, Harris's kid isn't the only one who's lost sleep over this."

I could relate to that, too—all those goddamn dots that never aligned properly.

I had been at it for over an hour, sitting at my computer, reading the final summary issued by the Ramsey County coroner, taking notes on Detective Downing's supplementary investigation reports. I wasn't so much interested in Downing's conclusions as in the names of all the people that he interviewed. Talk to them, I told myself, draw your own conclusions.

Erica arrived. She dumped her bulky winter coat, hat, and gloves on a chair near the door—"dumped" being the operative word.

"Wut up?" she said.

Wut up? my inner voice asked.

"Hey," I replied.

Erica slouched in a chair in the living area where she could get a good view of me working at the desk in the library area. Nina was one of the most beautiful women I had ever known, with amazing silver-blue eyes. Erica didn't have those eyes, but she possessed the rest of her mother's genes.

"What are you doing?" she asked.

"I talked the lead detective on the Harris case into letting me look at his case files."

"Have you figured it out yet?"

"Colonel Mustard in the library with a candlestick."

"I'm sorry I haven't had a chance to speak to you since last night."

"You were out late with the boyfriend."

"Malcolm is not my boyfriend. We met at Tulane—both of us from Minnesota, so we kind of bonded, but he's not my boyfriend."

"Okay."

"I've known him since we were freshmen, and he's always

been good company until . . . Well, you know what happened. I just wanted to help him, and since I couldn't, I mean not really . . ."

"You asked me to. It's okay."

"Is it?"

"Sure."

"Thank you. Karen says hi, by the way. Girl's always had a crush on you."

"Who's Karen?"

"You know Karen. We were on the fencing team together in high school, only she was saber and I was épée. You sometimes drove us to the meets."

"I remember," I said, although I didn't.

"I just had lunch with her. She's getting married the summer after she graduates, if you can believe that—an eighteen-month engagement."

My head snapped upward and I found her eyes. The gesture caused Erica to smile.

"Don't worry," she said. "It's not contagious."

"I didn't say anything."

"I love you, McKenzie."

Wait! What?

"Look at you. You're embarrassed. McKenzie, that is so cute."

"Stop it."

"You didn't know? After all these years? McKenzie, you're the father I never had. At least the father who didn't cheat on my mother and go to prison for dealing that I never had."

"Seriously. Stop it."

"You know why I love you? Because you've always treated me with respect. Always. My mother dated before she met you, you know, and those guys, they were all like 'Oh, aren't you pretty, aren't you smart; bet the boys chase after you.' But you never said those things, never tried to bond with me. You never—heck, you called me Ms. Truhler until I said Erica was fine. I knew you were sleeping with Mom, but you never did it at my house. At least you never stayed the night while I was there. Never hung around, never raided the refrigerator, never watched TV like it was yours. Never commented on my clothes or study habits or anything like that. Never offered advice unless I asked for it, never started a conversation with the words 'When I was your age,' and never took sides when my mom and I quarreled. Yet you were always there for me, just like you are now. Something else even more important—you were always proud of me no matter what I did, even when I convinced those TV ghost hunters that Mom's club was haunted. You have to admit, that was pretty funny."

"Yes, it was, although your mother didn't think so at the time."

"Which is another thing—she has a much better sense of humor since she hooked up with you; she's more relaxed, too. Anyway, my friends—half my friends have parents who are divorced, and they tell me horror stories about stepmothers and stepfathers and whatever, and I always feel left out because I don't have one to share. They're like, what about Nina's boyfriend, and I'm like, I wish he would marry the woman and adopt me."

I didn't know what to say, so I didn't say anything.

"Geez, your face," Erica said. "You are such a lost cause. I'd give you a hug, but wow . . ."

She left the chair and moved toward her bedroom. I called after her.

"Erica, I love you, too," I said.

"Too late. The moment's passed."

What a dumb ass, my inner voice said. Only I didn't feel like a dumb ass. I felt pretty good.

Malcolm Harris's mother was pretty. Not nearly as pretty as Erica's mother, but handsome enough that if she wanted company she'd have her share. She lived in New Brighton, which was neither pretty nor ugly, just sort of ordinary—a plain-Jane suburb located thirty minutes from both downtown St. Paul and downtown Minneapolis. She greeted me at the door with a smile, an odd thing to do, I thought, considering the circumstances.

"You're McKenzie," she said.

"Yes, ma'am."

"Malcolm said you agreed to help him, us, and let's have no more of that ma'am stuff. Call me Jayne."

She held the door open, and I passed through it. Her living room was in full-blown Christmas mode. Opened gifts were still stashed beneath a frighteningly realistic-looking artificial tree that stood in front of her big window, and there was holly and garlands hanging around door frames and arches; four stockings hung from the fireplace mantel.

"They said it was going to snow, but now it looks like it won't," I said just to be friendly.

"I met a meteorologist once who gave me a ten-minute lecture on all the science that goes into predicting the weather," Jayne said. "I think he was joking me. I think they just flip a coin. McKenzie, I didn't kill my husband."

"Now that we have that out of the way . . ."

"Let me take your coat."

I gave it to her. Jayne draped it over the back of a chair near the door and gestured at me to take a seat. She did the same.

"You spent a lot of time in the emergency room," I said.

"Just unlucky, I guess."

"Have you been unlucky since your husband was killed?"

"Nope."

"You can see how it looks."

"How does it look?"

"Like you were beaten up regularly."

"That's what Detective . . . What was his name?"

"Clark Downing."

"That's what Detective Downing thought, too. He kept asking me if I had anything to tell him. McKenzie, if I said I had been abused, that would be like admitting I had a motive for killing my husband, wouldn't it? So why would I say such a thing?"

"Good question, ma'am."

"Jayne."

"Jayne, it's entirely possible that someone who had the same suspicions about your situation as Downing might have killed your husband on your behalf."

"Then someone did me a favor."

"Your son doesn't think so."

The smile left Jayne's face. "No, he doesn't," she said. "To be honest, I don't either. It's just . . ."

Jayne moved from her chair to the mantel above the fireplace. Along with Christmas decorations, there were a lot of photographs, most of them of Malcolm. In one he was wearing Yankee pinstripes and a baseball glove. The one next to it had him posing with twelve other teenage ballplayers, all dressed in the same uniform, along with three grown-up coaches. The caption at the bottom read NEW BRIGHTON YANKEES. It was dated seven years ago.

"The reason Mal played baseball was because his father played baseball," Jayne said. "Frank pushed him into it, and Malcolm went willingly because—he loved his father. So did I until those last few years. We were happy, a happy family, until those last few years. Losing him the way we did—it's different than if Frank died in a car accident or from lung cancer or something like that. I don't even know how to describe the trauma it caused Mal. That's why I let you into my home, McKenzie, why I'm answering your questions. If it'll help him, give him some closure, let him get on with his life . . . I didn't kill Frank. Detective Downing probably doesn't believe me, but it's true. Let's start there."

"You were abused."

"Yes, but only during the last year and a half of our marriage. He never even raised his voice until . . . The first time he hit me, I was more shocked than hurt. I tried to hide it from Malcolm, hide it from everyone. I don't know how successful I was. Mal must have heard the arguments. 'Course, he was away at school most of that time."

"What happened?"

"I don't know for sure. It was as if Frank lost faith in humanity. Or himself. He worked for a large company that made furniture. When the housing market collapsed, the company downsized three hundred and fifty employees."

"Was he one of them?"

"No, but he worked in human resources, so he had to do the exit interviews, explain severance packages, all that. Since the employees never had a chance to confront the bankers and Wall Streeters who caused the collapse, or even the managers of the furniture company, they all vented to him. Frank became the face of their despair and received the brunt of their fury. It wore him out. If the company had done the layoffs all at once it might have been different, but they took over a year, firing people a few at a time. Somewhere along the line he assumed their anger; became angry himself. He took it out on me.

"Eventually he quit and went to work for the Szereto Corporation. I thought that would cheer him up. Szereto was a thriving company. Still is thriving. A friend of ours, Diane Dauria, is the president. Only his mood grew worse and worse. He became—he became very physical. I've spoken to people, and they told me that violence is something you learn; you need to be taught to be violent. He didn't have that in his background, his family growing up, yet somehow he learned."

"If you didn't kill your husband or have him killed . . ."

"McKenzie, please."

"What do you think happened?"

"I think he went to the park to meet a woman and she killed him."

"Why a woman?"

"They told me he was stabbed with a kitchen knife, and that just makes me think it was a woman. Besides, the last eighteen months—he wasn't satisfied with me, McKenzie. Frank wouldn't touch me except to hurt me. I suppose he could have found someone else, someone at Szereto maybe, and maybe he tried to hurt her . . ."

It was possible, I reminded myself. According to Downing's notes, Harris made a lot of calls to women that last year of his life, but also to men, mostly Szereto employees and job seekers. Downing couldn't prove any of the calls weren't job related—but how hard did he try?

"Do you suspect anyone in particular?" I asked.

"No. I mean, it couldn't have been someone I knew; I'm pretty sure of that—assuming he was cheating. Truth is, McKenzie, I have no idea why he went to that park. I'm just guessing. Those last few months, I avoided Frank as much as it was possible to avoid someone who lived in the same house."

"I understand."

"No you don't."

A knock on the front door interrupted our conversation. Jayne left her spot at the mantel and looked out the window. There was a decade-old black Toyota Camry parked in front of my Ford Mustang on the street, the engine running; the exhaust from the tailpipe curled upward and was snatched away by the wind. There were people in the car, although I was unable to tell who or how many.

Jayne went to the door and pulled it open.

"Critter," she said.

"Mrs. Harris," he replied.

She stepped aside, and a boy of college age moved into the foyer. He was wearing a winter coat zipped to his throat, but no hat or gloves.

"What happened to your face?" Jayne asked.

Critter's hand went to his cheek; fingers gently massaged a swollen nose and bruised lip.

"Believe it or not, I ran into a door," he said.

By then I had stepped behind Jayne. My presence seemed to startle him.

"I'm sorry," Critter said. "Am I interrupting?"

"Not at all," Jayne replied. "It's always good to see you." She gave him a hug just to prove it. "This is Mr. McKenzie. He's a private investigator that Mal hired to look into his father's murder."

Critter stepped out of Jayne's embrace. An expression of alarm crossed his face. He paused for a few beats to think.

"Malcolm hired you?" he asked.

"In a manner of speaking," I said. I had no intention of correcting Jayne's misconceptions.

Critter thought some more. Thinking seemed to come hard to him. After a few moments of awkward silence, Jayne spoke.

"What can I do for you, Critter?"

"Oh, yeah. I just came by to see if Malcolm wanted to hang out, you know, before he goes back to New Orleans."

"I'm sorry. He left about . . . must have been an hour or so ago. Said he was going to meet a girl. He had his skates with him, if that helps."

"The Oval, do you think?"

The Guidant John Rose Minnesota Oval, a 400-meter speed-skating track in Roseville, I reminded myself, probably the best ice in Minnesota. When Olympic hopefuls weren't using it, it was open to the public.

"I don't know," Jayne said.

"He's not replying to my texts."

"If he's skating, he might not know you're trying to reach him."

"Tell him we stopped by."

"I will. You know, he doesn't leave for school until January fourteenth, so you should have plenty of time to get together."

"Plenty of time. Bye, Mrs. Harris."

Critter left without looking at me. Jayne closed the door and stared at the wood as if she were deep in thought. I moved to the big window and, looking around the Christmas tree, watched as Critter moved down the shoveled sidewalk to his car. He opened the driver's side door after first pausing long enough to remove his cell from his pocket and take a pic of the front of my Mustang.

Clever boy, my inner voice said.

"Jayne," I said aloud, "who was that young man?"

"Christopher Meyer. A friend of Malcolm's. They played baseball together."

"They call him Critter?"

"His little brother couldn't pronounce his name when they were kids. It came out Critterfur, and the name stuck. Why do you ask?"

"He just took a photograph of my license plate."

Jayne left the door and hurried deeper into the room. Critter's car was driving off as she reached the window.

"Why would he do that?" she asked.

"So he can find out about me without my knowing."

"But—he could just ask, couldn't he?"

"You'd think so."

Jayne stared at the empty spot where Critter's car had been.

"He was always an odd duck," she said. "Nice, though. A nice boy. I know his family through Hotdish."

"Tell me about Hotdish."

"It grew out of the baseball team. Most of the parents, we

decided we enjoyed each other's company, so we kept meeting once a month even after the team disbanded. Potluck dinners, mostly. Barbecues."

"Supposedly you were with them when your husband was stabbed."

"Supposedly?" Jayne looked at me as if she were thinking of something that she didn't want to say. "They're my friends."

"Yes, ma'am—Jayne."

"Like I said before, I'm willing to go through all this again if it'll help Malcolm, but I'm getting tired of people accusing me of murder. Truthfully—look at me, McKenzie. Truthfully, there were times when I did want to kill Frank; there were nights when I dreamt of killing him. Only while I might have wanted to kill my husband, I would never have killed Malcolm's father."

"Okay."

"I don't expect you to understand what I'm talking about."

"I've been involved in this case for a day," I said. "I'm just stumbling around looking for something that will take me somewhere else."

"Is that an apology?"

"An explanation."

"I'll accept that—for Malcolm's sake. One thing, though, for what it's worth . . ." She gestured at the window, and I followed her gaze to the space where the Toyota Camry had been parked. "Critter's face. I've used the excuse myself, so I know—nobody runs into a door."

I thanked Mrs. Harris for her time, courtesy, and patience and went to the Mustang. I started it up yet did not drive off. Instead I worked my cell, sending Erica a text message because she usually refused to answer when someone actually called—something about phone conversations being so twentieth century.

R U skating @oval with Malcolm?

Her reply came thirty seconds later: *no skating @depot with mal why*

The Depot was an indoor ice rink built into what was once the Chicago, Milwaukee, St. Paul & Pacific Depot Freight House and Train Shed in Minneapolis, I reminded myself. About half a mile from the condo.

I texted: *Met kid looking for Malcolm doesn't seem happy— might have been the something stupid he hit yesterday.*

Erica's reply: *?*

Wouldn't hurt to stay close to home, I told her.

beware of strangers with candy I get it

THREE

The reception area's outer wall was made of tinted glass. I looked through it, watching the vehicles below moving at a brisk pace along Interstate 394. It was midafternoon, though, and they would slow considerably as rush hour approached. I wondered if that might not have been the real reason Harris lost it. New Brighton to St. Louis Park and back on our highway system—he could have been stuck in traffic for as much as two hours a day if not longer, enough to drive anyone into a rage.

Behind me a receptionist answered phones and directed visitors to their destinations inside the offices of the Szereto Corporation. If there had been Christmas decorations hanging there or along the corridors, they had been well scrubbed away by the time I arrived. All I found was comfy chairs and plenty of reading material on the tables, all of it business related, and a flatscreen TV mounted on the wall tuned to CNBC. The market had closed down 237 points, and the pundits were forecasting catastrophe as we approached the new year. 'Course, the market had been up 118 points the day before, and they had predicted the same thing.

I heard a woman call my name, and I turned toward her. She was older and stern-looking and, like the receptionist, was dressed in chic business attire. She spoke in a clipped just-the-facts tone of voice that reminded me of the nuns who taught at St. Mark's Elementary School when I was a kid. I had been a great disappointment to them.

"Mr. McKenzie," she repeated. "Ms. Dauria will see you now. This way."

She spun abruptly and began walking. She didn't stop until she realized I wasn't following her.

"Something, yes?" she asked.

"Do you have a name?"

Her expression suggested that she rarely heard that question. "Does it matter?" she asked.

"Of course it matters."

"Groot," she said. "Candace Groot. I'm Ms. Dauria's personal assistant."

I made sure I was smiling when I offered my hand. She seemed surprised by both gestures.

"Call me McKenzie," I said. "No mister required."

She smiled in return, but it had a tentative quality as if she were trying it on to see if it fit.

Being the boss's right-hand woman, she might not have the chance to wear it very often, my inner voice told me. *Being her friend could prove useful.*

"Candace," I said. "That's an uncommon name."

"Not when I was born. Call me Candy."

It took me a few beats to wrap my head around it—calling a woman her age by what some might consider a stripper's non de plume—but I did what I was told.

"Have you been here long, Candy?"

"I was Mr. Szereto's personal assistant when he founded the company. And his son's. And now I assist Ms. Dauria."

"Actually, I meant Szereto's offices. But good to know."

Candy smiled some more and led me down one corridor and up another toward a corner of the building.

"We finished remodeling about a month ago," she said. "That's why everything looks brand-new. Do you like it?"

"Very much."

"I like it, too. It was so dark before. Ms. Dauria wanted to brighten up the place and make it as comfortable as possible. Our employees might be a little too comfortable if you ask me, but whatever works."

Candy strode the corridors as if she owned the place, or at least had rights to it. People nodded as we passed, yet she didn't seem to notice them. 'Course, that might have been because she was so engrossed in telling me about the birth of the Szereto Corporation forty-three years ago and how she got her job not because of her business degree but because she could type ninety words a minute.

"That was on a manual typewriter, too, not even electric," Candy said. "I'm probably the only person in the building who knows what Wite-Out is."

"Working here so long, I bet you know where all the bodies are buried."

"I should hope so. I buried most of them."

She smiled at her own joke and led me into an office that resembled the reception area. There was an open door on the far side, a desk and chair strategically located near it so that Candy could block anyone from entering without permission. She passed me through the door with the words "Ms. Diane Dauria, Mr. McKenzie."

Dauria moved toward me with her hand extended.

"A pleasure, Mr. McKenzie," she said.

If Jayne Harris was New Brighton, then Dauria was Uptown, probably the most fashionable neighborhood in Minneapolis. At first glance, her black silk certainly appeared business-office appropriate, yet the way it molded to her figure demanded comparisons to every woman standing within fifty feet; comparisons that would clearly favor her.

"It was kind of you to see me," I said. "Especially on such short notice."

Dauria shook my hand; her flesh was soft, yet her grip was firm.

"Whatever I can do to help," she said. "Thank you, Ms. Groot."

Candy left the office but did not close the door. Dauria moved behind her large glass desk. There was a sleek PC on top, along with an elaborate telephone system and a Sheaffer Ferrari fountain pen—but no paper. I sat in a chair across from her. A window-wall was at her back. If not for the slate gray clouds, I would have been looking directly into the sun.

Dauria made a production out of looking at the jeweled watch on her wrist. I don't think she wanted to give me a sense of her wealth so much as to remind me that her time was far more valuable than mine—don't waste it.

"Mr. McKenzie, you said—"

"McKenzie is fine."

"McKenzie it is. You may call me Diane."

"Thank you, Diane."

"You said on the phone that Malcolm Harris asked you to find out what happened to his father, but you didn't say what you planned to do about it."

"There's not much I can do, Diane. The man's going to stay dead no matter what I learn."

"Considering the circumstances, I believe your . . . should we call it a flippant attitude? I believe it is out of place."

"I apologize," I said, although I didn't really mean it. "Sometimes we use humor to mask the seriousness of things."

"I ask again—what will you do if you learn the truth? Will you inform the police?"

"Probably. I'm sure they'd like to know."

"Yes, yes, of course." Diane glanced at her watch some more and then returned her gaze to me. "Tell me what you want as directly as possible."

"I have questions . . ."

"Obviously."

Behind her chair was a credenza stacked with photographs. I was surprised to see a framed copy of the New Brighton Yankees. I gestured at it.

"Are you a member of the Hotdish?" I asked.

"I am. Didn't you know?"

"Jayne Harris told me that you were friends, only I didn't make the connection."

"Does it matter?"

"Frank Harris wasn't just an employee; you knew him personally because of Hotdish."

"Yes, although we kept it out of the office."

"How did you come to hire him?"

"One of my first duties when I was made president of the company was to dismiss our human resources director. As you said, I knew Frank through Hotdish, knew of his work for his previous employer, so I asked him to apply for the position."

"This was . . ."

"As I said, it was right after I was made president, so it had to be two years ago."

"Just twelve months before he was killed."

"Yes. Unfortunately, that's become one of the anniversaries we now use to mark the passage of time."

"Did Harris get along well with his co-workers?"

"As far as I know."

"Did he get along well with any co-worker in particular?"

"If he did, I never heard."

"Would you have?"

"My assistant, Ms. Groot—she keeps me pretty well informed. McKenzie, Detective Downing asked the same questions when the incident took place. I'm afraid I have no better answers now than I did then."

"You never know. Time and memory—sometimes things look much clearer from a distance."

"If you say so."

"Did you know that Frank was abusing his wife."

"Not . . . not when I hired him. When I found out, I was angry enough to fire him but couldn't think of a way to manage it without leaving Szereto open to a wrongful termination lawsuit. He did a good job for us, especially when you consider what happened before. Time and memory make it hard for me to reconcile one man with the other."

"What happened before?"

"Szereto business, not yours."

"Fair enough."

"Make no mistake, McKenzie. My feelings toward Frank— God, I hated him for what he did to Jayne. There was just nothing I could do about it. I suggested to him once, in private, that he should think about working somewhere else. He told me he would leave when he was good and ready. He was the HR director. He knew my hands were tied."

"Tell me about the Hotdish."

Diane reached behind her for the photo of the New Brighton Yankees.

"It was the kids," she said. "We went to all their games, their practices—usually drove them there. That's what parents do, isn't it? We discovered in a very short period of time that we enjoyed each other's company and started doing things together, barbecues after the game; that sort of thing. When the season ended, the final season, we fell into the habit of meeting once a month. Sharing our lives. It was the members who helped me move to Edina after I was promoted. It was Katie's doing mostly. She kept us together."

"Katie?"

"Katherine Meyer."

Diane thrust the photograph toward me; it was the first time I had a close look at the Yankees. She tapped a finger on the second ballplayer on the left kneeling in the first row. I recognized him immediately. Critter Meyer.

"That's her son," Diane said. She moved her finger three players over in the second row. "Here's Malcolm. This beautiful young lady"—she tapped the ballplayer kneeling directly in front of him, the one with a rich pumpkin-colored ponytail flowing out from the back of her baseball cap—"is my daughter, Sloane."

"Your daughter?"

"There were only three girls playing in the league back then. Sloane was one of them. The Yankees desperately needed her, too. The first year, when most of the team was in the seventh grade, they only won three games. When Sloane joined the team in the eighth grade, they finished ten-and-six and missed the playoffs on a tie-breaker. The next year they went undefeated and won the league championship. She was named MVP. Pitched and played short. My little girl. The boys didn't want her on the team at first. Which truly upset Katie, one of the reasons I like her so much, calling out the team for being prejudiced. Same with Philly." She tapped the photo of an African American kid standing at the end of the back row. "Jalen Phillips is his real name. Back then I think there might have been fewer African American kids playing baseball in New Brighton than girls. Katie expected the boys to treat him like a teammate, too, so they did. Anyway, when the boys saw Sloane throw . . . and bat . . . and run . . . She was fourteen for fifteen in stolen bases that final season. Half of the boys wanted to date her; the other half treated her like a sister. It was kind of fun to watch."

Diane spoke with such pride, and her smile was so broad, that I found myself smiling, too. But then I love stories like that.

"Is Sloane still playing?" I asked.

"No. In high school they make the girls play softball, and Sloane didn't care for that. Same in college. She's a junior now, majoring in women and international development at St. Catherine University in St. Paul. She wants to change the world for the better and won't take no for an answer."

I found myself chuckling.

"You think that's funny?" Diane asked.

"Not at all. I was just thinking—I've never known a ginger you could push around."

"That's because they're teased when they're young. They grow up tough. When she slid into second base, it was always cleats high. You know what I mean by that?"

"Sure. I played ball myself. For a young woman who demands to be taken seriously, it makes a powerful statement."

"It does indeed."

I noticed Diane's eyes search my left hand, third finger for a ring that wasn't there. It gave me a pleasant jolt that grew in intensity when I noticed that she wasn't wearing a wedding band, either. It aroused in me a golden-blond memory of a woman, the one who came and went before Nina. In many ways Nina was a miracle, the rebound girl who stayed.

"You interest me, McKenzie," Diane said.

Do I need to remind you, my inner voice said, *that you're spoken for?*

No, you don't, I told myself.

"You and the other members of the Hotdish," I said. "When did you become aware that Harris was abusing his wife?"

Whatever Diane had been thinking was pushed to the back of her mind. She spun in her chair, returned the photograph to its spot on the credenza, and spun back again.

"Some suspected right away," she said. "The more Jayne denied it, the more they suspected. But me? I'm often oblivious to what's going on with other people, their emotions. It's a personal failing, I know. Once I found out, though—I don't know why

Frank beat Jayne. I don't know why she let him. It's incomprehensible to me. My husband cheated on me fifteen years ago. I divorced him on the spot. If he had tried to beat me, I might have killed him. Certainly I would have had him arrested. There's no compromise in these matters."

Now we know why her daughter is so tough, my inner voice said.

"What did you think when you learned that Frank had been killed?"

"He got what was coming to him."

"Besides that."

"Are you asking if I believe Jayne was responsible? She was not. That's the one thing I know for sure. She was surrounded by Hotdishers at the time."

"Were you among them?"

"No, I—" Diane became very still. "I was out of town. I believe Detective Downing made inquiries just to make sure."

I did a quick review of Downing's notes in my head. Something about Chicago—I'd have to check.

"What about the other Hotdishers?" I asked.

"Most of them were at the party that night. Those that weren't, like me, they were cleared by the police. I'm surprised you don't know that."

"Actually, I do. I just wanted to hear what you had to say."

"You don't consider me to be a suspect, then?"

"When you have no suspects, everyone becomes a suspect. All I know for sure is that Harris was killed by someone he knew, by someone he had arranged to meet."

"I assume you believe that person works for the Szereto Corporation."

"Not necessarily. Diane, you work in an extremely competitive industry."

She leaned back in her chair and regarded me cautiously as if she were unsure what I was getting to and didn't like it—

being unsure. She picked up the pen; it was something to hold while she considered my statement.

"That's why it's fun," she said.

"Is there much corporate espionage?"

"Now I understand where you're going. To answer your question—yes and no. Sometimes the struggle for customers can become very aggressive, and industrial spying often affords high gains and little risk to those who practice it, because more often than not it goes undetected until a knock-off is introduced to the marketplace. Even then it's extremely difficult, if not impossible, to trace the origin of the product. However, it's nothing compared to the tech industry, where entire companies can rise and fall based on who launches what products first."

"Yet there's money to be made."

"Are you suggesting that Frank could have been involved in the theft of proprietary information, that he might have attempted to sell it to our competitors and that somehow this contributed to his murder?"

"I am."

"Nonsense. For one thing, he wasn't privy to any of our restricted areas. Believe me, security protocols were quite effective back then. They're even better now. Unless you have clearance, you're not allowed anywhere near R&D, and those employees that are have to check their smartphones at the door. Besides, he wasn't the type."

"Wasn't he?"

Diane didn't have an answer for that. I asked, "From the time Harris started working for you until now, have any of your competitors come up with products or marketing schemes that made you wonder?"

"Time and memory, again. Yes, there have been a couple of things that made me suspect . . . McKenzie, we have people, all they do all day is evaluate competitive products, competitive claims, and marketing materials, searching for possible patent and copyright infringements, and they haven't found anything actionable that could be traced back to Frank."

"Okay."

Diane played with her pen some more.

"McKenzie, what if I asked you to leave this matter alone?" she asked.

"I'd have to ask you why."

"I don't want my friends upset."

"If you're referring to Malcolm and Jayne, they're already upset, and they're the ones who asked me to investigate."

"Jayne didn't."

How does she know? my inner voice asked. *News must travel awfully fast in the New Brighton Hotdish.*

"Perhaps not," I said. "However, she seemed okay with it when we spoke, which makes me wonder if you might not have another reason for asking me to quit."

"Is this how you spend your time, making obscene suggestions?"

"Pretty much."

Diane stood so abruptly I was startled. A moment later, Candy appeared. She spoke loudly. "Ms. Dauria, you're needed in the conference room."

Diane glanced back at the jeweled watch wrapped around her wrist.

"Thank you, Ms. Groot. McKenzie, I'm afraid I must end this." She circled the desk and offered her hand again. "I'm sorry I wasn't more helpful."

"Perhaps you'll allow me to speak with you again at some later date."

"If I have the time. I'm a working girl, you see."

"I thought you were *the man*."

"Which means I need to work harder than most men. Mr. McKenzie, I cannot have you disrupting my workforce with your questions, either."

With that Diane moved toward the door. She spoke as she passed Candy. "Please see Mr. McKenzie to the elevators."

She was out of the office and moving down the corridor when I spoke to her assistant.

"Was it something that I said?" I asked.

"You brought up a subject that's very difficult for us."

"You know what we were talking about?"

"Of course. This way, McKenzie."

Candy was a lot less talkative on our way back to the elevators near the reception area. I couldn't have that. If I was unable to call on Diane for help, I might need hers.

"Ms. Groot," I said. "Candy—I owe you an apology. Frank Harris's son asked me to investigate what happened to his father. I was so concerned with his feelings that I didn't consider what effect my questions might have on others."

Candy squeezed my arm. I don't know if she meant it maternally or otherwise.

"Did you know Frank Harris?" I asked.

"Of course."

"What did you think of him?"

"I didn't care for him. It seemed . . . He did a good job, at least that's what I was told. But it seemed to me as if he wished he were somewhere else. Like him or not, though, he was one of us. What you need to understand, McKenzie, is that tragedy has befallen the Szereto family before, and it hurts to be reminded of it. You can understand that, can't you?"

"Of course, only if it's not too painful, may I ask—what tragedy?"

"You don't know?"

"No, ma'am."

"Mr. Szereto. The son, not the father. He was murdered two and a half years ago."

What did she say?

"Murdered?" I asked.

"Uh-huh. He was so young, too. His wife was pregnant at the time."

"Can you tell me about it?"

We were standing next to the bank of elevators. Candy pressed the down button.

"Not much to tell, I'm afraid," she said. "He was president of the company right before Ms. Dauria took charge. One day, well, one night, actually, he was shot to death while he was sitting in his car at a stoplight. The police never found out who did it."

"Why was he killed?"

"If they knew that, then they'd know who killed him, wouldn't they?"

She had a point.

"Did you know him well?" I asked.

"Practically watched him grow up working for his father."

"What about you? Do you have a theory why Szereto was killed, who killed him?"

Candy's lips curled into a thin smile, only there was no joy in it. At the same time, a bell pinged and the doors of the elevator slid open.

"Good afternoon, McKenzie," she said.

FOUR

The killing of Frank Harris might have been worth only six
paragraphs in the *St. Paul Pioneer Press,* but the murder of
Jonathan Szereto Jr.—that was covered by the *Pioneer Press,*
the Minneapolis *Star Tribune,* the *MinnPost,* all the local TV
stations, and Minnesota Public Radio. Money will do that. I noticed, though, that all the reports I found on the Internet were
filed within twelve days after the shooting. Which meant that
the cops had developed no new information since then that
would have kept the story alive—at least none that they had
been willing to share.

I called Detective Downing, catching him just as he was
about to call it a day.

"I wonder if you could do me a favor," I told him. "There was
a homicide committed in St. Louis Park two and a half years
ago. An unsolved homicide. Will you reach out to the lead investigator on the case, see if he'll speak to me?"

"What homicide?"

I told him what my online research had told me—
approximately 8:30 P.M., Thursday, June 22, Jonathan Szereto
Jr., the forty-three-year-old son of beauty industry pioneer

Jonathan Szereto Sr. and president of the Szereto Corporation, was driving home from an undisclosed location.

"The police determined that he had left his offices at 5:36 P.M.," I said. "Yet they have no idea where he was for the ensuing three hours or what he was doing. Just like with Frank Harris."

"Probably not just like him, but go on."

"Szereto stopped at a traffic light less than a mile from his office. An unidentified vehicle pulled next to his. A witness out walking his dog said he heard two dull pops that he thought might have come from inside the second vehicle, but when he didn't hear the sound again, he ignored it. He didn't believe anything was amiss until the unidentified vehicle sped off after the light changed while the car carrying Szereto remained at the intersection."

"Was he the one who called it in?" Downing asked.

"No. The driver of the car that came up behind Szereto and was caught waiting through two red lights called it in. He blew his horn a few times and then went up to Szereto's window wondering if he had passed out or something; saw the blood. Szereto had been shot in the head and the throat with a nine-millimeter handgun. Very messy. From what I read, the St. Louis Park PD never came up with a viable person of interest. The press speculated that it was a random shooting like when that schoolteacher was shot a while back for no particular reason."

"This is connected to my case how?"

"You have to admit it's an interesting coincidence."

"In what way?"

I explained the math.

"Szereto was killed two and a half years ago, at about the same time that Harris began abusing his wife. Six months later, Diane Dauria was named president of the Szereto Corporation, replacing Szereto. Almost immediately, she dismissed the company's director of human resources and hired Harris—

they were both members of the New Brighton Hotdish, you see. One year later, Harris was killed."

Downing laughed at me. Can't say I blamed him.

"And you think what?" he asked. "That Dauria asked Harris to kill Szereto so Dauria could get a promotion—and then paid him off with a new job before killing him a year later—because why exactly?"

"I haven't worked out all the details yet."

"Well, here's one—I can place Dauria in Chicago at the time of the Harris stabbing. She was conducting a seminar with a chain of salons or whatever they're called that carries their merchandise; something about new product innovations. It's in my notes."

"I know. Doesn't mean she didn't have it done while she was gone, though."

"It sounds to me, McKenzie, like you're grasping at straws."

"Clark, I went through your supplementals very carefully. Your investigation was thorough as hell. Grasping at straws is pretty much all that's left. So far this is the only thing I could find that seems amiss. Can I use that word again? Anyway, just for my own peace of mind . . ."

"Yeah, mine, too. I'll call you back."

"Thank you."

"Are you sure there aren't any other unsolved homicides we should be looking into?"

"I'll let you know."

I was starting dinner when Nina came home. She stopped inside the doorway and inhaled deeply.

"That smells good," she said. "What is it?"

I answered as she discarded her winter coat and boots: braised boneless pork ribs simmering in a gravy laced with chili powder; mashed potatoes seasoned with onion salt, black pepper, butter, cream cheese, sour cream, and chives; plus green beans and pecans sautéed in chicken broth and maple syrup.

"You are such a good cook," she told me.

I turned the heat down to a simmer on everything and wrapped my arms around her.

"There are a few other things I'm pretty good at, too," I said.

"What do they say in Missouri? You'll have to show me."

"I can do that. Do you need to go back to Rickie's tonight?"

"Nope."

"After dinner . . ."

"What's wrong with before dinner?"

"Now that you mention it . . ."

Erica walked through the front door. She was leading Malcolm by the arm because he had trouble seeing where he was going; his head was tilted back, and he was pinching the bridge of his nose.

"We're almost there," Erica said.

"This is so embarrassing," Malcolm told her.

"Don't be such a child."

"I'm not a child."

"Yes, you are."

"Shut up."

"You shut up."

Erica led Malcolm up the steps into the kitchen area and halted at the sink. She wet a wad of paper towels with cold water and pressed it against his nose. He took the towels into his own hand and lowered his head.

"Is it still bleeding?" she asked.

"I think it stopped."

"It doesn't look broken."

"It hurts, though."

"Uh-hum," Nina said.

"Hi, Mom. Hi, McKenzie. Are we interrupting anything?"

Nina stepped out of my embrace.

"Gosh, honey, whatever gave you that idea?" she said.

"Mom, this is Malcolm. Mal, my mother."

"Hello, Ms. Truhler." The paper towels gave Malcolm's voice a muffled quality. "It's a pleasure meeting you."

"Call me Nina. What happened to you?"

Malcolm looked at Erica as if he were afraid she would answer the question. She didn't.

"Nothing," Malcolm said. "Just a silly accident."

"Like what happened to your hand?" I asked.

"I didn't want to come here. Erica made me."

"You're the one who said you didn't want your mother to see you like this," Erica said.

I took a chance.

"Was the accident caused by Critter Meyer?" I asked.

Malcolm started speaking—"How do you know"—and stopped.

"I'm a semiprofessional private investigator," I said. "Remember?"

"It's not what you think."

"I honestly don't know what to think. Help me out."

Malcolm didn't answer.

"Erica?" I said.

She raised both her hands in surrender. "Leave me out of it," she said.

Nina grabbed Erica's wrist and lowered her hand to get a good look at her knuckles. They were swollen. She pulled Erica over to the sink, turned on the cold water, and pushed the girl's hand into the flow.

"I don't know about McKenzie," she said, "but I'm starting to lose my temper—something I hardly ever do."

Erica smiled at her mother's words. "Hardly ever?" she asked.

"Rickie . . ."

"Mom, I'm in kind of a difficult spot here."

She made promises, my inner voice said.

I stepped closer to Malcolm.

"I'm only going to ask one more time," I said.

"I was in a fight, okay?" he said.

"With Critter?"

"Yes."

"What was that about?"

"It's personal."

"I'm sure it is."

"You got into a fight with my daughter," Nina said.

"Not with her. I mean, she was there."

"That's what I meant. It's why *I'm* taking it personally."

"Stop yelling at me. People are always yelling at me."

I stepped between Nina and the kid; I was pretty sure that she might have punched him if I hadn't. I deliberately kept my voice low and calm.

"Explain it to us," I said.

"I knew he was looking for me. You did send the text," Malcolm said. "I ignored it, and then we met up at this coffeehouse on Silver Lake Road, him and some other friends."

Friends?

"That doesn't tell me what the fight was about," I said.

Malcolm glanced at Erica. She didn't say a word.

"It was"—Malcolm turned his head so Erica couldn't see his face—"about a woman."

"My daughter?" Nina asked.

"No, a different woman. You don't know her."

I took another chance.

"Sloane Dauria?"

Malcolm's eyes grew wide with—was it surprise or fear? Probably both, I decided.

"Sloane, no, why?" he said. "What do you know about Sloane?"

"I know she's pretty fast."

"What's that supposed to mean?"

"Fourteen stolen bases in fifteen attempts your championship year."

"Oh, yeah. I remember."

"What did you think I meant?"

"I don't know."

"What does any of this have to do with Rickie?" Nina asked.

"Nothing."

Nina held up Erica's hand, now dripping with water.

"Then how did she get hurt?" she asked.

Erica freed herself.

"There were three of them," she said. "Only one of him, so—I hit the one who was closest, just the way McKenzie taught me."

I winced at the answer, and not just because Nina glared at me as if I were the cause of every problem that had ever existed in the world. I had contributed only three lessons to Erica's education: I taught her how to play Texas Hold 'Em, pick locks, and throw a punch. In my defense, I hadn't actually expected her to do any of those things.

"I didn't need your help," Malcolm said.

"The patriarchy is alive and well and standing in my kitchen," Erica told him.

"C'mon, Rick."

"Know what? Next time I'll just stand by and watch them pummel you about the head and shoulders."

"Why were you fighting over Sloane Dauria?" I asked.

"You were fighting over some other girl while you were out with my daughter?" Nina asked.

"We weren't fighting cuz of Sloane," Malcolm said. "I mean, she was part of it, but only because—arrrrrggggg. Can't you just leave me alone?"

My inner voice said, *There are too damn many kitchen knives lying around.* I took hold of Nina's shoulders and turned her away. She didn't like it, yet she didn't resist, either. I guided her to the sofa in front of the fireplace in the living room area.

"Let the children work it out among themselves," I said

She didn't reply. I think it was because she didn't trust herself to speak. The one aspect of Nina's life that you don't mess with—ever—is her daughter.

We sat with our backs to the kitchen area. After a couple of beats Nina attempted to speak, but I put a finger to my lips. The thing with living in what amounted to a single room, the acoustics were wonderful. Even though the kids were now whispering, we could hear them plainly; it was as if they were sitting next to us.

"I shouldn't have gotten you involved in my problems," Malcolm said.

"It's okay."

"Now your mother hates me."

"She hates all the men I'm involved with."

"Are we involved?"

"Mal . . ."

"I know, I know. Best friends forever."

"We are involved, though, you and I. McKenzie is, too, because of me. You can't keep secrets from him, you know. Not if you want him to help you."

"What happened today, that has nothing to do with my father. This thing with me and Critter, it goes back way before . . . before Dad was . . . before he was killed."

"What thing?"

"Rickie, can we not talk about it? It was such a long time ago."

"Not so long that Critter has forgotten."

"Yeah, well, I'm trying to forget."

"How come all this time you've never mentioned Sloane Dauria to me? Who is she?"

"Someone I played baseball with on the team in New Brighton. She was really good."

"Is she pretty?"

Oh-oh, my inner voice said.

"Yeah, she really is."

"Prettier than me?"

"No one is as pretty as you."

Nice save, kid.

"Besides, Critter hangs around with her all the time," Malcolm said. "I mean, he's always at her house."

"Does that make you jealous?"

Sssssssss . . .

"What? No. If anything, he should be jealous of me. He sees you standing next to me; he has to think his whole life sucks."

Not bad, not bad . . .

"I'm just teasing with you," Erica said.

"I have to go, but, Rickie—New Year's Eve, there's a party, some of my teammates from when I played ball, this group my mom is part of, if you're not doing anything . . ."

"I thought you said you weren't going to that party."

"I wasn't, but now my mom is making a big deal out of it. Anyway, I was wondering . . ."

"Oh, Mal. I wish I could. I have to work. The club, my mom's club that she named after me, New Year's Eve is huge, and she needs me to help out. Maybe if you had asked sooner . . . Thanks for asking, though. I appreciate it."

" 'Kay."

"I'll see you before the party, though."

"Absolutely."

"And we'll get together during the weekend."

"Looking forward to it."

I turned my head just enough to watch Erica lead Malcolm to the door. They hugged but didn't kiss, and then he was gone. Erica closed the door and leaned against the wood, supporting her weight with one hand.

"Mom, do you need any help New Year's Eve?" she asked.

"You can help hostess, if you like."

"Thank you."

"How's your hand?" I asked.

Erica wiggled her fingers as she moved toward us to prove it was undamaged.

"Tell me what happened," I said.

"Not much to tell. We were at this coffeehouse in New Brighton. The Bru House, I think it's called. When we left, Critter—I didn't know who he was then—he and two other guys showed up. Critter pushed Mal, and Mal pushed him back. They didn't even speak to each other at first, just started pushing. I know you don't want to hear it, Mom, but that was kinda fun. I mean, it's fun to know I can really hurt a guy if I have to. The one I hit, he cupped his face like it was going to fall off, and then I kicked him in the knee like McKenzie said I should. He limped back to the car, and the other guy just sort of stepped off while Malcolm and Critter started throwing punches at each other. Critter said, 'What are you doing?' and Mal said, 'I'm not doing anything,' and Critter said, 'Don't lie to me. I was at your mom's.'"

What does that mean? my inner voice asked.

"That's about all the conversation they had," Erica said. "The thing is, though—even while they were hitting each other, they didn't seem like they were that angry. It was like they were just going through the motions, you know? Like it was something they felt they had to do. Then these other guys came out of the coffeehouse and broke it up, and I drove Malcolm's car here because he didn't want to go home right away. Anyway, thank you, McKenzie. For teaching me."

Erica retreated to her bedroom, closing the door behind her.

"Thank you, McKenzie," Nina said. "For teaching her."

"There are a couple of moves I could teach you, too, if you're still interested."

Nina patted my knee. "Not while Rickie's home." She moved toward the kitchen area. "When's dinner?"

Dammit!

FIVE

Detective Sergeant Margaret Utley had a suspicious nature. She agreed to meet me per Downing's request, except not at a neutral location. Instead, she selected one of the four substations that the St. Louis Park Police Department actually labeled "cop shops." We spoke in an interrogation-slash-conference-slash-break room over foam cups filled with really awful coffee.

"What do you have for me?" she asked.

"I was hoping you had something for me."

"That's not how this is going to work."

"How is it going to work?"

"You're not going to see my case files; I don't give a damn how they do things in New Brighton. But if you can help me, then maybe I can help you."

"Quid pro quo."

"Now we're speaking the same language."

"I have an unsolved homicide of a white suburban male, not into drugs, not in the life, which means the odds of him being murdered were quite slim. You have an unsolved homicide of a white one-percenter, also living the squeaky clean, which means the chances of him being murdered were even less. Both worked for the same company—"

"Not at the same time."

"True. However—"

"However, the Szereto Corporation has employed thousands of workers in its forty-three years of existence. It currently has over four hundred full- and part-time employees. The odds that two of them were involved in violent death within eighteen months of each other are not as statistically improbable as you seem to think, such is the world we live in."

"When I worked the job you have, I never took a coincidence lightly regardless of how statistically probable or improbable it might have seemed at the time, and neither do you."

"Why would you assume that, McKenzie?"

"When I called to set up the meet after Detective Downing gave me your name, you could have told me to go . . . entertain myself. You didn't."

Utley regarded me carefully.

"My experience, someone that kills and gets away with it—often they feel empowered to do it again," she said.

"Meaning?"

"You're right. It is possible that the person or persons unknown who killed Jonny Szereto might have been working for the company. It's possible they might also have killed Frank Harris."

"Which brings us back to where we started."

Detective Utley showed me the palms of both her hands as if she expected me to keep speaking, so I did.

"During your investigation, did you speak to Diane Dauria?" I asked.

"Vice president in charge of research and development."

"She was vice president. She was made president of the company six months after Szereto was tagged."

"Which means she benefited from his death. Whaddya know, McKenzie? You might be useful after all."

"Did you speak to her?"

"Of course. She was in Chicago at the time of the murder."

"She was in Chicago when Harris was killed, too," I said. "What do you think the odds are, statistically speaking?"

"Depends on how often she goes to Chicago. Okay, McKenzie, here's one for you. Jonny Szereto was not squeaky clean. He was a country-club drunk who tried to fuck everything in a skirt that he could make stand still. I have statements suggesting that when Jonny took over after the old man died, he turned the company into his own private whorehouse, threatening to terminate vulnerable female employees, single mothers, young women carrying huge student loans, unless they gave it up— blackmailing them into trading sexual favors for their jobs. The economy being what it was back then, what it still is . . ."

I needed to let that sink in for a moment as my inner voice started calling the man names that you don't often hear even on HBO. I found myself flashing on what Diane had said about Harris—*He got what was coming to him.*

"Was Dauria among them?" I asked.

"She said no. Nearly all of the women I interviewed said no. They claimed that they had not been abused and had no knowledge that anyone else had; they claimed they didn't know what I was talking about. Some were straight-up angry about it. They accused me of slandering the Szereto name. Except a chosen few—apparently Jonny was very selective in choosing his victims, picking only on those that were"—by the sound of her voice, Utley was loath to speak the word even as she said it—"weakest. The women who confirmed the rumor begged me to keep it to myself. They were afraid their husbands, boyfriends, families wouldn't understand."

"I don't blame them for that."

"Neither do I, although if just one of them had had the nerve to step forward . . ."

"You know how the system treats rape victims."

"Yes, I do."

"Especially if there's no indication of violence; if it's just he said, she said."

"I know."

"Who told you this was happening?"

"Originally? It was the director of human resources, guy named Stuart Mason, but only after I leaned on him. Apparently a couple of the women complained, went to his office for help. He had their names and stories in his files."

"What did he do about it?"

"Not a goddamn thing."

Now you know why Dauria fired him, my inner voice said.

"You see my problem, then," Utley said.

"The names of the women . . ."

"No. You don't get that. Not from me."

"Did any of them live near the intersection where the shooting took place?"

"I know what you're going for. The man leaves his office, and three hours later he's found dead only a mile away—maybe he spent the time forcing himself on one of his employees. I checked, and there were a few who lived in the general vicinity; more than a few. None of them admitted to being one of the bastard's victims, though."

"How 'bout someone who didn't admit it?"

"A distinct possibility."

The look in Utley's eye, I knew better than to push the matter any further.

"Mason, then," I said. "Where can I find him?"

"Szereto?"

"No. Dauria fired him the minute she took charge of the company."

"Good for her."

"Makes me think she knew what was going on."

"I don't know. She seemed genuinely surprised about it when I interviewed her. If she had . . ."

"That could be a motive, too. Protecting her co-workers . . ."

"Or it could have been any of the women that Jonny raped, whether they lived nearby or not."

"Or their husbands. Or their boyfriends."

"Or—it could have been Jonny's wife."

"Did she know what her husband was up to?" I asked.

"She said she had no idea."

"Does that make her the last to know or simply the last one to admit it?"

"Which brings us to Jonny's mother—Evelyn Szereto. Turned out that she and Jonny had a big blow-up in front of witnesses about how he was running her husband's—his father's—business into the ground just days prior to the murder. She said, and I think I'm quoting accurately, 'I can get rid of you in a heartbeat.' "

"Did Evelyn know about the rumors?"

"She denied it, too, at first. When I told her I had already interrogated the human resources director, she admitted that he had informed her about the complaints."

"I don't suppose you know where Evelyn was when her son was shot."

"I do. She and her daughter-in-law were having a three-hour dinner at Club Versailles on Lake Minnetonka. Do you know it?"

"One of those places where you need a black credit card before they'll seat you at the bar."

"According to both of them, Vanessa had just learned that she was pregnant, and she and Evelyn were chatting about how their lives were going to be forever changed at just about the time someone stuck a nine-millimeter in Jonny's face, the mother celebrating with six-hundred-dollar champagne and the daughter-in-law drinking designer water. Afterward, Vanessa drove them home. Turned out they all lived together."

"Cozy."

"And awfully convenient," Utley said.

"You have too damn many suspects."

"Tell me about it. Now you've added Diane Dauria to the list, and I can't place her at the scene any more than I could the others. There were no traffic cameras in the vicinity. According to my only reliable witness, who admits he's not a car guy, the shooter's vehicle may or may not have been a dark-colored Toyota. That's all I have."

"How come none of this made the papers, the evening news?" I asked.

"I wasn't about to tell anyone, and neither was the ACA; not unless it led to an indictment. Why would we? Ruin how many lives for no reason? As for the Szereto Corporation, ask yourself, would you want it to get out?"

We both took turns sipping our coffee in the silence that followed. Finally Detective Utley said, "I should get back to work."

"Me, too."

Yet neither of us moved.

I had to say it. "Detective Downing is upset that he hasn't cleared the Harris homicide."

"Are you asking if I've lost sleep over the Szereto case? No, I haven't, but McKenzie—first day on the job, I was taught you can't choose the victim."

"I was taught the same thing."

"I want the killer."

I nodded as if I believed her.

I found Stuart Mason on LinkedIn. He was working for an investment firm in Golden Valley, only three miles from Szereto's corporate offices. There was nothing in his profile that suggested he had been associated with the problems over there or that he had been fired. I went to his office without calling first for an appointment. The receptionist directed me to his door as if people dropped in on him unexpectedly all the time. His assistant was less accommodating, a practiced bureaucrat who relished the opportunity to control your life if ever so briefly, daring you to respond with resentment or anger or, God help you, with sarcasm. She thrust a sheaf of papers attached to a clipboard at me and told me to fill in the blanks. I wrote "McKenzie" where it said NAME, scribbled "Jonathan Szereto Jr." in large letters across the top page, and handed back the clipboard. The office assistant took one look and glared at me as if I were a jackrabbit that had somehow managed to invade her carefully cultivated garden.

"It's a personal matter," I said.

She responded by taking the clipboard into the office located directly behind her desk. A moment later she reappeared. She motioned me through the office door. I moved past her. She closed the door behind me.

A man was sitting behind a desk covered with files. He was wearing a dress shirt and dress slacks, but no tie or jacket. He pointed at the clipboard. "What is this?" He glanced down where I had written my name. "McKenzie."

"I'd like to talk to you about your time at Szereto."

"I'm bound by a confidentiality agreement."

"I've already spoken to the St. Louis Park Police Department."

"I will neither confirm nor deny anything they have to say."

"I've also spoken with Diane Dauria."

"That lesbian bitch?"

The "bitch" part didn't surprise me, but "lesbian"?

Who cares? my inner voice said.

"I take it you don't think well of her," I said.

"I took care of the paperwork, her contract, payroll, bene-fits, all of that—gave her the papers to sign. When she finished I went to congratulate her on her promotion, only before I could even get the words out she fired me. Fired me. After all I did for Szereto. Had security escort me from the building."

"Why?"

I had hoped the question would speed him along, yet it seemed to have the opposite effect. Mason leaned back in his chair and regarded me carefully.

"Who are you?" he asked.

Several fibs sprang to mind, some of them tried and true, but I figured a man in Mason's profession would probably know a liar when he saw one. I decided I'd get further if I told the truth—sort of.

"I'm investigating the murder of a Szereto employee," I said. I emphasized the word "investigating" because it made me sound official.

"Jonny Szereto?"

"No. Someone else."

"There's a second one?"

"Frank Harris. Did you know him?"

"No, but—I know the name. He's the one they hired to re-place me. He was a friend of that lesbian bitch. At least that's what I was told back when I still had friends over there who would talk to me. When did this happen?"

"About a year ago."

"A year?"

"The cops were unable to solve the crime, so now I'm look-ing into it."

"They couldn't find out who killed Jonny, either—fuckups."

I felt a chill of anger climb up my spine. Having been in har-ness myself, I don't like it when people criticize the police, even when they richly deserve it, but I let it slide.

"Who do you think killed Szereto?" I asked.

Mason grinned at me.

"Could have been a lot of people," he said.

"The women he abused?"

"You heard about that, huh?"

"I don't think it's a secret."

"Sure it is. The cops know because they're the cops, because they read my files, but no one else except maybe some of the people the cops talked to. They were asking a lot of questions, you know? To most of the employees, though, the industry—it's a deep, deep, deep dark secret."

"Were you responsible for that?"

"Partly—and that lesbian bitch fired me for it. Do you think it was easy keeping all that shit quiet? Keeping those women quiet? I should write a book. Be a bestseller like *Fifty Shades of Grey*."

"Why don't you?"

"That damned confidentiality agreement."

"You're talking to me."

"I'm not telling you anything you don't already know."

"The names of the women . . ."

"Uh-uh. The police didn't tell you, I'm not gonna. What has this to do with whatshisname, Harris, anyway?"

"I'm trying to find out if there's a connection. Tell me—when the women came to you, what did you do?"

Mason regarded me for a few beats while his internal voices argued over whether or not he should tell the story. From the look in his eyes, he clearly wanted to. So I gave him permission.

"This is just between you and me," I said.

"The first time, I took it to the boss."

"Jonny Szereto?"

"What you gotta understand, McKenzie, my job is to serve the interests of the employer, not the employees—what I told that woman cop. HR serves employees, too, of course, for purposes of retention and morale, but only because it's good for the company. At the end of the day, the employer always comes first."

"You took the complaint to your boss even though the complaint was about him?"

"That's what I was paid to do," he said.

"What happened?"

"I told him one of the secretaries, she was all teary-eyed, accused him of bringing her into his office, forcing her to her knees, and making her service him."

"What did he say?"

"He said to fire her."

"Did you?"

"I told him if I did that, she might take it to the cops, go public. I told him this was the kind of thing that could destroy a company overnight, especially a company where I think maybe ninety-five percent of its customers are women. Also, at the time, there were rumors that the company was for sale, that some European conglomerate was looking to buy, so a scandal, not in Szereto's best interests. Jonny just waved me off, told me to handle it."

Mason grinned again; swear to God, like he was enjoying the telling.

"You have to admire the man's audacity," he said.

I felt like bitch-slapping him upside the head. Instead, I asked, "Did you handle it?"

"Not at first. At first I was like, if I ignore it, maybe it'll go away. Then a second woman came forward. And a third. One woman, a girl really, even though she already had a kid in daycare, she said how Jonny brought her into the office, locked the door, and told her she was a substandard employee and he was going to fire her unless she shaped up. What he meant by that was she should slowly remove all of her clothes, do a kind of striptease, you know, and show him her shape. Then he made her lean against the glass wall of his office, her hands pressed against the glass so anyone driving along the freeway could look up and see while he fondled her tits and pussy. Afterward he penetrated her from behind, and when he finished he made her clean him off with her mouth. Isn't that amazing?"

Go 'head, my inner voice said. *Beat the hell out of him.*

"So the problem wouldn't go away," I said aloud.

"I knew this couldn't go on, so, like I told the police, I took it to the boss's boss."

"Who was that?"

"Mrs. Szereto, his mother. She's the chairman—chairwoman of the board of directors."

"I thought Szereto was a family-owned company."

"It is. Well, two-thirds of it is family owned. The rest of the shares are publicly traded. The board of directors—it's what they call a paper board. It meets once or twice a year to approve the company's financials, dividends, whatever is required by law. Mrs. Szereto waves all the shares she owns, and everyone else pretty much does whatever she says."

"What did Mrs. Szereto say when you went to her?"

"She said she would take care of Jonny, and I should take care of the women."

"What did she mean by that?"

"Some were promoted, some were transferred, some resigned; they all got money. Lots of money."

"Do you think that made it all right?"

"I was just doing my job, protecting the company."

"Did Mrs. Szereto take care of her son?"

"All I know is that they had a huge fight that very day in the conference room."

"Then what?"

"Jonny got himself killed, but"—he held up his hand like a cop stopping traffic—"that was like three weeks later, so don't go around saying I accused the old lady. Okay?"

It happens all the time—you want to say something but you

don't know what until much later, when the perfect words come to you. By then, though, it's too late. What I should have told Mason was that I wished he had been in the car with Jonny Szereto, that three shots were fired instead of two, and that one of them drilled him right between the eyes. Except I didn't think of it until I was already in the parking lot and walking to my Mustang.

SIX

I have friends who live on Lake Minnetonka, but not many. That's where Minnesota's one percent hang out, and even though there are those who consider me to be a member of the fraternity, I never feel comfortable there. Call it my blue-collar upbringing asserting itself.

I found Mrs. Szereto's big house at the end of a long private driveway surrounded by several acres of snow left undisturbed except for the tracks of various woodland creatures. It had been decorated so tastefully for the holidays that I expected to turn around to see camera crews taking its photograph for magazine covers and postcards. I parked next to a four-car garage and walked to the door. It was cold enough that the thin layer of ice crunched beneath my feet; a north wind blew through my hair.

I rang the bell. It was because of the brisk wind that I rang it again without waiting the polite length of time. The inside door was pulled open. A man stood there, a muscle-bound thirty-something trying to pass for a twenty something in a tight, thin, short-sleeve T-shirt and jeans. My first thought—didn't he know it was cold outside? My second—he didn't look like a servant. He looked like someone's angry boyfriend.

"Whaddya want?" he asked.

"I'm McKenzie. I'm here to see Mrs. Szereto?"

"Which one?"

"The chairwoman of—"

"I was just messin' with you." He opened the outer storm door. "Hurry in, then," he said. "We're not paying to heat the whole outdoors."

It was something my father might have said, but it didn't make me like him any better. I stepped past him. He shut the door behind me. I stamped my feet.

"I don't want you here," he said. "If I had my way—I'm just saying."

"That might bother me if I knew who you were."

"That's none of your goddamned business. I know why you came around, and I don't like it. That's none of your goddamned business, either. I told Mrs. Szereto so. But she's—you just watch yourself, that's all I got to say." And then, "Keep your shoes on," he told me.

It was an unexpected courtesy, especially given the circumstances. In Minnesota in winter, visitors are usually asked to deposit their shoes and boots at the front door.

"Thank you," I said.

Still, I wiped them vigorously before I followed him into an expansive living room. It was also well decorated; it reminded me a little bit of the holiday displays in the Mall of America.

"Mrs. Szereto, whatshisname is here," he shouted.

"McKenzie," I said.

"Whatever."

A woman entered the room. She was tall and thin with short white hair; her face was made up as if she were expecting someone to take her photograph. Her clothes looked like something advertised in next month's *Vogue*, yet her eyes were as old as Babylon. I knew from my research that she had been a model; a full twenty years younger than her husband when they married and twenty years older than her son when he died. Which made her, what? Sixty? Sixty-five?

"Are you McKenzie?" she asked.

"Yes."

"I'm Mrs. Jonathan Szereto."

She offered her hand and I shook it. The thirtysomething watched us. Mrs. Szereto threw a glance at him over her shoulder. I didn't know enough to decipher their private code, yet something in her smile must have relayed specific instructions, because he announced, "I have things to do." He left the room, though not before pausing to straighten a pillow that didn't need straightening. The look he gave me—you didn't need to be a code-breaker to translate its meaning. "Be very careful," it said.

"Housekeeper?" I asked.

"Jack McKasy," Mrs. Szereto said. "He's my man-about-the-house; takes care of things for me and Nessa, does what needs to be done, runs errands. He has rooms above the garage." Her face brightened. "Housekeeper, though. I'm going to call him that; hear what he says. Bet he doesn't like it."

She reached out her hand. I removed my coat and handed it to her. Mrs. Szereto draped it over the back of a chair.

"I must say that I was quite intrigued by your phone call. That, however, is not why I agreed to meet with you. Should I tell you why I agreed to see you? It's because I know who you are, McKenzie. From the newspapers."

"Ma'am?"

"I was a good friend of Reney Rogers; played poker with her every Wednesday at Club Versailles for years. I liked her very much."

So did I, my inner voice reminded me.

"I cried and cried when I learned that she had been raped and murdered. I didn't stop crying until I read that you found the man who did it. Tell me, McKenzie, how did it feel when you shot him?"

"Can't say I felt much of anything."

"Now you want to kill the man who murdered my son."

I didn't know how to respond. If that was what Mrs. Szereto was hoping for, saying no might cause her to toss me out of her house, and I would lose the access to the Szereto Corporation that I was hoping for. If I said yes, she'd probably know I was lying. The truth is, I've killed people both as a police officer and whatever you would call what I do now, and it's taken its toll. I often have trouble sleeping, and when I do sleep I sometimes have distressing dreams. I find that I'm occasionally irritable, too, and prone to angry outbursts for no particular reason. In moments of solitude, I actually mourn the people I've shot, even the ones who were trying to shoot me. Except for the man who murdered Reney Rogers. Killing him didn't bother me one damn bit.

"Well?" Mrs. Szereto said.

"I'd like to find out who did it before I make any promises."

"You do want to see the person punished?"

"Yes," I said, although after speaking with Stuart Mason, I wasn't sure that was true.

Mrs. Szereto nodded her head as if she found the answer acceptable.

"Some people think I might have killed him," she said. "Detective Sergeant Margaret Utley of the St. Louis Park Police Department—do you know her?"

"We've met."

"She didn't say it to my face, but I know she considers me a suspect. McKenzie, do you think it's possible for a mother to murder her only child?"

"Yes."

Mrs. Szereto folded her arms across her chest and stilled herself. An electrified fence of hostility spread from her eyes.

"You do?" she said.

Uh-oh, my inner voice said. *You had better say something smart or she's going to fry your ass.*

"Some sons need killing," I said.

She took a measured step toward me.

You call that smart?

" 'Course, that's what wives are for," I said.

She halted and slowly dropped her arms to her sides. The barrier lowered with them.

"If you knew Nessa . . ."

The squeal of a young voice interrupted her. A moment later a boy dashed into the room. He could not have been much more than two years old. He flattened himself against the wall just inside the doorway. A woman entered. She might have been Mrs. Szereto forty years ago; her golden hair was even cut short like the older woman's. She was hunched over, pretending to be some kind of animal.

"Arrrrrg, where are you?" she said.

The boy giggled. The woman pivoted toward him.

"Arrrrrg, there you are."

She gathered the boy in her arms and started kissing his cheek and neck. He laughed as if it were the most fun he'd ever had.

Mrs. Jonathan Szereto said, "McKenzie, this is Mrs. Jonathan Szereto."

By then, the younger woman had flipped the boy over and was holding him upside down by his ankles. She spoke to me from between his sneakers.

"Hello. My mother-in-law told me you were coming over."

Mrs. Szereto gestured at the boy.

"And this young rapscallion is Mr. Jonathan Szereto the Third."

"Hi," I said.

I shook the boy's hand. The fact that he was upside down at the time made him giggle some more.

"It must get very confusing around here," I said.

"We're forever opening each other's mail," the younger Mrs. Szereto said. "It'll be easier if you call me Vanessa."

(71)

"Thank you."

"You can call me Evelyn," the older Mrs. Szereto said.

I bent over and looked at the boy, holding my head sideways. "What should I call you?" I asked.

"Mommy is a bear," he said.

"A very pretty bear."

Geezuz, my inner voice said. *You just can't help yourself, can you?*

"Arrrrg," Vanessa growled. She swung the boy by his ankles and carried him from the room. "Time for you to hibernate."

"What's that?" the kid asked.

"Nap."

"Noooooo."

"Cute boy," I said when they were gone.

"Unfortunately, he'll grow up to be a man," Evelyn said.

"Not necessarily. Some boys never grow up."

"Like my son?"

I turned. Evelyn was standing so close to me that for a moment she was all eyes. I was startled enough to take two steps backward. Evelyn lowered herself onto a sofa that looked as if it cost as much as my car. She patted the cushion next to her. I sat. She turned toward me, propping herself up against the back of the sofa with an elbow. The V-neck of her blouse fell open slightly, and I caught a glimpse of her lace bra. I think I was supposed to, the way she smiled when she saw my eyes flick down and up again.

What the hell? my inner voice wondered.

"I used to model," Evelyn said. "I was very successful at it."

"I believe that."

"I went by the name Eve back then. It was how Jonathan and I met, at a photo shoot for one of his products. He was smitten with me."

"I believe that, too"

"He took me to dinner that very evening, and so on and so forth."

"Okay."

"Do you know what I mean by 'so on and so forth'?"

"I was told that touching the model is off-limits."

"The rule applies to the photographer, not the client."

"That's convenient."

There was something purring in her laugh, a sensual something, and I wondered how long it had taken her to get the sound just so.

"McKenzie, am I making you nervous?" Evelyn asked.

"Yes, you are."

She laughed some more and squeezed my thigh.

She's playing you, my inner voice said.

You think?

I wonder why.

Sex?

No. Something else.

"Nice to know that a girl still has it after all these years," Evelyn said.

She surprised me by leaving the sofa and taking up residence in a chair on the other side of the coffee table.

"Better?" she asked.

"Only marginally."

"You're cute. Don't worry, McKenzie. I'm taken."

I flashed on Jack McKasy; my inner voice said, *Hmmm.*

"Oh?" I asked aloud.

"My grandson is the only man in my life now."

"Ahhh."

"My daughter-in-law is available, however. She also modeled. She was twenty when she met my son at a photo shoot, family history repeating itself. She's twenty-five now. And very wealthy. One day soon—well, not too soon, I hope—she'll have more money than God. Rich, young, and beautiful. Sounds irresistible, doesn't it?"

"Hard to resist, anyway."

"You said she was pretty."

"Yes, I did."

"You're thinking about sex now, aren't you?"

"What makes you say that?"

"Men—that's all you have on your minds. They say a man thinks about sex every seven seconds."

"Not true. Speaking from experience, when I'm playing hockey or watching a ball game, or reading a book, I can go as many as three or four minutes without thinking about sex."

"I'm impressed."

"It's one of my proudest achievements."

"My son thought about sex constantly. I think now that he might have been addicted to it. McKenzie, I know what he was accused of. I believe those accusations. I didn't at first. I told the detective that they weren't true, but I knew. Jonathan . . . shocked me by some of the things he did. Do I look like someone who's easily shocked?"

"No."

"He shocked me. For a long time I couldn't think about any of this, much less talk about it. Now, so much time has passed . . . Jonny was sick: a terrible thing for a mother to say, I know. I hated him for what he did to those women. He was also my son, so I loved him, too."

"Stuart Mason said you covered up for him."

"Paid to cover up for him. There's a difference. Well, maybe there isn't. It was a difficult situation. I knew Jonathan had to go—from the company, I mean. He couldn't be allowed to run the company, but his name, my husband's name—in the beauty industry, fashion industry, the name is everything. It was the name I was protecting. I didn't kill him, though, or have it done, I don't care what Detective Sergeant Margaret Utley might suspect. I couldn't have done that. No. And Nessa—having seen her, met her, do you think it's possible that lovely young woman could have murdered her husband?"

"You'd be amazed at what people can do given proper motivation."

"You're a cynic, McKenzie."

"Really, I'm not. A cynic is someone with a high opinion of people who becomes disappointed when they don't live up to his expectations. I'm rarely disappointed in people."

"Is that because you have such a low opinion of them to start with?"

"I'm just saying most people are pretty dependable."

"I can use a man like you."

You can?

"In what capacity?" I asked.

"There you go, thinking about sex again."

No, I wasn't. Was I?

"No," Evelyn said. "What I want— My grandson—he's two years old now. McKenzie, I believe the most important things happen to us while we're young. Successes and failures, significant emotional events—they're what turn us into the people we become. What will happen to my grandson, I wonder, if he grows up amidst rumors that his mother or grandmother murdered his father? Do you think that might affect his life? Maybe ruin his life?"

"What do you want me to do?"

"Precious few people know about Jonny, what he did, including the people at the corporation, and I've worked very hard to keep it that way. If it ever got out . . . Yet even so, a lot of people suspect I killed my own son, or Vanessa killed him, or that we conspired to kill him together, take your pick. It's a lie."

"Okay."

"I want you to prove it."

"Me?"

"McKenzie, I want you to clear my name—clear it for my grandson's sake. I'd offer you money, except that you don't do these things for money, do you? No one paid you to find Reney Rogers's killer."

"That's true."

"Well, then?"

"I won't make a promise I can't keep."

"When we spoke on the phone you told me about young Malcolm Harris, about trying to learn who killed his father. What promise did you make him?"

"Only that I would look into it."

"That's acceptable to me. Besides, didn't you say there was a possibility that Jonathan's murder and Frank Harris's murder were connected? Isn't that why we're sitting here?"

"Yes."

Evelyn showed me the palms of her hands.

"Did you know Harris?" I asked.

"I met him once. Him and his wife. At my party. I always throw a New Year's Eve party for our employees, those in our corporate offices. We spoke for ten minutes at the most. I doubt I would have even remembered him except that his wife"— Evelyn's fingers went to her throat—"she was wearing a dress with a very high collar, but I could see the bruises on her neck anyway. He was another man who abused women, wasn't he?"

"That's what the cops think."

Evelyn looked up and away as if she were trying to fix something in her mind. After a moment she shook her head.

"You came here to ask for a favor," she said. "What is it?"

"I need access."

"To . . . ?"

"The Szereto Corporation; your employees. I spoke to Diane Dauria, but I doubt she'll let me interview anyone else over there unless . . ."

"Unless I tell her to."

"Yes, ma'am."

"Help me and I'll help you. It's that simple."

Why do I have the feeling you're making a deal with the devil?

"Okay," I said.

"I'll speak to her, then."

"Speak to whom?" Vanessa Szereto asked. She moved across the room and sat in the chair next to Evelyn's, tucking her feet beneath her the way some women do.

"I was just about to invite McKenzie to the party."

"You should."

"My annual New Year's Eve party tomorrow night for the employees, shareholders, important vendors, anyone connected to the Szereto Corporation. We hold it here. I could introduce you around, make sure people know you have my blessing."

"Blessing for what?" Vanessa asked.

"Frank Harris, one of our employees, was murdered a year ago."

"I remember. Poor man."

"McKenzie thinks his death might be connected to Jonny's murder."

I watched Vanessa's face for some sign of guilty knowledge.

"Do you think that the killer might be at the party?" she asked. "That is so Agatha Christie. Will you unmask him the way it's done at the end of her books?"

Not the reaction you were expecting, my inner voice told me.

"Probably not," I said.

"You should come anyway. It's always a lot of fun. We'll have live music."

"We start early," Evelyn said. "About six o'clock, so employees who have other commitments can make an appearance and then leave. Unfortunately, those who stay—by midnight half of them will be thoroughly intoxicated. I end up sending them home in shuttles I hire for the occasion."

That sounds promising, my inner voice said. *Alcohol and loose lips. On the other hand, Nina won't like it. 'Course, she'll be busy at the club—and it's not like you have to stay until midnight.*

"That's very kind of you," I said.

"I'll count on your presence, then," Evelyn said.

"Please do."

"Nessa, you should wear your strapless red silk. I bet McKenzie would like that very much. Wouldn't you, McKenzie?"

"I'm sure your daughter-in-law would look fine in anything she chooses to wear."

Vanessa chuckled at the compliment. "Don't mind my mother-in-law," she said. "She's been trying to fix me up ever since . . . for a couple of years, now. It annoys her that I've chosen to live the life of a single mom."

"I can take care of the boy," Evelyn said. "At your age you should be taking care of yourself."

"I always have."

"McKenzie. I demand that you dance with Nessa at the party."

"It would be my pleasure," I said.

"And so on and so forth."

"Evelyn," Vanessa said.

"What did I say?" Evelyn asked.

I rose slowly from the sofa.

"The call to Dauria," I said. "You'll make it today?"

"As soon as you leave," Evelyn said.

I retrieved my coat and gave the two women a Minnesota good-bye, meaning I took my own sweet time at the door thanking them for their courtesy and telling them how much I looked forward to seeing them again. It wasn't a matter of being polite. I just didn't want them to know how discombobulated they had both made me feel.

After the final good-bye, I slipped out of the front door. Evelyn called to me.

"Oh, by the way, McKenzie—the party is black tie."

I walked to my Mustang, slid inside, and started it. It had Intelligent Access, meaning its sensors could read the key fob in my pocket from three feet away, allowing me to unlock the door and start the engine with the push of a button. I sat there for a moment and revved the 435-horsepower V-8 engine because I liked the sound it made. Movement caught my eye, and I turned my head toward it. Jack McKasy was leaning against the garage, his arms folded across his chest, and watching me. He was dressed only in his T-shirt and jeans, and I wondered how long he had been standing there and how much longer he could continue standing there before frostbite set in.

I revved the engine again.

Jack didn't budge.

Maybe he's already frozen solid, my inner voice said.

The automatic heater kicked in—I keep it set at sixty-eight degrees—and soon the Mustang was toasty warm. I tapped the link for KBEM-FM radio; Moore by Four spilled out of the speakers, filling the interior with its cover of "Duke's Place."

Still Jack didn't move.

One of you is an idiot, my inner voice said.

I powered down the window.

"Hey, Jack," I said. "Is it true that guys think about sex every seven seconds?"

He dropped his hands and straightened up.

"What's that supposed to mean?" he asked. What he meant was "Are you insulting me?"

"See you tomorrow night," I said.

He didn't like that, either.

I closed the window and drove off.

Fine, you're the idiot, I told myself. But at least you're not the one standing outside in the cold.

SEVEN

Diane Dauria didn't flat-out refuse to see me. Since it was important to Mrs. Szereto that we get together, she said she was hopeful a meeting might be arranged sometime in the future when an opening could be found in her exceedingly busy schedule although, off the top of her head, she couldn't imagine when that might be. Meanwhile, she would make her personal assistant available to me.

I found Candy Groot sitting alone in the employee cafeteria and sipping a beverage from a tall cardboard cup with a plastic lid. It was a spacious room with plenty of natural light, wooden chairs and tables, carpeting on the floor, and several chandeliers. There were so many food stations located along the walls offering such a wide selection of cuisine that it reminded me of a shopping mall food court. All of them were closed by the time I arrived save one that provided gourmet coffee, light sandwiches, pastries, and snacks.

Candy watched me cross the large room to her table. I waved at our surroundings.

"Very plush," I said.

"We care about our employees, although—Mr. McKenzie, I decided I don't care for you."

"I'm sorry to hear that, because I like you just fine."

Candy gestured at a chair opposite her, and I sat.

"You're disruptive," she added.

"Sorry 'bout that."

"Going over Ms. Dauria's head the way you did—that was unforgivable."

"Look at it from my point of view."

"I just don't know what you expect to accomplish."

"I know about Jonny Szereto. I know that he abused women in this company."

Candy's eyes clouded. There was some lightning in them, followed by thunder.

"Now what?" she asked. "You want them to revisit their pain, their embarrassment, their shame?"

"No."

"What do you want from them? What do you want from me?"

The rain fell. Candy closed her eyes against the tears and grimaced as if she hadn't meant to say those words and wished she could take them back. In that moment, I understood why. She had been one of Jonny's victims.

Goddammit, my inner voice shouted.

Candy lowered her head, shook it a few times, and brought it up. She brushed the rain away with the back of her hand.

"I'm sorry," she said. "I don't know why I did that."

Because the pain is always lingering nearby and some jerk just reminded you of it.

"I cried at his funeral, too," Candy said. "Do you believe it?"

I didn't say if I did or didn't.

"What exactly are you looking for?" she asked.

"A connection between Jonny Szereto and Frank Harris."

"Does there have to be a connection? Must one thing be part of the other?"

"No, but . . ."

"But what?"

"If there is a connection—listen, it's not just about Harris's son. Jonny's son, too. Mrs. Szereto is afraid of the harm it might do him growing up not knowing the truth. The rumors he'll hear instead."

"Is that why she's letting you do this?"

"It's why she *asked* me to do this."

"Whether you find out who killed Jonny or not—how much truth do you think Evelyn will tell her grandson?"

"Only what she thinks he'll need to get by."

"A child should never suffer for the sins of his father, yet he will. The children of all those . . . people . . . will pay for it."

"Someone needs to."

"Should I tell you the truth, McKenzie? Should I tell you what Jonny did to me, the filthy names he called me while he was doing it? Forty-two years I've given to this company, to the Szereto family, from the day I graduated college until now. Should I tell you what that meant to him?"

"Why didn't you quit?" I asked. "Why didn't you call the police? Why didn't you burn the sonuvabitch to the ground?"

I regretted the questions immediately. They made it sound as if I blamed her for what had happened. I knew better than that. I dealt with rape victims when I was on the job. I was taught how to behave, how to "chaperone" a victim. I was taught that rape was the ultimate violation, just one step short of homicide. I was taught about the fear, shame, anger, shock, humiliation, and guilt that a woman experiences. I was taught about her inability to sleep and the nightmares she'll have when she does sleep, the erratic mood swings and the feelings of worthlessness that will come later. Yet there I was, piling on.

I reached across the table and took Candy's hand in mine.

"I didn't mean it the way it sounded," I said.

"I ask myself the same questions, though. I tell myself that I didn't want to hurt the company. That I was protecting Mr. Szereto's name, that good and sweet man. Only there's more to it. I never married, McKenzie. Szereto was all that I had or ever will have. I can't even imagine being somewhere else, getting another job at my age. Jonny knew it, too, and used it against me."

"I'm so sorry."

She looked down at my hand holding hers and shook it away.

"Do you want to know something?" she asked. "Every morning when I look into the mirror, I smile because I know that Jonny's dead. I wish I had killed him. I hope you never find the person who did."

"I understand."

"No man understands."

Fair enough.

"I've been instructed to assist you," Candy said. "Tell me how."

"I'd like to speak to your HR guy."

"Woman. Our director of human resources is a woman."

"Okay."

Candy stood.

I stood.

"I've been told to stay with you, not to let you out of my sight for a moment," she said.

"So you can report everything back to Dauria. I get it."

"*And* to Mrs. Szereto."

That, I admit, caught me by surprise. It made me feel like I wasn't trusted.

The director of human resources was sitting behind her desk. Her name was Annabelle Ridlon, and like Candy, she was dressed in a fashionable outfit. I had noticed that all of the employees I saw while making my way to her office were stylishly dressed, mostly in black, and I mentioned it.

"The Szereto Corporation has an image in the beauty industry of chic sophistication, and the president wants the employees to reflect that at all times," Ridlon said. "We do not dress casually here."

"If a woman came in wearing a pair of skintight two-hundred-dollar jeans with strategic rips in them?"

"She'd be sent home."

"It's the way the boss likes it," Candy said.

"Ahh."

"What can I do for you, Mr. McKenzie?" Ridlon asked.

Candy half sat, half leaned against a round table off to the side of Ridlon's desk where she could watch us both at the same time. It was as if she knew something funny was going to happen and wanted to make sure she didn't miss it.

"I would like to read your files," I said.

"No."

"Especially those containing complaints from women—"

"No."

"When Jonathan Szereto Jr. was president."

"Hell, no."

"Mrs. Szereto said—"

"I don't care."

"Ms. Ridlon—"

"Mr. McKenzie. Any HR professional understands how essential it is to uphold employee privacy."

"You're not a doctor. You're not a priest or a lawyer. You're under no obligation to maintain confidentiality."

"Hell I'm not."

"Everything in your files is discoverable."

"Are you a police officer? Member of a government agency? Do you have a warrant?"

"Look—"

"No, you look, McKenzie. What you're asking for—I don't have the time to list the many legal and ethical issues involved. I'm just telling you, you're not going to get it. Not from me."

I gestured toward Candy.

"Ms. Groot will confirm that I am inquiring with the permission of the chairwoman of—"

"If Mrs. Szereto were standing right where you are now, then probably I *would* take the time to list the many legal and moral issues involved, and when I finished I'd bet she'd take my side. In any case, I'm not going to give up the files. I'll make them fire me first."

"May I sit down?"

Ridlon gestured at the chair in front of her desk. I sat.

"I like you a lot more than the last HR director I spoke to," I said.

She shrugged as if she couldn't have cared less.

"May I ask a general, nonspecific question?" I said.

"If you don't mind a general, nonspecific answer."

"I know what happened here while Jonathan Szereto Jr. was president, what he did—"

"None of that is public record."

"And what the former HR director did about it—"

"If Stuart Mason discussed any of these matters with you, he's in violation of the nondisclosure clause in his contract."

"Although I don't know the identity of any of the women involved." I added that last part because Candy was listening and I wanted to make sure she knew that I was on her side. "Now, I need to make some assumptions."

"Assume away," Ridlon said.

"I assume that Frank Harris had access to all of Mason's files, that he knew which women complained of . . . Let's call it harassment for lack of a better word."

"Let's call it rape for accuracy's sake."

"Could he have hurt them the way Jonny hurt them, thinking that since they gave in once they might give in again?"

"If Mr. Harris had abused his position, I've seen no evidence of it; nothing to suggest that he victimized anyone. This isn't a Ma and Pa operation, McKenzie. Mr. Harris was working with assistants, associates, and they tell me that while he often seemed distant, he behaved with the utmost professionalism. That's probably why Ms. Dauria hired him without considering other applicants. Because she knew he could be trusted."

That's right, my inner voice reminded me. *Dauria hired him. 'Course, she didn't know about Jayne at the time.*

Ridlon seemed to read my mind.

"Could he have kept his criminal activities secret—assuming he was involved in criminal activities?" she asked. "I think not. In any case, no one came forward to complain after he died; no one sought redress or threatened to sue the firm."

"Perhaps his victims were embarrassed."

Ridlon regarded me for a few beats with such intensity that I knew she was trying to determine what kind of man I was.

"I couldn't say," she said. "In any case, our security protocols have been updated since Ms. Dauria took over. Now all employees who use company computers or phones, or GPS-enabled company cars, are subjected to technological surveillance. We can track the specific content employees produce at their workstation down to the individual keystrokes. In addition, we've added social media clauses to employee contracts that allow us to monitor their personal Web sites, Facebook pages, and Twitter accounts. We do this to root out employees involved in industrial spying and corporate espionage. One woman—we had to let her go when she posted on her Facebook page that she was thrilled to be collaborating on a special project. She said she couldn't reveal what she was working on, but wrote 'Watch out, Gillette.' In essence, she announced to the world that the Szereto Corporation was involved in designing the next generation of women's razors."

"I would never have guessed that."

"In her personal information she listed her specific credentials and for whom she worked. Add that to her post—granted, the privacy settings on her account limited her remarks to only her friends, about two hundred I think it was. But McKenzie, if we're monitoring our employees' activities, what's to stop our competitors from doing the same? I would wager that nearly everyone in the beauty industry has an organized system for collecting information on their rivals. They'd be foolish not to."

"What does this have to do with anything?"

"We're always searching for communications that undermine the company's business strategies and public image, but we see everything. If Mr. Harris had abused his position, someone would have complained, even if it was only to her girlfriend on Twitter—and we would have known."

"Okay."

"Okay?"

"I'd be happy to give you twenty minutes on paranoid, power-happy employers versus the individual employee's right to privacy, but I doubt you'd want to hear it."

"Every employee of the Szereto Corporation is an ambassador for the Szereto Corporation."

"Yeah, well, I have a feeling you've given me all the help you're going to."

"Funny, I wasn't trying to help you at all."

I stood. Ridlon stood. I noticed for the first time that she was taller than I was by about three inches. I offered my hand. She shook it.

"Believe it or not, I'm grateful for your time."

"In that case, as a wise man once said, don't go away mad . . ."

"Just go away," Candy Groot said.

Candy walked me to the elevator.

"What's next?" she asked.

"I think I've spread as much joy and sunshine around here as I can for now."

"Meaning?"

"Meaning I'm leaving."

"Good."

"Tell Ms. Dauria that I still need to speak with her."

"Why?"

Because, my inner voice told me. *It isn't only Szereto that connects Frank Harris and Jonny. It's her.*

The elevator doors opened, and I stepped inside.

"I'm sorry for your troubles," I said. "I really am."

Candy didn't answer. Instead, as the doors closed, I saw her take up her cell phone and start making a call.

Not long ago, something called the American Highway Users Alliance ranked the fifty worst traffic bottlenecks in the country. Minnesotans were outraged—outraged!—that we didn't make the cut. How could there be a worse snarl than the one that occurred when three lanes of westbound I-394 traffic were reduced to one lane so it could merge with three lanes of southbound I-94 traffic as it slowed to 35 mph and passed through the Lowry Hill Tunnel? At the best of times with weather not a factor, it was a ten-minute delay. At drive time with rain or snow added to the equation, it could take an hour or more. And it was snowing.

I joined the long, slow crawl back into Minneapolis almost immediately after I left the Szereto parking lot, KBEM-FM turned up loud, the windshield wipers keeping time. The same vehicles in front and behind the Mustang stayed with me for several miles. Because I hadn't expected the traffic to change, it wasn't until I put the bottleneck behind me and managed to merge with the vehicles heading north on 35W that I realized I was being followed.

A black Acura.

Staying close, accelerating and slowing as I accelerated and slowed.

I shifted lanes.

It shifted with me.

Who? my inner voice asked. *Why?*

The freeway lights were already on; at that time of year in Minnesota, night falls like a hammer around 5:00 P.M. Yet I couldn't make out the driver's face in the rearview. My first thought—Jack McKasy. My second—whoever Candy Groot called while I was boarding the elevator.

I flashed on what Detective Utley had told me earlier—her only reliable witness was sure the shotgun blast that killed Jonathan Szereto Jr. had come from inside a dark-colored Toyota. Yet it could have been an Acura, I told myself. Ever since the automotive industry decided that mpg was more important than character, most cars were given nearly indistinguishable aerodynamic designs. Since this one sped through a red light to remain on my rear bumper when I took the Washington Street exit . . .

No, no, no, my inner voice chanted. *You're being paranoid. You haven't done anything worth getting shot over. Yet.*

I moved to the right-hand lane.

The Acura stayed with me.

I slowed for a stoplight.

The Acura twisted into the left-hand lane and halted with a jerk next to me.

Its passenger window started to power down.

I didn't linger long enough to see who was behind the window or to get a good look at the driver. Instead, I threw the Mustang into reverse and stomped on the accelerator.

Tires spun on the freshly fallen snow, caught, and squealed as the Mustang leapt backward.

I stopped twenty feet behind the Acura and waited.

Nothing happened.

There were no flashes of gunfire. No telltale popping sounds. Although the Acura did engage its turn signal.

I watched carefully, the wipers counting the seconds like a metronome.

When the light finally changed, the Acura hung a left and drove onto the freeway entrance ramp, heading back in the direction it had come.

Behind me, someone tapped his horn. I put the Mustang into a forward gear and drove toward my condominium.

The coverage in the underground garage where I parked was iffy. It wasn't until I was on the elevator heading up to the seventh floor that I was able to call Detective Downing.

"What?" he wanted to know.

"Could you quick run a license plate for me?"

"I was just about to go home."

"It's important."

"Why?"

"It belongs to a black Acura that was following me. I'm thinking it might have been the same car that was used in the Jonathan Szereto shooting."

"You're kidding, right?"

"No."

"An Acura isn't a Toyota."

"They look alike."

"They do not."

"In the dark? To a guy who doesn't know cars?"

Downing hesitated for a few beats and said, "I'm beginning to wonder if I should have checked your references more thoroughly."

"I'm neither paranoid nor delusional as far as I know."

"Uh-huh. I'll get back to you."

He did, fifteen minutes later. I was in the condo and sucking on the business end of a Summit Ale when he called.

"The Acura belongs to Jerome Geddings," Downing said. He recited a street address.

"Why does that name sound familiar?" I asked.

"It's in my files. Geddings is a member of the New Brighton Hotdish. He was one of them that alibied Jayne Harris on the night her husband was stabbed."

"My, my, my."

"McKenzie, what does this mean?"

"I have no idea, but the coincidences—they're starting to pile up."

I went to my notes, partly to confirm what Downing had told me. Jerome Geddings was indeed a founding member of the New Brighton Hotdish and had signed a statement swearing for the record that he was among those who were with Jayne when Frank Harris was attacked. I searched a couple of social media sites for information. A business profile announced that he worked quality assurance for a tech firm in Apple Valley. That didn't sound like a job where you could just get up in the middle of a shift and wander off. Even if he could—Apple Valley was located on the other side of St. Paul, about as far away from St. Louis Park as you could get and still be in the Twin Cities. Fact remained, though, he did follow me. Why? How would he even know who I was? Candy Groot was on her phone when I left the Szereto offices—did she call him? Why, again? She had no connection to the Hotdish, did she? Maybe she called Diane

Dauria, and Dauria called Geddings and told him to do what? Scare me? Shoot me? Find out where I lived? I found myself humming an old Michel Legrand song:

... like a circle in a spiral, like a wheel within a wheel,
never ending or beginning on an ever-spinning reel ...

The Hotdish was the obvious common denominator, so I returned to Downing's list of witnesses who had vouched for Jayne Harris and checked them out one at a time. Like many people these days, they had all posted a frightening amount of private information on Web sites such as Facebook and Linked-In. With the notable exception of a few interests and hobbies like caving and paranormal investigations, they all seemed pretty ordinary to me, with middle- to upper-middle-class occupations—account supervisor, IT development manager, graphic designer, RN at Allied Hospitals and Clinics, adult education management professional, senior data architect, financial analyst—two divorces, and not a single arrest among them. Obviously they knew Frank Harris, yet none of them seemed connected to Jonathan Szereto Jr. except Dauria.

One name stood out. Katherine Meyer, the person Dauria said was the chief instigator of the group. She labeled herself as a "marketing and advertising consultant—poet."

I glanced at my watch—6:57. Nina was at the club; I didn't expect to see her until much later tonight. God knew where Erica was; she had been purposely vague about where she was going and with whom starting when she turned eighteen. The girl valued her independence.

I made a call. Katherine Meyer answered on the third ring.

"Mrs. Meyer," I said. "My name is McKenzie."

"Call me Katie. I wondered if I was going to hear from you."

"News travels fast in the New Brighton Hotdish."

"We're a close-knit group."

"I'm not disturbing your dinner, am I?" It's a question that most Minnesotans ask when making phone calls between 5:00 and 7:00 P.M.

"Not at all." Katie spoke so quickly that her sentences sounded like one long word. "I was just about to run over to Cub. I am so low on flour and sugar. I'm hosting a New Year's Eve party tomorrow night, and oh my God, so much to do."

"I'm wondering if you could spare a few minutes to talk to me?"

"To talk about Frank Harris? Yes, yes, I know, I know. My son, Critter? He said he met you at Jayne's house, and Jaynie and I had the most delightful conversation, talked for it seemed like hours and hours. Kids today, all they do is text, but when I was young, it was like I had a phone glued to my ear. My father was always yelling at me to hang up. Afraid he'd miss an important call. Now everyone has their own private phones. Even children. First and second graders. If you don't return a text or a missed call in like five minutes, oh my God, people wonder if something terrible has happened. Either that or they think you're snubbing them. It's funny how things change from generation to generation, don't you think?"

"Mrs. Meyer. Katie—"

"I don't have time to talk, McKenzie. I really don't. I have so much shopping to do, and then I have to bake. Cakes and pies. Pillsbury, you know how it has an annual bake-off which pays a million dollars to whoever comes up with the best dessert? I thought I'd give the winning recipe a try. Might not be worth a million, though. We'll see. I'll settle for half a million."

Katie chuckled at her joke, but only for a moment.

"But you want to talk. Okay . . . umm . . . Diane said you were over to Szereto. Was that because it was the last place where they saw Frank alive? Like on the TV? 'Course, he was alive when they found him in the park, so . . . What a world. Diane—well, you can't go by her. That woman. I love her to pieces. Smart, oh my God, only she has no sense of humor that I've ever seen. She's so pretty and thin I told her once she must have a painting hidden in her attic but she. Didn't. Get it. You have to explain jokes to her. Just ruins them. You want to talk, though. Only not over the phone like we're kids—you hang up first, no you. Umm. Oh, I know. Tomorrow. How 'bout—I'm meeting a client at eight thirty. I'm a freelance writer. Well, writer, creative director, account executive, producer, whatever you need. How 'bout—there's a coffeehouse on Silver Lake Road? Do you know New Brighton? The Bru House. North of 694. East side of the road. You can't miss it. They sell a frittata muffin, oh my God. Does ten thirty work for you? In the morning, I mean? I doubt my meeting will last that long; the client wants to shut up shop at noon, give his employees a jump on the holiday, only you never know, do you?"

"Ten thirty would be great."

"Okay, okay. I'd have you over to the house, but you might be a homicidal maniac. Am I right?"

"Well, no—"

"I'm kidding. Besides, the place is a mess. I haven't even started cleaning yet. Do you think I'm going to get any help from my husband? From Critter? I can't talk now. I'm already halfway out the door. Okay, okay. Tomorrow then. Ten thirty, right? Good-bye, McKenzie."

I had done very little talking, yet I felt out of breath when the call ended. I had learned one thing, though, without asking—everyone in the Hotdish seemed to know who I was and what I was doing.

Maybe Geddings was acting on his own, my inner voice suggested.

No, I told myself. He might have known my name, but not what car I drove.

Unless Critter told him.

Hey, that's right. The kid took a picture with his phone. Still . . .

Erica opened the door, closed it, and walked past me without saying a word.

"A pleasant good evening to you, too," I said.

"McKenzie"—she slumped in a chair without taking off her coat—"I'm confused."

"About what?"

"About men."

"Isn't this a conversation you should be having with your mother?"

"Have you met Robin? You haven't, have you? He is so cute. Waitresses fawn over him and I'm sitting right there, that's how cute. He's funny, too. And you don't get into the engineering department at Notre Dame without being smart. Something else. He likes me. He really likes me, I can tell."

"Okay."

"Meanwhile, Malcolm is a screwup even during the best of times. I'm just saying."

"Okay."

"I don't understand love."

"Join the club."

"The guy Karen is marrying, what a jerk. Why would you marry someone you knew was a jerk? Why would you even go out with him?"

"She probably doesn't see him that way."

"Why doesn't she? She's graduating in the top ten percent of her class."

"Karen or you?"

"Both of us. What does that have to do with anything?"

"The heart—"

"Don't. Okay? Shut up about the heart. The heart is the least reliable organ in the human body. McKenzie—you weren't always rich."

"No. I was a blue-collar kid from St. Paul all the way down to my white socks."

"You wore white socks?"

"It's a metaphor."

"Would you have hooked up with Mom if she weren't well-off?"

"Of course. Have you *seen* your mother?"

"Would she have hooked up with you if you weren't a millionaire?"

"I don't think she knew I was rich when she pushed that guy down the stairs."

"Is that really a true story?"

"Yep. I was chasing a guy out of the old Minnesota Club, and his partner was on the landing above me. When he tried to interfere, your mother gave him a hip-check, and down the stairs he rolled. That's when I knew she was the girl for me."

"When did she know you were the guy for her?"

"I have no idea. I'm not even sure I am the right guy. Could be she's just letting me hang around until the real thing comes along."

Erica stared at me as if she were wondering if I actually believed that.

"You make her laugh," she said. "I've known her fifteen years longer than you have, and during that time she hardly ever laughed."

"Is that because I'm humorous or peculiar?"

"Heck if I know." She stood. "Robin makes me laugh. All the time. So does Malcolm. 'Course, Malcolm—he's just a friend. I couldn't even think of dating him while I was dating Robin. That would be . . . I don't know."

Erica retreated toward her bedroom.

"Gawd!" she said.

EIGHT

So far it had been one of the softest winters on record, with temperatures as high as twenty degrees above average. We had come to within an inch of having a brown Christmas. It snowed again the following day, but instead of the foot we were promised, the Twin Cities was dusted with only three inches—try using that as an excuse for being late to work. Yesterday's snowfall? Barely enough to pretty up what was already on the ground. The street crews hadn't even bothered to plow it.

I found a spot in the parking lot in front of the Bru House and walked inside. Like just about every other retail business, the place had been decked out for Christmas. Friendly conversations, soft music, and the aroma of coffee and fresh bakery greeted me at the door.

"McKenzie?" a woman said. She was wearing black-rimmed glasses.

"Yes."

"I knew it was you. Critter said you were tall, and Jayne Harris said you were handsome, so I knew it had to be you. Jayne said you look like Bradley Cooper the actor, but she exaggerates. Should we sit over here by the window? Oh, wait. You haven't ordered yet. Why don't you get your coffee and I'll guard the table. Sometimes this place gets awfully crowded."

"Can I get you anything?"

"I have a cup. Thanks for offering, though. It was very kind of you. I'll be right over here. By the window. See?"

The table had two chairs and a view of the parking lot and Silver Lake Road beyond. It was littered with a large cardboard coffee cup with lid, a paper plate holding half a muffin, a well-scribbled legal pad, and an open laptop. Five minutes later, I sat across from the woman. The legal pad and computer had been placed into a shoulder bag, and the muffin had been consumed, but the cup remained. I extended my hand.

"McKenzie," I said.

"Katie Meyer. Oh my God, I didn't say before. You probably thought I was this crazy person accosting strange men in coffeehouses."

"I really didn't."

Her coat was hanging off the back of her chair, and she was wearing a powder blue dress shirt with a button-down collar and a light brown cardigan with tiny dark blue dots. The sweater seemed distressed to me, with a couple of unraveled knits, zigzagging threads, and some pilling, and I thought, Is that a thing now? Then I realized. "Katie," I said. "Your sweater is inside out."

"Oh my God." She immediately pulled it off and started rearranging it. "You must think I'm such a ditz. My client—I wore it like this during our meeting. 'Course, we've worked together many times over the years. He knows me. Probably telling everyone—that Katie . . ."

She put the sweater back on, this time right side out.

"Better?" she said.

Five foot two, eyes of blue—the lyric to the old song came to me as I regarded her over the brim of my coffee cup—with a figure the fashion police labeled petite; I doubted she weighed a hundred pounds. Add that to her effervescent personality and cheerful smile—I was convinced she was still carded in every club and bar she walked into. I told her so.

"At my age?" she said. "Besides, I don't hang out in bars anymore, although . . ." She leaned across the table. "This one time I went into a bicycle shop because I was buying a helmet for Critter, these two college boys, they started hitting on me, telling me I should join them on this tour, this *overnight* bike trip." Katie brought her hand to her mouth. "I was old enough to be their mother." She dropped her hand. "Oh my God, don't ever tell anyone I told you that."

"Why not? It's a pretty good story."

"People will think I was milfing."

"Milfing?"

"You know what a MILF is?"

"I hardly think . . ."

The light in her eyes went out just like that. The blue became dark and cold, and Katie said, "People blame women for all kinds of things that are not their fault."

I didn't know what she was thinking, and I didn't ask.

"I'll keep your secret," I said.

"Promise me."

"I promise."

And the light returned.

"Besides, women of a certain age should only be involved with men of a certain age," Katie said. "Don't you think?"

"Life is short. I'm not sure you shouldn't take what you can get."

"It's all right for men to say that, only society holds women to a different standard, always has, always will."

"I know a young woman who would be happy to tell you where society can go in no uncertain terms."

"Have you met Sloane Dauria?"

"I was thinking of someone else, but based on what her mother told me, yes, Sloane, too."

"Wonderful girl and a real beauty. Super serious, though. Like her mother. Oh my God."

Katie glanced around the room, adjusted her glasses, and leaned forward again.

"I feel so wicked."

"Why?"

"People know me here. They know I'm a happily married woman with two kids—one of them in college no less. Yet here I am having coffee in an out-of-the-way coffeehouse with a man. It just makes me feel so—'course, my husband knows I'm here. You know what he said when I told him I was going to meet a strange man that Jayne said looks like Bradley Cooper in a coffeehouse? He said, better that than a motel. I remember when he used to be romantic. We're all so old now. Although I don't feel old. Do you feel old?"

"Sometimes."

"I bet we're the same age, too."

"Except you don't look it. You look like you're a graduate student, which is probably what those kids in the bike shop thought, not that you're a MILF."

Katie stared at me for a few beats.

"You're trying to be nice," she said. "Well, thank you."

"You're welcome."

"About Frank—Frank Harris. Wasn't that terrible? A terrible thing. And now you're trying to help Malcolm and Jaynie, too, I guess. That's what we're going to talk about, isn't it?"

"Yes."

"The police"—her eyes clouded again—"have done nothing."

"They've tried."

Katie stared at me as if she were debating whether to argue about it. Her eyes brightened; she lowered her head so she was looking at me over the top of her glasses and spoke in a Yoda voice. *"Do. Or do not. There is no try."* Her hand went to her mouth, and she laughed behind it. "Oh my God—where did that come from? I don't even like those movies. I mean, they're okay . . ."

This is one emotional woman, my inner voice said.

"Diane Dauria told me that you founded the New Brighton Hotdish," I said.

"Oh, that's just silly. How can one person found a club?"

"Was it your idea?"

"Noooooah. What happened—I'm a freelance writer, mostly advertising, but some journalism, too. I worked at Carmichael Lynch, Campbell Mithun, but when Critter was born—do you know how Critter got his name?"

"Jayne Harris told me."

"Critterfur—that still cracks me up. Anyway, when Chris was born I decided to go freelance so I could stay home with the youngsters. Agency work—the hours can be so brutal, no kidding—and back then, freelance, if you had a track record, experience working in the agencies, you could do pretty well. I did. 'Course now, the economy, the agencies downsizing, laying off staff, everyone that used to be a copywriter, art director, suddenly they're working freelance out of necessity, which has flooded the market, making it tougher to earn a living. Anyway . . ."

Katie adjusted her glasses and took a sip from the cardboard cup.

"Anyway, I had pretty flexible hours while the kids were growing up, so I would go to the ballpark early, wherever we were playing that week, and scope out a picnic table or bring one of my own and set up something for the players, snacks and juice boxes, that sort of thing. They were fourteen years old that final season, thirteen and fourteen, freshmen in high school. Now look at them. College juniors every one, scattered hither and yon. Only the parents—it started getting pretty elaborate, especially that last year. We started having dinners at the ball-parks, the other parents bringing all kinds of dishes, which was way better than doing fast food because that's what happened, the games starting at six and everyone rushing to get there after work and then ending after seven, seven thirty, and us running out to get burgers or tacos or something because it was too late to cook a decent meal. We kept at it even after the season ended, the championship season, because we liked each other and the food was really good, some of the members showing off, always trying to outdo each other and the rest of us—McKenzie, you can't bring a bag of tortilla chips and a jar of salsa when some-one is bringing fifteen pounds of baby-back ribs and someone else has a slow cooker filled with jambalaya."

She paused to take a deep breath and another sip of coffee. "What do you want to know?"

"The truth about Frank and Jayne Harris."

"You want to know the truth?"

"The group being so close for so long, you must know each other's secrets."

"The truth and secrets, too? McKenzie, I'm pretty naïve when to comes to stuff like that. I always have been. When I was a sophomore in college, well, sophomore and the beginning of my junior year, I dated a grad student who was studying child psychology, and I loved him. Everybody loved him. He was kind and generous and caring, and he made me laugh right up until he was arrested for—he was a pedophile, McKenzie. He abused the kids he worked with while getting his degree, he had child pornography in his apartment, and I didn't know. I spent a lot of time in that apartment, McKenzie. I didn't see anything, I didn't—even today, we're talking twenty-five years later, and I still don't believe it. I mean I believe it—the evidence was pretty overwhelming, but I still wonder—how come I didn't know? Now you're asking about Frank and Jaynie. I saw the bruises, I saw the cast on Jayne's arm, but she and Frank said they were accidents, and I believed them just like I believed my boyfriend. Why wouldn't I?"

"What about the others?"

"The members of Hotdish that weren't as dumb as I was? Whatever they thought they kept to themselves. Or at least they kept it from me."

"I find that hard to believe."

"So do I. Why are men so cruel?"

I don't think she expected a reply, so I didn't offer one. I didn't have a satisfying answer anyway.

She removed her glasses and became still, her eyes locked on her hands, her hands wrapped around the coffee cup, thinking thoughts that twisted her mouth into a kind of angry pout. I gave her as much privacy as I could, turning my attention to the window. Traffic on Silver Lake Road was light. I noticed a black Acura drive past. I didn't give it much thought until it cruised by a second time and pulled in to the Bru House lot. I was able to read the license plate, confirming that it was the same car that had followed me the evening before. I told myself it would be nice to have a gun and then dismissed the notion. Too many people carry guns these days, including me.

The Acura parked at a diagonal in the only empty slot on the side of the building. I could see its passenger-side taillight from where I sat but nothing else, which meant the driver shouldn't be able to see me; wouldn't see me actually leaving the coffeehouse until I stepped into the lot and walked to my car. I waited for someone to enter the building, yet no one did.

Katie's head came up; she put her black-rimmed glasses back on. For a moment she actually looked her age.

"I'm sorry," she said.

"S'okay."

"I don't know why I've been so emotional lately. The holidays, I guess. Throwing a New Year's Eve party, what was I thinking? But no. No, no. You know what? It's you, McKenzie. You're the reason I'm upset, dredging up painful stuff like you are. Jayne's upset, too. She wishes you would stop what you're doing. So does Diane. As for Malcolm, poor Malcolm—what happened to his father, I can see how that might be upsetting, and not knowing why it happened . . . it must be so very hard for him. I saw him a few times during summer vacation, gave him a big hug. He seemed to be handling it better than he did when it first happened; he was smiling a lot and joking around with Critter and the other boys. Now, though . . . Christmas is what does it. For some people it's the most depressing time of year. More people kill themselves during the holidays than at any other time, did you know that?"

"Actually, that's not true."

"It isn't?"

"People are offered some protection around Christmas by the proximity of their families, and also it's winter, and no matter how hard the winter, people tell themselves things will get better. I call it the promise of spring. When spring comes along, though, and people with suicidal thoughts see that nothing has changed . . ."

"More people commit suicide in the spring?"

"Yes."

"How do you know this?"

"I used to be a police officer. I used to respond to a lot of those kinds of calls."

"That must have been hard."

"It was."

Katie stared for a few beats as if she were trying to reconcile that version of me with the person sitting across from her.

"What were we talking about?" she asked.

"You're upset."

"Yes, I am, and usually I'm not, upset I mean. Usually I'm the opposite of upset. My friends, my family, they like to make fun of me because they say I'm so cheerful all the time. It's very annoying. I can be earthy when I want to, really."

"Earthy?"

Katie leaned in close, said, "I use the F-word all the time," and nodded her head solemnly.

"I'd love to read your poetry sometime," I said.

"Dark, dark stuff," she said. "Makes Sylvia Plath look like Shel Silverstein." She pulled her head back and laughed. "No, it doesn't. What do I have to be dark about?"

"Jayne Harris," I said. "I can understand her being upset, dredging up bad memories near the anniversary of her husband's murder, as you said, although—she did seem to appreciate that I was trying to help her son. Diane Dauria, though, has me baffled. Why does she care if I try to find out who killed Frank?"

"I don't know. Maybe she did it and she's 'fraid of getting caught, have you ever thought of that?"

"Yes, I have."

An expression of horror crossed Katie's face.

"Oh my God, McKenzie, how can you think that? Diane is just the nicest person ever, even if she is the most serious. Besides, she wasn't here when it happened. She was in Chicago. The police said."

"You're the one who brought it up."

"I was kidding. I was—I'm sorry. I'm really sorry. It isn't something you should joke about, is it?"

Pretty much what Dauria said, my inner voice reminded me.

"The rest of Hotdish—what are they saying about it?" I asked.

"I doubt most of them know what's going on. Heck, I don't even know what's going on. Probably it'll come up tonight at the party, but . . . We're friends, McKenzie, except it's not like we live in each other's pockets. It's a social thing, after all. Some of the families have dropped out over the years, a couple of others have joined in; friends of friends. Dwayne Phillips, he and his son, Jalen—they called him Philly—they were members, but then they quit right after the championship party. I heard they moved to New Ulm a couple of weeks after the game; didn't even bother to say good-bye. Kinda sad. 'Course, they were African Americans. Philly was the only person of color on the team. Could've been the only family of color in New Brighton for all I know; we're not nearly as diverse as we could be. They might have been uncomfortable around us. I liked them, though. Liked them a lot. Nice people. And the others. Sometimes everyone shows up at the monthly Hotdish, sometimes it's only a couple of families, depending on what's going on. We all have our own lives to live is what I'm trying to tell you. People still care about what happened to Frank, don't get me wrong. Only it's starting to be a long time ago and they don't care as much."

"Then how do you explain the fact that I'm being followed by members of your Hotdish?"

Katie blinked at me from behind her glasses.

"No," she said. "What? Being followed?"

"Ever since I took the case."

"That's, that's—why?"

"You tell me."

"McKenzie, I told you that Jayne and Diane are upset, and so am I, but we all want to see Frank's killer arrested."

Katie's expression and body language suggested that she was genuinely shocked by my announcement. Either that or she was the best actress I've come across in a long while. Because I wasn't a hundred percent sure either way, I stood up.

"Wait here," I said.

"McKenzie . . ."

I slipped on my jacket but did not zipper it.

"Don't move," I said. "I'll be right back."

I left the table and went out the front door of the coffeehouse, staying close to the wall; Katie watched me through the window, a puzzled expression on her face. I circled around the far side of the building, keeping it between the Acura and me. I moved cautiously past the drive-thru and came up on the black vehicle from its side, hoping the driver wasn't letting his attention wander, that his eyes were firmly fixed on the front of the Bru House. I managed to get next to the car without him noticing.

I yanked open the driver's door. His head pivoted toward me. Not Jerome Geddings, I told myself. A young man instead. College age. An expression of alarm on his face.

Geddings's son, my inner voice announced, *driving the old man's car.*

I said it aloud. "Does your father know what you're doing?"

"What are you doing?" he wanted to know.

I grabbed his arm and pulled him out from behind the steering wheel.

"Who are you?" he asked.

"You know who I am."

"I wasn't doing anything. I was just sitting here. You have no right."

"Shut up."

I pulled him away from the vehicle, hip-checked the door closed, and shoved him toward the Bru House.

"Who do you think you are?" he said. "You can't do this." He turned toward me. I noticed he was favoring his right knee. "I'll call the police."

I gave him the look, the one that dared him, just dared him, to do something stupid.

"I'm not afraid of you," he said, although I noticed he didn't raise his hands like he wanted to make a fight of it.

"You want to talk to the cops?" I slipped the cell from my jacket pocket. "Fine, let's talk to the cops."

"Wait," he said. "What are you doing?"

"Calling the police."

"Wait a sec."

"Make up your mind."

"McKenzie . . ."

"See, you do know who I am." I moved him along. "Come on. There's someone I want you to meet."

I took the kid's arm when we entered the coffeehouse, spun him until he was facing Katie, and gave him another shove. He nearly fell in the woman's lap but caught himself in time. Katie adjusted her glasses as she stared at him.

"Steven?" she asked

"Mrs. Meyer," he said. "I wasn't doing anything."

"He was waiting for me in the parking lot," I said. "I caught him following me yesterday, too."

Geddings's eyes darted from me to Katie as if he wanted to deny it but was afraid of being caught lying in front of her.

"Steven, is this true?" Katie said.

"You know it's true," I told her. I reclaimed my chair. "How else would he know to come here unless you told him?"

"I didn't—"

I held up a finger.

"Or someone else in the Hotdish told him," I said. "Jayne Harris knew you were meeting me. How 'bout Diane Dauria?"

"I don't know what to say," Katie told me.

"How 'bout you, kid? What do you have to say?"

"Nothing."

"Steven," Katie said.

"I was just sitting in the car waiting for my friends. We come here for coffee, you know that. It's our hangout."

"That's true, McKenzie. Critter comes here all the time, too."

"Were you here when Critter got into a fight with Malcolm Harris?" I asked.

"Chris and Malcolm were fighting?" Katie said. "Why?"

"Mrs. Meyer . . ."

"The young woman who was with Malcolm," I said. "Were you the one she punched and then kicked in the knee?"

Geddings's fingers flew to a spot just to the left of his chin where I was sure the blow must have landed.

"She caught me by surprise," he said.

That's our girl, my inner voice said.

"Why were Chris and Malcolm fighting?" Katie asked.

"I don't know."

"Yes, you do," I said.

"I really don't," Geddings said. "Mrs. Meyer, honestly. You'll have to ask Critter."

"Why were you following me?" I asked.

"I wasn't."

"You knew my name."

"I was guessing."

I turned toward the woman. "See what I have to deal with?" I said.

"Leave me alone," Geddings said.

"You were following me," I said.

"Why would I?"

"Because someone told you to. Who? Was it Diane Dauria?"

"This is nuts,"

"What does she want to know?"

"You're crazy."

I asked Katie, "Do you think I'm crazy?"

"I don't know what to think."

"Fair enough."

"Can I go now?" Geddings asked.

What was I going to do, slap him around? Waterboard him until he told me what I wanted to hear?

"Beat it," I said.

Katie reached out and took Geddings by the wrist.

"How's your mother?" she asked. "How's her cold?"

"Better. She said she'll be at the party tonight for sure."

"Tell her I'm going to call later."

Geddings saw something in her expression that made him swallow hard.

"Yes, ma'am," he said. He left in a hurry.

"Nice boy," Katie said.

"I'll have to take your word for that."

"You didn't need to be so mean."

"I get cranky when people lie to my face."

"He said he wasn't following you. He said he was here to meet his friends."

"You believed him?"

"I've known Steven since he was twelve years old. Yes, I believe him."

"If he was waiting for his friends, why did he just leave?"

I threw a thumb at the window. Katie adjusted her glasses yet again as she gazed out just in time to see the Acura pull onto Silver Lake Road and drive off.

"You frightened him," she said.

"He frightened me."

"I don't understand anything that's going on."

"I'm going to take your word for that, too. I'm doing it for the worst possible reason, though."

"What's that?"

"Because I think you're adorable and I'm sexist enough to let it make a difference."

Katie's hand flew to her mouth.

"But only to a point," I added.

"Oh my God," she said. "You know what? I think Jayne is right. You do look a little like Bradley Cooper."

I started the Mustang, told my onboard computer to call Erica, and canceled the call when I remembered she rarely answers her phone. Instead, I pulled out my own phone and sent a text: *I want to meet with Malcolm. Arrange it.*

Malcolm and Erica were sitting opposite each other on stools at the island in the kitchen area when I returned to the condominium. There was a box of vanilla wafers and a plastic tub of cake frosting between them. I watched as they took turns dipping wafers into the frosting, sliding them into their mouths, and chasing them with swigs from the same two-liter bottle of orange pop, apparently rendered germ-free by—was it love? Say it isn't so, I told myself.

"Seriously?" I said.

"Live in a college dorm for a while, this becomes a delicacy," Erica said. "Try it."

I did, and thought, This is pretty good.

Stop it! my inner voice said. *Don't encourage them.*

"Not particularly nutritious, though," I said aloud.

"Sometimes I do Nutella with apple slices," Erica said.

"Much better."

"What do you want to talk about?" Malcolm asked. "Rickie said you wanted to talk."

"I met a friend of yours today."

"Who?"

"Steve Geddings."

"Steven?"

I gestured at Erica to make sure I had her attention.

"That's the name of the guy you punched in the face the other day," I said. "If you see him again, watch yourself. He hasn't gotten past it."

"That's because I'm a girl."

"What did Steven want?" Malcolm asked.

"He didn't say," I told him.

"I don't understand."

"He's been following me."

"Why?"

"I don't know why. He followed me yesterday and again today when I went to see Katie Meyer."

"You spoke to Mrs. Meyer?"

"We had coffee at the Bru House. I like her very much. She seems to genuinely care about her friends. That, apparently, includes you."

"What did she say?"

"That's not terribly important."

"Yes, it is."

"What's important—why is Geddings following me?"

"How should I know?"

"You and I aren't going to get along very well if you keep this up."

Malcolm slipped quickly off his stool and turned toward me. "Are you calling me a liar?" he asked.

"Let me guess. You're outraged by the allegation."

His fists clenched, unclenched, and clenched some more.

"Mal," Erica said. "McKenzie's trying to help you."

"I really am," I said. "I'll keep at it, too, if you would just explain why so many people don't want me to help you."

"Who?" Malcolm asked. "Who doesn't want you to help?"

"Apparently, Critter and Steven Geddings for a start. Tell me about the fight again."

"I told you—that has nothing to do with my father."

"The fight at the Bru House. What about the one before that?"

"Before that?"

"Someone punched Critter," I said. "Punched him several times. His nose was swollen, and his lip was bruised."

"I don't know anything about that."

"When we met, your knuckles were scraped and bloody."

"I hit a wall."

"Because you were angry with your mother?"

"Yes."

"Because she said to get over what happened to your father?"

"Yes. McKenzie, I mean it. This thing with Critter has nothing to do with my father."

"What does it have to do with?"

"It's personal."

"Then why is Geddings following *me*?"

"I don't know." Malcom thought about it, then spoke in the form of a question. "Maybe they're hoping you'll lead them to me?"

"Really? They're searching for you? Are you that hard to find?"

"I don't know."

"Why would they be looking for you?"

"I don't know. I keep telling you. I don't know why they're following you. It doesn't make sense to me."

"Tell me about your mother."

"What about her?"

"She wants me to stop trying to help you, too."

"I know. She doesn't think any good will come of it, and . . . and she said it makes her sad."

"Why?"

"I heard the stories, McKenzie, about my father hitting my mom. She never told me, but I heard. Sometimes I think that's all he left behind when he died, the stories."

"What about Dauria?"

That made him pause.

"Diane?" he said.

Diane? my inner voice repeated.

"She also made it clear I should go away," I said.

"Why would she care?"

"I don't know. Why would she care?"

The look in his eyes suggested that he didn't have a clue.

"Sit down," I told him. "Relax."

Malcolm returned to his spot at the island. Erica passed him the box of vanilla wafers. He took one, but not to eat. It was just something to hold.

"Something else you should know." I took the stool next to Erica. "There's a possibility that your father's murder is connected to a second killing."

Malcolm froze in place, not moving a muscle except for what was required to snap the cookie in half. His eyes grew wide, and his voice climbed two octaves.

"What killing?" he asked.

"A couple of years ago—"

"Where?"

Erica reached across the table and touched his hand. He pulled it away.

"In St. Louis Park," I said. "The former president of the Szereto Corporation."

"The beauty company?" Erica asked.

"Yes."

"Where Mal's father used to work?"

"Yes. A man named Jonathan Szereto Jr."

"Oh," Malcolm said.

"What do you know about it?" I asked.

"Nothing, really. It's just—what you said just caught me by surprise is all."

"You're not surprised anymore?"

He dropped the remains of the vanilla wafer on the countertop and brushed the crumbs from his hand.

"I don't know why I reacted that way." Malcolm was smiling at Erica when he said, "This whole thing has me pretty messed up."

Erica smiled back.

She stopped smiling when she noticed Malcolm's eyes lock on something over her shoulder. She turned to look. Nina had emerged from the master bedroom and moved across the living area. She was wearing a fitted scarlet gown that accentuated the imagination, and for a moment I was back in the Minnesota Club watching her shove a miscreant down a flight of stairs. She had worn a different dress then, only it was the same color, and it stopped my heart. I had no idea what she was looking for—I mentioned the dress, right?—but she apparently found it, turned, and walked back into the bedroom. Malcolm followed her every step of the way.

Erica reached across the island and punched him hard on the shoulder.

"Oww," he said.

"Were you perving on my mom?" Erica asked.

"No. What? No, I wouldn't do that."

"Erica," I said.

"What?"

"I was perving on your mom."

"Gawd. You're both disgusting."

"Who's disgusting?" Nina asked. She was now walking through the kitchen area while fixing an earring to her earlobe.

"Men," Erica said.

"Can't live with them, can't live without them. If you're coming with me, you'd better change."

"I should leave," Malcolm said. He said it to Nina, not Erica.

Erica grabbed his arm and pulled him toward the door. I nearly stopped them to ask more questions, but didn't. They made their good-byes, and Erica all but shoved him out. She walked past us on the way to her room.

"Honestly, Mother," she said.

She went into the bedroom, slamming the door behind her.

"What did I do now?" Nina asked.

"You became the most beautiful woman in the room."

"That hasn't been true since Rickie turned sixteen."

"She doesn't know how pretty she is. She only knows how pretty you are."

"I'm not that pretty; never have been."

"I beg to differ."

Nina hugged me. I hugged her back. For the fourth or fifth time that day I reminded myself how lucky I was.

"What are your plans for tonight?" she asked.

"I have a few things to do, but I promise to be at your side when the ball drops."

"That's all I ask."

"I have a question, though."

"What?"

"Do I look like Bradley Cooper?"

"No. Not at all."

NINE

I arrived fashionably late to Evelyn Szereto's New Year's Eve party—which meant I was forced to park well down her private driveway. I was wearing black dress shoes, and my feet chilled long before I reached her front entrance even though the temperature was in the low thirties—cold nearly everywhere else but practically balmy in December in Minnesota. A man wearing a tuxedo opened the door for me, said "Good evening, sir," took my trench coat, and handed me a ticket with a three-digit number. Clearly he was help hired for the evening. What annoyed me, his tux looked better on him than my double-breasted job did on me.

There was no one at the door working security; no one checking my name off of a guest list. I saw Jack McKasy, though, standing at the bottom of the staircase and scrutinizing the proceedings with a keen eye. He looked better in a tuxedo than I did, too.

When his gaze fell upon me he grimaced like a man who had just lost a bet. He jerked his head as if he wanted me to come toward him, so I did.

"Mrs. Szereto said if you showed up she wanted to talk to you," Jack said.

"Where is she?"

"Upstairs."

I attempted to move around him and climb the stairs. He pressed a hand against my chest. There was a lot of strength in the hand, and it stopped me cold.

"No one goes upstairs," he said.

"You said—"

"When she comes down you can talk to her. No one goes upstairs. That's the rule."

"I certainly don't want to break any rules."

"Don't fuck with me, McKenzie."

"Why would I do that?"

"Mrs. Szereto said you killed a guy. That's doesn't scare me."

"How long have you worked for Evelyn?" I used her first name so Jack would think we were closer than we were.

"What do you care?" he asked.

"Just wondering. She seems to confide in you, trusts you."

"I've been here about three years if you gotta know. It was the kid who hired me, Jonny."

He refers to Jonny as a kid, even though he was at least a decade older, my inner voice told me.

"Jonny wanted me to take care of the grounds, the house," Jack added. "Do whatever heavy lifting needed to be done cuz he sure as hell wasn't going to do it, get those soft hands of his dirty. Sometimes I ran errands, drove him around. After he got killed, I stayed on. The ladies, they know they can depend on me."

"You're the only staff member?"

"They have people that do the cleaning, the laundry; a cook that comes and goes. I'm the only one that lives in."

"You have a room above the garage?"

"You have a problem with that?"

"Not at all."

"Yeah, well, people look at you when you say that like it's

something terrible. Like you're one of them serfs from the Middle Ages. One guy, he told me I was an indentured servant. I didn't even know what that was, had to look it up. Only it's the nicest apartment I've ever had; I don't care if it is above the garage. These are the nicest people I've ever worked for, too. You don't fuck with them, McKenzie, or I'll fuck with you, I don't care how many people you've killed."

"I'll keep that in mind."

"You'd better."

I wandered. Mrs. Szereto's house was much larger than I realized when I visited the day before. 'Course, I had been in only one room. There seemed to be about twenty, each of them painstakingly decorated in the colors of Christmas. It reminded me of the James J. Hill House, the mansion built by the railroad tycoon on Summit Avenue in St. Paul. Nina made me go with her to listen to ghost stories on Halloween a few years ago. We got lost.

People flowed from one room to the other like a meandering river, searching for faces they recognized and then stopping when they found one, forcing the river to alter course around them. The men all wore tuxedos or elegant suits; the women were attired in gowns and posh party frocks, most of them black, many looking as if they had never been worn before. They looked very festive among the overstated Christmas decorations. A woman in red vest and green tie, who didn't look old enough to drink, found me in the crowd and offered a glass filled with champagne from the tray she carried. I took the champagne and said, "Thank you." She smiled in return, and I wondered if she thought I looked like Bradley Cooper, too. Probably not.

I sipped the champagne, wishing it were ale—you can't take me anywhere—and wandered some more. I discovered a huge room that had been converted into a dance hall with a prefabricated wooden floor and a temporary stage where a seven-man orchestra was channeling Count Basie. The floor was filled with couples dancing as if they knew how to swing and others who moved as if they only listen to rock and roll. Straight-back chairs lined the walls. Candy Groot was sitting in one of them, an empty champagne glass in her hand. I walked up to her. She saw me coming and turned her head away.

No one's happy to see you tonight, my inner voice said.

"Ms. Groot," I said.

"Mr. McKenzie." She stood and looked at me. "I want to apologize for my behavior yesterday. I was very rude."

"Please, Ms. Groot—Candy. The fault was all mine. I am so sorry if I caused you even a moment of pain. I promise it was not my intention."

She stared as if she weren't quite sure what to make of my remarks. She reached out a hand and rested it on my arm.

"It wasn't you who caused me pain," she said.

"I'm sorry just the same."

Candy stared some more and smiled a sad sort of smile. It bothered me, thinking that I was responsible for the sadness.

"Thank you," she said. "You're very kind."

My response was to give her hand a quick squeeze. She lifted the hand from my arm and ran her fingers under the lapel of my tux.

"Very nice," she said.

"This ratty old thing?"

Candy thought that was funny. She was wearing a black velvet dress with a hem that touched her knees.

"You look lovely," I said.

"Thank you."

"Not dancing?"

"Waiting for Ms. Dauria to arrive and then Mrs. Szereto's speech."

"Mrs. Szereto is giving a speech?"

"Every year she comments on the state of the company; tells

people what percentage of their salaries they'll be receiving in profit sharing. That's when the party really takes off. You'll notice that everyone is pretty much behaving themselves now."

"Actually, I hadn't noticed."

"They're all drinking Mrs. Szereto's champagne. After the speech is when the bars open. There's one in nearly every room. The place will be like a zoo."

I can hardly wait, my inner voice said as I drained my glass.

"You know how in *The Great Gatsby,* Gatsby threw these huge, elaborate parties yet rarely attended them himself?" Candy asked. "That's Mrs. Szereto. She'll make a grand entrance, give her speech, chat briefly with a few of the executive staff, and then poof, she'll be gone."

"She doesn't like to socialize with the help?"

"Actually, I think she does it for the benefit of the help. They won't need to be afraid of misbehaving in front of the chairperson."

"What about the president?"

"Ms. Dauria has a fairly benign attitude about it all—what happens in Mrs. Szereto's house stays in Mrs. Szereto's's house. Why are you here, McKenzie?"

"Evelyn invited me."

"That doesn't answer my question."

"Seeing what there is to see. You'd be surprised how much of what I do is a matter of just showing up."

"You know my feelings on the subject."

"I do."

Candy took my hand as if she wanted us to be friends despite our differences.

"Let's get some more champagne," she said.

We made our way out of the ballroom. Fellow employees nodded at her and said "good evening," and Candy nodded and said "good evening" in reply, yet she didn't pause to speak to anyone, and no one seemed intent on speaking to her until our path was blocked by a woman wearing shoulder-length hair that she had colored Marilyn Monroe blond to hide the gray and a shiny, low-cut black dress that screamed "think of sex."

"Candace, dear." The woman gave Candy an air kiss on both cheeks and stepped back. "How good to see you."

"Ms. Randall."

Randall turned her attention toward me.

"And who might you be?"

Candy was still holding my hand. She lifted it for the woman to see.

"He's with me," Candy said.

"No doubt, no doubt." Randall ran her fingers under the lapel of my tux just the way that Candy had earlier. "I bet he's expensive."

I didn't know if I should be insulted or flattered, so I just smiled and nodded my head

"Good evening," Candy said. She meant to lead me away. Once again, Randall blocked our path.

"Wait," she said. "I need to speak to Evelyn."

"I'm sure she'll be down at any moment."

"In private."

"Good luck with that."

"My, my, haven't you become the liberated vixen, speaking disrespectfully to your elders."

"You got the elder part right, anyway."

"I need to speak to Evelyn."

"Then go speak to Evelyn."

"I want you to arrange it."

"No."

"Candace, dear—"

"Pamela, dear. I don't work for you."

"Maybe you shouldn't be working for the Szereto Corporation, either."

Candy snorted—actually snorted—and pulled my hand. This time she succeeded in leading me away. I glanced at Randall over my shoulder. She didn't seem angry so much as confused.

"Look at you," I said. "Standing up and talking back."

"There was a time when I wouldn't have had the nerve to do that."

"I like it. Who was that woman?"

"Pamela Randall. She's one of the minority shareholders."

"I don't pretend to know anything about business, but aren't you supposed to be nice to shareholders?"

"She's a mercenary. She not only owns shares in Szereto, she has a strong position in Barek Cosmetics. I think she might even be on the board of directors."

"Is that smart?"

"You wouldn't think so. If one stock is doing well at the expense of the other, the best you could hope for is that they'd balance out. If the entire industry suffers, all of your investments will suffer. On the other hand, Randall has been involved with Szereto for quite a few years now, and my impression is that she's very, very smart. She must have a plan."

"Can she get you fired?" I asked.

The way she reacted, Candy seemed to find the question funny, although she didn't tell me why.

Eventually we found another young woman with a tray of champagne glasses. We each took one, clinked glasses, and sipped. Candy did not release my hand until a kind of low murmur from some of the other guests drew our attention toward the front door, and then she dropped it like a preteen whose parents had just walked into the room.

Diane Dauria stepped through the door, followed by her daughter; I recognized Sloane by her dark red hair. Coats were removed, and I couldn't help but notice that Diane was wearing a clinging black gown trimmed with silver and tailored to display her impressive contours. Sloane, on the other hand, was dressed as if she were afraid someone would notice she was a woman, in a formless gray number that covered her body from throat to ankles. The disguise didn't work.

Sloane found me watching. Her eyes narrowed like a cat's. She moved carefully to her mother's side, also like a cat, and spoke into her ear. Diane glanced at me, nodded, and said something in return. I was enough of a lip-reader to make out my name.

Mother and daughter proceeded to cross the room to where Candy and I were standing. It took them a while; Diane kept pausing to shake hands and occasionally hug an employee, often taking the time to introduce Sloane. The smile on her face told one and all that she was very proud of the girl.

When Diane finally reached us, she embraced Candy. She called her Ms. Groot.

Candy said, "I haven't seen Mrs. Szereto since the party began, but we went over her speech earlier. She's prepared."

"Good." Diane hugged Candy again. "I don't know what I would do without you. I know you've met Sloane."

"Of course I have."

Sloane and the older woman hugged like old friends.

"Candy, hi," Sloane said.

"Look at you," Candy said. "Your mother needs new pictures in her office, because you get prettier every year."

Sloane blushed at the compliment—actually blushed. I found it refreshing.

"McKenzie," Diane said. She made no attempt to either hug me or shake my hand, and her smile suddenly seemed pasted on. "I'm surprised to see you here. Please tell me that you're not crashing the party."

"Mrs. Szereto invited him," Candy said.

"Why?"

I answered by saying, "You're missing the Hotdish New Year. Katie Meyer told me she was making a million-dollar dessert."

"I'm going later," Sloane said. "First chance I get to blow out of here."

Diane gave her daughter a look. I didn't know if it was because she had revealed her plans or her disdain for the Szereto affair.

"I don't really know anybody here," Sloane added in self-defense. "McKenzie, how do you know about the Hotdish party?"

"I had coffee with Katie this morning. She had wonderful things to say about you, by the way—I hope she doesn't mind me telling you that. Your mother did, too, but you'd expect it from your mom."

Sloane gazed at Diane as if she didn't expect it at all.

"What wonderful things?" she asked.

I improvised. "How smart you are; that you refuse to let society's expectations push you around. Is it true that you once stole second base fourteen times out of fifteen tries in a single season?"

Sloane didn't even grin when she said, "I was fifteen for fifteen—the ump missed the call," which told me that she not only meant it, she was still outraged by the injustice of it all.

She extended her hand and I shook it.

"I know who you are, McKenzie," Sloane said. "I know what Malcolm asked you to do. Mom's not happy about it, and neither are Critter and some of the others, although I can't imagine why. Me, I hope you do find out who killed Malcolm's father.

Bad things happen, you need to do something about it, don't you? Otherwise they'll keep happening."

"Most people don't think about it that way."

"I'm not most people."

Clearly not, my inner voice said.

Sloane released my hand.

"I'm going to drink some champagne," she said, "because I'm legal now, Mother, but not too much, because I have to drive to New Brighton and then to my apartment in St. Paul."

Diane pursed her lips as if it were an argument she had already lost.

"Do you live near St. Catherine's?" I asked.

"Yes. Actually, it's closer to the University of St. Thomas."

"I grew up in that area."

"Then you know all the bars."

Diane grimaced.

Sloane hugged her shoulder. "I'm kidding, Mother," she said. She stepped between me and Diane, draped an arm around Candy's shoulder, and led her away. "We should leave so my mom can say nasty things to McKenzie in private." While glancing over her shoulder at her mother, Sloane added, "Candy, do you know where we can get some good dope?"

"You'll have to excuse my daughter," Diane said.

"Not at all. I like her very much. Because I like her, I'm starting to like you."

"I don't know what to say to that."

"Children are not responsible for their parents. But parents *are* responsible for their children. If Sloane is all she seems—it says something about her mother."

"That's one of the nicest things anyone has ever said to me. Dammit, McKenzie. Sloane was right. I was going to be nasty."

"Not now?"

"What will it take for you to go away? Money?"

"It'll be a lot easier, Diane, if you don't assume I can be bought."

"Everyone can be bought."

"There you go, making assumptions."

I wasn't pretending to be virtuous. Truth is I had never put myself up for sale, even in those days before the reward, for no other reason than I was afraid that someone would actually buy me. Instead, I prided myself on living on my salary. 'Course, it's easier now because the return on my investments pays me nearly $175,000 a year, of which I'm likely to spend a third.

"Diane, I'm not your adversary," I said. "I'm not trying to cause you grief."

"I keep telling myself that. I tell myself that Mrs. Szereto is your patron. I tell myself—should we be honest with each other?"

"That's always a good policy."

Not always the best policy, though, despite what you might have heard, my inner voice added.

"I liked the look of you," Diane said. "When you first arrived in my office, the way you carried yourself, what you said about Sloane without having met her; even your questionable attempts at humor. A woman my age in my position, it's difficult to meet a man who's acceptable."

You're acceptable? Wait till Nina hears . . .

"However, the questions you're asking are upsetting my friends and co-workers," Diane said. "It's disrupting my place of business. That's unacceptable."

Oh well.

"Two men are dead," I said. "Murdered. That is also unacceptable. Don't you think?"

"You seem intent on making me the villain of this piece."

"Not at all. I'm just curious."

"About what?"

"Since we're being so honest—tell me, Diane, which murder don't you want me to solve? Frank Harris's? Or Jonny
Szereto's?"

Her anger was volcanic, yet it was contained in her eyes.
Unless you were watching carefully, you would not have known
how dangerously close she came to erupting. I had no doubt she
would have gone off on me if we had been any place except
where we were. She said as much.

"I refuse to make a scene," Diane said.

"Please, not on my account."

"We were starting to get along so well, too."

She eased back into the river of guests and drifted away,
shaking hands and hugging and having kind words for everyone but me.

A moment later, Annabelle Ridlon was at my side. She was wearing a midnight blue dress that displayed more cleavage than
you'd expect from a woman who was tasked with combating
sexual harassment in the workplace. Her heels gave her a half-
foot height advantage over me.

"How to win friends and influence people," she said. "Mc-
Kenzie, you should write a book."

"Hmm?"

"I was watching you and Dauria. It seemed to me she was
trying very hard not to punch you in the mouth."

"You noticed that, huh?"

"Part of my job description is knowing when people are in
the throes of powerful emotions."

"What do you do when you see that?"

"Mostly I try to stay the hell out of the way."

"Is that what they teach you in human resources school?"

"Actually, my master's is in industrial psychology, but yeah.
It's much easier to deal with people when they're calm and

relaxed. One of the things I do is try to make them feel calm and relaxed."

"When I was a cop, I rarely dealt with people who were calm and relaxed. If they were, they wouldn't have needed me."

"I often deal with the same dynamic."

"Speaking of which, you weren't particularly cordial the last time we spoke, yet you're being awfully gracious now. Given your boss's apparent animosity, aren't you afraid of being labeled a traitor to the cause?"

"I wasn't angry with you the other day, McKenzie. I was merely being firm. If you had asked about our healthcare or 401(k) programs, I would have smiled and made very pleasant small talk, like now. Besides, technically I work for Dauria; she's the one who hired me, but I answer to Mrs. Szereto. It's the way the system was set up after—"

"After Jonathan Szereto Jr. was killed."

"You're awfully blunt."

"Blunt enough, Annabelle, to tell you that you look great tonight."

Ridlon fanned her face with the flat of her hand. "Oh, I do declare," she said. "It doesn't bother you that I'm so much taller?"

"Not at all. I like tall women. But then I've always been ambitious."

That caused her to throw her head back. "McKenzie, what a great line," she said. "I'll have to give that to my husband."

"Are you taller than he is, too?"

Ridlon held her hands about six inches apart.

"By that much even without heels," she said. "The first time we met, he asked me to dance. I looked down at him thinking, Really? He just grinned that bad-boy grin of his and told me that fortune favors the bold." Ridlon fanned herself some more. "What's a girl to do?"

"Where is your husband?"

Ridlon glanced right and left.

"He went to get something manly to drink," she said. "That's the word he used—manly."

"I was told the bar doesn't open until after the speech."

"He's awfully resourceful, my husband."

"Do you know everyone here?" I asked.

"Lord, no. The Szereto Corporation is family owned, emphasis on family. Mrs. Szereto wants everyone to believe that we're all in this together. That's why she likes to throw the party at her home. On the other hand, there are over two hundred and twenty employees in our manufacturing and distribution facility in Owatonna and another hundred and sixty in our corporate headquarters in St. Louis Park. It's becoming more difficult to maintain that philosophy."

"Especially if you're reading everyone's mail."

"Funny."

"What exactly does Szereto make, anyway?"

"Honestly, McKenzie. Didn't you even bother to visit our Web site? We're involved in hair care, facial care, body care, and cosmetics. We sell our products through beauty salons, some chains, but mostly independents, from here working east through Wisconsin, Illinois, Michigan, Indiana, Ohio, and New York and then up and down the coast from Maine to North Carolina. We're not Revlon or Estée Lauder, but we have a strong presence in the industry, and it's getting stronger. We were all concerned when a European conglomerate attempted to buy the company two and a half years ago, but the family refused to sell. I heard a couple of other offers have been made since, but Mrs. Szereto won't even listen to them."

"Good for her."

"I think so, too."

A man worked his way through the crowd to Ridlon's side. The top of his head barely came to her chin. He was carrying two glasses. He gave one to his wife.

"Scotch, Annabelle," he said. "One ice cube as usual. I selected it myself."

She sipped the drink, closed her eyes, and sighed like she'd swallowed lifesaving medicine.

"I love you so much," she said.

"I know."

Ridlon opened her eyes.

"McKenzie, my husband," she said.

We shook hands. I noticed he was drinking his Scotch neat.

"How did you manage that?" I asked.

"Bartender was a woman," he said. "Women find me irresistible."

His wife chuckled.

"Besides, I slipped her ten bucks," he added.

She laughed out loud.

We all turned our heads when we heard the applause. It started slowly from another room and grew in intensity as Evelyn Szereto stepped across the threshold into the room where we were standing. She worked the crowd like a politician, shaking hands, giving hugs, bestowing the occasional kiss to a special cheek as she made her way past us. Vanessa followed closely behind, a beaming smile on her young face. She was dressed in a strapless red silk gown with a clinging bodice that seemed to defy the laws of both gravity and motion. She saw me, tilted her head just so, and gave me a wave.

Ridlon looked down at me.

"McKenzie," she said, "you really are ambitious."

We followed Mrs. Szereto into the ballroom. She mounted the stage, followed by Vanessa, to greater applause. Even the musicians seemed happy to see her. She spoke into a microphone that the bandleader had given her.

"Good evening," she said.

Her voice floated over the crowd. Half responded with "good evenings" of their own.

Mrs. Szereto gestured at Vanessa and said, "Welcome to our home."

Applause.

"We want you to think of it as your home, too—except none of you are allowed to stay overnight, and we don't want you raiding the refrigerator like last time. I'm talking to you, Kent."

A heavyset man near the stage laughed and waved his hands as if he wouldn't think of committing such a criminal act.

"It's been a fabulous year . . ."

Applause.

"And next year is going to be even better."

More applause.

"I know what you're all anxious to hear—you want to know about the three new products that we've introduced to the marketplace."

Groans mixed with applause. The crowd knew that Mrs. Szereto was teasing them.

"They're all doing gangbusters. The salons can't keep them in stock. Especially the new face cream for our more . . . mature clientele." She smoothed her cheek with one hand. "Not that I use it."

Laughter and applause.

"But you don't want to hear that. What you really want to know is—what's what about the new product we're introducing on Valentine's Day?"

More moans and groans.

"Our testing tells us that it's going to be huge, like a man once said. Huge. But you don't want to talk about that, either. You want to know—how are our competitors faring?"

The moans sounded more like deep, frustrated sighs.

"Unfortunately, it's been a challenging economy, and sales seem to be down across the industry. Barek Cosmetics in particular is suffering. My spies tell me their profits are down nine percent."

I was surprised by how gleefully the Szereto employees accepted the news. I nudged Ridlon and asked about it.

"When the company was founded in the seventies, Mr. Szereto and Brian Barek were partners," she told me. "Only they had a falling-out, and Barek started his own business. While Mr. Szereto insisted on courting an upscale customer base, Barek dumbed it down to the common denominator, selling his crap through drugstores and supermarkets, whoever was willing to stock it. Over the years, Barek Cosmetics has become the face of the enemy, the people we don't want to be."

"I can see that you're all terribly upset by the news," Mrs. Szereto said. "Of course, what you really want to know . . ." She smiled, pausing for dramatic effect. "The Szereto Corporation had one of its best years ever despite the economy. Not quite as good as last year, but a huge jump from the year before. We had net income of $377 million."

Applause interrupted her. She waited.

"And we had net profits of $43,656,000."

More applause, louder.

"How much is that?"

Mrs. Szereto pointed at Kent.

"Eleven-point-five percent," he said.

"How much are we paying this guy?" Mrs. Szereto asked.

"It's eleven-point-five-eight percent."

The response was loud and rowdy. Above it all, Mrs. Szereto added, "That's how much your bonuses will be, your profit sharing. Eleven-point-five-eight percent of your yearly salaries." Her employees already knew that, though.

Ridlon's husband hugged her waist and leaned in.

"Can we buy a boat?" he asked. "Huh, Annabelle? Can we, can we?"

She thought that was awfully funny.

"I want to thank all of you—all of you—for your dedication, for your hard work, for your commitment to the standards of excellence that my husband instilled in this company so many years ago," Mrs. Szereto said. "I want especially to thank Diane Dauria for the straight course she has been steering since taking command of this ship."

I was surprised by the crowd's reaction to Mrs. Szereto's compliment. Apparently Diane was far more popular than I would have supposed—at least for the evening.

"I also want to thank the nerds in product development. Time and time again we've been first to the marketplace with the best and most innovative products. You guys are geniuses. When companies like Barek Cosmetics accuse us of unfair business practices, I take that as a compliment on your ability to anticipate the needs of the market long before anyone else. Terrific job."

More applause.

"Unfair business practices?" I asked.

"Every time we introduce a new product, they accuse us of stealing their trade secrets," Ridlon said.

"Now all of you—including Kent," Mrs. Szereto said, "eat, drink, and be merry, for tomorrow . . . tomorrow you all have the day off. I expect to see you all back hard at it, though, Monday morning."

The crowd gave Mrs. Szereto a nice ovation, but it lasted only until she left the stage, went over to Kent, and gave him a hug. The ballroom emptied as employees proceeded to the bars and food tables, Ridlon and her husband among them. I drifted to a bar. They didn't have a beer I liked, so I ordered bourbon. The drinks were free. There was a tip jar, though, and I threw in a ten.

I eavesdropped on the conversations around me. Most employees seemed pleased with the size of their bonuses, although a few suggested in low voices that they deserved better. A voice that was not low, however, suggested that the amount was ridiculously high. It came from a man standing in the corner near the bar. He had black hair combed back with gray at his temples and over his ears; yet someone else who wore a tuxedo better than I did. Pamela Randall stood in front of him as if she were trying to shield him from the other guests. Or maybe it was the other way round.

He waved what looked like a double whiskey and said, "It's our damn money the bitch is throwing around."

She said, "Now's not the time."

I drifted toward them, pretending to be invisible, so I could hear better.

"Eleven-point-five-eight fucking percent—who gives out numbers like that? Nobody."

"Would you please lower your voice?" Randall said.

"It's fiscally irresponsible, those kinds of numbers. It comes right out of our dividends. We, the minority shareholders, we should sue. Corporate malfeasance is what it is."

"Stop it, Neil."

"You're on the board. Did you vote for this?"

"Yes, I did."

"Why?"

"Because my measly six and a half percent wasn't going to beat Evelyn's sixty-six percent, so why make a thing of it?"

"Fifty-six percent. She only controls fifty-six percent now."

"Do you really think Groot is going to vote her ten against Evelyn?"

Wait, my inner voice said. *Candy owns ten percent of the company?*

"You do this every year, Neil," Randall said. "Whine, whine, whine. This is how they run the company. This is how they've always run the company. More to the point, this is how they ran the company when you bought your stock. Get over it. We're all making money."

"We would have made a damn sight more money if we had sold to the Europeans when we had the chance."

"There's no way Evelyn was going to sell the family business."

"The son was keen on the deal."

"It was never going to happen. Besides, I have something bigger in mind."

"I've seen that look before. Oh, you do have something going on, don't you? What? Tell me."

"No. Now shut up and dance with me."

"I don't feel like it."

"Dance with me now or you don't get to dance with me later."

The couple moved into the dance hall, and I thought, That was an awfully effective line Randall came up with; made Neil do her bidding just like that. I hope Nina never uses it.

I drifted from one room to another and saw Sloane sitting alone at a small table with a white linen tablecloth littered with New Year's Eve party favors. Her elbows were on the tabletop and she was squeezing her face between her hands, yet even then she couldn't make herself look ugly. She jumped up when Diane entered the room and moved quickly to her side. She said something in the older woman's ear. As she spoke, Diane glanced at her expensive watch and nodded her head. Sloane hugged her mother tight and went off in the direction of the front door. Diane watched her go.

I glanced at my own watch as I approached—9:55 P.M.

"Off to the Hotdish party?" I asked.

Diane flinched. "McKenzie, you startled me."

"I'm sorry."

"I'm surprised that you're still here."

"Evelyn wants to speak to me." Again I used her first name on purpose.

"What about?"

"I don't know."

"You don't know or you won't tell me?"

"Normally I enjoy it when people are annoyed with me. Yet somehow with you . . ."

Diane pulled her hands behind her back, which stretched the material of her gown across her breasts. There was nothing carnal about it, though. She was a peacock merely displaying how repulsed she was by my presence.

"Mrs. Szereto is still in the ballroom," she said. "Talk to her and go."

TEN

A tight knot of people surrounded Mrs. Szereto, yet her eyes found me when I entered the room. She gestured with her head. I followed the gesture to Vanessa. She was sitting in one of the chairs against the wall and speaking with a man who seemed to be studying the single teardrop pearl that hung between her breasts. I might have expected that from a hormonal kid, except he was a solid decade older than Vanessa was, and you'd think he'd have seen pearls before. I glanced back at Evelyn. She gestured more emphatically. I set my drink at the foot of an empty chair and moved toward the young woman. She smiled at me.

"McKenzie," she said.

I extended a hand.

"May I?" I asked.

Vanessa took the hand.

"Of course. Excuse me," she told her displeased companion. We moved toward the stage. "Thank you for the rescue."

"It's my pleasure."

"Tell me, though. Are we dancing because you want to or because my mother-in-law insisted?"

"I'm doing it because you're a lovely young woman and I want to know more about you."

"Ha."

The band swung into an extended cover of "Autumn Leaves," the female vocalist singing the original French lyrics followed by Johnny Mercer's English translation. Vanessa and I claimed a corner of the dance floor near the stage. The couple I heard complaining earlier were in the opposite corner.

"Do you know who those people are?" I asked.

"I don't know the man," Vanessa said. "The woman is Pamela Randall. She's on the board of directors."

"I overheard them earlier. They're not happy about the size of the bonuses Szereto is handing out."

"I don't care."

Vanessa slipped into my arms. We moved in a tight circle, holding each other close—but not *too* close. At the second turn I noticed Jack McKasy leaning against a wall. He was staring as if he were hoping his heat vision would burn me to a crisp.

"He doesn't like me at all," I said.

"Jack? That's because you're doing what he probably wants to do."

"What's that?"

"Dance with me."

"I take it you don't have that kind of relationship."

Vanessa's head fell back, and she looked at me with a shocked expression. "I wouldn't be involved with him," she said.

"What about your mother-in-law?"

"That's an awfully provocative thing to ask."

"Just trying to learn how things work."

"It's difficult living in the same house, yet we both try hard to maintain a certain level of privacy and discretion."

"What does that mean?"

"It means I can't answer your question. I can tell you one thing, though . . ."

"Yes?"

"Sometimes Evelyn calls him 'Happy Jack.' "

"When?"

"When do you think? What you need to remember is that Evelyn's husband has been dead a lot longer than my husband."

"From our conversation yesterday, she seems quite concerned about your social life."

"She means well, only— The woman has been very, very good to me and my son, but the men she's introduced me to—I have heels with higher standards than she does."

"The man I saved you from, was he one of them?"

"Couldn't you tell? I'm done with older men, though."

I had no reason to be disappointed by Vanessa's declaration, yet I was.

Watch it, my inner voice told me.

"Do you know what Evelyn told me this morning?" Vanessa asked. "She said what I needed was for a man to fuck me good and proper. And so on and so forth. That's a direct quote, by the way. The first part, not the second."

Now it was my turn to look shocked. Vanessa laughed at me.

"What surprises you, McKenzie? That she would say such a thing or that I would repeat it?"

"Both."

"Evelyn can be quite earthy when she wants to be. So can I."

"That's the second time I've heard that word today."

"Tell me, McKenzie. What do you think of recreational sex?"

"Is this a trick question?"

"Not at all."

"I suppose if the participants are both on the same page . . ."

"I'm not asking about *the participants*. I'm asking about you."

"When I was a kid, I was both a devout believer and a frequent practitioner. Not anymore."

"What do you believe now?"

"I believe in love."

Vanessa rested her forehead against my chest. She spoke into my shirt.

"So do I. I always have. Try explaining that to Evelyn."

Her head came up, and she looked me in the eye.

"I loved my husband," she said. "Jonny betrayed me in the worst way possible, and I still loved him. What does that say about me?"

"Nothing bad."

"I don't believe in fate or destiny, McKenzie. I believe our lives are shaped by the choices we make along the way and the consequences of those choices. I was a naïve twenty-year-old fashion model who fell in love with a man twice her age. I don't regret that decision, only what Jonny made of it. Now I'm faced with more choices, some of them forced on me by my mother-in-law. I choose love. I will find it again. I won't rest until I do. What else do you want to know?"

I wished the song would end. I wished it would end so I could put as much distance as possible between myself and this beautiful, intelligent, charming, and heroic young woman who moved so effortlessly in my arms. I thought I should get out of there. It seemed to me a fellow could get into some very serious trouble there. Yet the song kept playing and we kept dancing.

For a while I kept my eyes off of her. In the far corner, Pamela Randall was grinding against her partner like a needy debutante with a boy her parents didn't approve of. Near the door, Evelyn was still holding forth with her courtiers.

"What does your mother-in-law think of your decision?" I asked.

"If she doesn't like it, she can move."

"Move? I thought this was her house."

"No, it's mine. It's all mine; I own everything. Most people don't know that, the employees, the shareholders. What happened—I barely knew my father-in-law, McKenzie. He seemed like a nice man, everyone says he was, but he was old and in ill health when I met him. Jonny and I had been married for only a few months when he died. Anyway, he was twenty years older than Evelyn and had always assumed that he would go first and she would inherit. Except Evelyn was—is—a beautiful woman and young. He believed that she would probably remarry after he passed, and he didn't want a stranger—her second husband, obviously—taking possession of everything he built. He drew up a will when his son was born stating that Evelyn would be made very comfortable—he left her millions, McKenzie—only he made sure that everything else, the company, this house, all of his other property, would go to Jonny. Evelyn knew this. She told me later that she didn't mind. She thought it was very fair what Mr. Szereto did, leaving it all to her son. I expected the same thing, especially after I became pregnant. Except Jonny was . . . killed . . . before he got around to it, before he drew up a will or put anything in trust. So I inherited it all, me and my son."

"Yet Evelyn is chairperson of the board," I said.

"Better her then me. I wouldn't even know where to begin to run a company this big, to run a company of any size. I was an English major in college; I didn't even graduate. If Evelyn wants to—McKenzie, don't get the wrong impression. I love my mother-in-law. Like I said, she's been very good to me. If she wants to be in charge, if she wants to run things, let her. If people assume that she owns the company, that's fine with me, too. As far as I'm concerned, it's all hers until my son is ready to take over. He will take over, too, McKenzie. I have a will. I have trusts set up. Everything goes to Jon."

"When the Europeans attempted to buy the Szereto Corporation, it was you who said no, then, not Evelyn?"

"It was me. Evelyn was delighted to hear it, too. Especially when I let her vote my proxy. It proved to her that I intended to make sure that my father-in-law got his wish, that the company would remain in the family. It was a turning point in our relationship. Up until then I wasn't sure she approved of me. Now we get along very well. We're both devoted to my son and to Szereto."

"What about Candy Groot?"

"What about her? Oh, wait. I forgot. The codicil. A couple of years after my father-in-law died, Evelyn found a handwritten codicil in his papers where he wrote that he wanted ten percent of the company to go to Candace. He said he could never have built Szereto without her. Jonny wanted to challenge it in court even though Evelyn was adamant that the codicil was legitimate. I don't think she wanted to see ten percent of the business go to an outsider, either, but she was determined that all of her husband's last wishes be respected. It got pretty ugly for a while there, too, between the two of them . . . and then . . . So much happened so fast, McKenzie—Jonny's death, the police investigation, the inheritance, my son's birth. Whoever said 'That which does not kill us makes us stronger' was a fool."

The song ended. We stopped dancing. Vanessa looked me in the eye.

"Tell me you have a girlfriend," she said.

"I do."

"Tell me that you love each other more than anything."

"We do."

"That's what I want."

I kissed her cheek.

"That's what I want, too," I said.

When I turned around, both Pamela Randall and Mrs. Szereto were gone, but Jack McKasy was still there; he hadn't moved from his spot against the wall. Only now Candy Groot was with him, speaking animatedly. Jack nodded his head, yet his eyes remained fixed on us.

I thanked Vanessa for the dance and went searching for Evelyn. Jack shook his head as if dislodging a daydream and spoke sharply to Candy. Candy replied in kind. Jack turned and left the ballroom. I went through the other door. Candy watched me. She had a drink in her hand. She downed the contents and followed after Jack.

The crowd had thinned somewhat; many of the guests had heard what they had come to hear and moved on. What remained was still formidable, however. It took some time to search the many crowded downstairs rooms. In one of them I discovered Randall sitting at a table strewn with cone-shaped hats and noisemakers. The gentleman she had hushed earlier sat across from her; two other couples sat on either side. Our eyes met.

"Looking for that dreary little secretary?" she asked.

I knew who she meant, yet I made myself look puzzled just the same.

"The woman who owns ten percent of the Szereto Corporation?" I asked. "That dreary little secretary?"

"It's given her delusions of grandeur," Randall said. "Please join me." She rapped the tabletop with her knuckles. "May we have a moment, please?"

The other guests rose from the table and left the room without comment as if they were used to being summarily dismissed by the woman. Randall patted the chair next to her. I sat. At the same time I threw a thumb in the direction her friends went.

"Power happy?" I asked.

"It's my weakness, dear. I love to have the little people jump when I want them to jump."

"Yet Candy kept both feet firmly on the ground."

"She neglected to introduce us. I'm Pamela Randall."

"McKenzie."

"McKenzie." She said my name as if were something she wanted to taste to see if she liked it. "You're not Candy's friend, though, are you? You work for Evelyn."

"If you say so."

"Either her or—tell me, McKenzie. Did you enjoy your dance with the little princess?"

"If you mean Vanessa Szereto, yes, I did enjoy it. Very much."

"Poor beautiful young rich girl, tragically torn from the love of her life, single mother cut adrift in the cold, cruel world—do you picture yourself as the hero riding to her rescue?"

"She hardly needs rescuing."

"What exactly are you doing for Evelyn?"

"We're back to that, are we?"

"Does it involve deliberately eavesdropping on private conversations?"

I didn't say.

"I saw you at the bar," Randall said.

I merely shrugged.

"You might as well tell me, dear," Randall said. "By this time tomorrow, I'll know everything there is to know about you."

"Except what I'm doing for Evelyn."

"We'll see. So, Candy's friend. That surprises me. Very cold, that one. Dry as day-old toast."

"Ms. Randall—"

"Call me Pamela."

"Pamela, are you always this—what's the word?"

"Bitchy?"

"Close enough."

"Only on special occasions."

Her smile brought a pleasant glow to her face that reminded me inexplicably of a candle set in a mason jar on a table in a dimly lit coffeehouse with a trio strumming guitars and singing folk music from a tiny stage. There was something comforting about it that I couldn't reconcile with her catty behavior.

"I'm confused, dear," Pamela said. "I don't like being confused. Things seem to be going on with the Szereto Corporation, and I don't know what. I'd like to get the truth. I'm not sure Evelyn is giving it to me. You see, I'm an outsider. I wasn't there at the beginning, not like Candace Groot. When I bought into the company after my husband died, Mr. Szereto was already an old man, his best years behind him. And I stayed in, actually increased my position during the amusement park ride that was his son, Jonny. I was content back then to remain a silent partner like the vast majority of shareholders in the vast majority of businesses. But I'll be damned if I'm going to sit quiet now while my investment goes down the tubes because of some Szereto family tradition or misplaced loyalty to a dead man."

"Didn't the Szereto Corporation just have one of its best years ever?"

"What do they call it—the calm before the storm?"

"Seems like a good time to sell, then. Take your profit and put it in Barek Cosmetics. Oh, wait. They lost money this year."

"Aren't you a clever boy?"

"Isn't it a conflict of interest to be on the boards of competing companies?"

"They don't compete so much as complement each other, Szereto appealing to a higher demographic and Barek, admittedly, selling to the low end."

"I wouldn't know about that. In any case, as a member of the Szereto board of directors, isn't it your privilege to call for a meeting and demand answers?"

Pamela thought that was awfully funny.

"Demand answers from Evelyn?" she said. "You don't know her very well at all, do you, dear?"

"Truthfully, I met her for the first time yesterday."

"Well then, let me give you a piece of advice; take it or leave it as you will. I don't know yet what you're doing for her, but whatever it is, watch your back."

Pamela waved her hand, dismissing me just as she had the others. I stood. She surprised me a little when she also stood and offered her hand. I shook it.

"I look forward to meeting with you again," she said.

"It would be my pleasure," I said, although I really didn't mean it.

I kept searching for Evelyn Szereto. Eventually I discovered myself in the largest kitchen I had ever seen.

"What are you doing here?" Candy Groot asked.

There were about two dozen people in the kitchen, most of them dressed in white smocks and laboring over stoves and ovens, yet she was the only one to notice me.

"I'm looking for Evelyn," I told her.

"She's indisposed."

"Is she?"

Candy spoke with the grave dignity of a drunk attempting to act sober.

"As I informed you earlier," she said, "the woman does not attend her own gatherings."

"She asked to speak with me."

"You may converse with me instead. Feel free."

I could see past Candy to a staircase on the far side of the kitchen that apparently led to the second floor. I set my hands on her shoulders and smiled as I slowly rotated her out of the way.

"Perhaps later," I said.

I started for the staircase; to hell with Jack's rules. Candy took hold of my arm. She looked at me with intense eyes that I bet were blurry inside, and I thought, A tightly wound spring letting go. Why should that surprise me?

"McKenzie," Candy said. "Do you like black-and-white movies?"

The question caught me off guard.

"Yes, I do," I said.

Candy wobbled a little bit. She tightened her grip on my arm to steady herself. It occurred to me that she was an attractive woman. In the past few days I'd met several attractive women who had pushed past the sixty-year barrier, and I wondered if that was a thing now, women aging so well. Or had it always been that way but being both young and self-centered I hadn't noticed before? In any case, I thought it boded well for mine and Nina's future.

"Some of the people I work with," Candy said, "especially the younger people, they say they won't watch black-and-white movies; they say they have never even seen one. I like them, though, the black-and-white movies you see on TCM, with heroes and villains clearly delineated, and the good guys always triumphing over the bad guys simply because they are good. Yet the real world—it's in color, isn't it, the real world?"

"It certainly is."

"I don't know what to do with myself."

I didn't know how to respond to that. Was it an invitation? It could have been, the way her wide, wet and shiny eyes stared at me. Or was it merely the lament of a lonely woman searching for someone to confide in?

"Candy, what are you doing here?" I asked.

"In the kitchen? At the party?"

"No, here. Here. In Minnesota in winter. I was told that you own ten percent of the Szereto Corporation. That makes you a wealthy woman. Beaucoup bucks, right? What the hell are you doing here? Why haven't you retired? Why haven't you taken your money and run off to an island somewhere; catch some rays on a white sand beach while sipping cold drinks with paper umbrellas served by tall men with ready smiles? Why don't you go get your groove on instead of doing Diane Dauria's bidding; instead of taking shit from people like Pamela Randall?"

Candy took a deep breath that sounded like a sob. "I tried to tell you before," she said. "It's all I have."

"But it shouldn't be."

"Don't you think I know that?"

"Candy . . ."

"I need another drink," she announced.

Clearly that wasn't true, yet she released my arm, turned, and walked out of the kitchen in search of one just the same. I made no effort to stop her.

I climbed the staircase. I was near the top when I heard Evelyn's voice.

"Stop what you're doing," she said. "I mean it. Stop—don't, don't do that—my guests . . ."

Despite her words, the sound of her voice suggested that she wasn't in distress, so instead of going into full-blown cop mode and bounding up the rest of the staircase, I moved cautiously.

"I said—no—stop it, Jack . . ."

I peeked around the corner.

Evelyn was standing in the corridor, her back against the wall, her eyes closed, while Jack pressed his body hard against hers. She was making no attempt to escape. Jack's mouth was nuzzling Evelyn's ear; his hand was between her legs, the hem of her expensive gown bunched up around her waist. I couldn't actually see Jack's hand from where I was standing, although Evelyn's halting moans gave me an idea of what he was doing with it.

He said something, only his words were muffled by Evelyn's hair.

"Things couldn't be going better," she said. "Why ruin it?"

Jack mumbled a reply that I also couldn't hear except for a name—he called her Eve, the name Evelyn used when she worked as a model.

"I promised you, didn't I?" Evelyn said. "Just not—oh, there, there, right there, oh, oh . . . Happy . . . Happy Jack . . ."

I spun around and retreated down the staircase back to the kitchen, thinking there were some things that you just can't unsee.

Whatever she wanted to talk about, my inner voice told me, *Monday will be soon enough.*

I arrived at the front door just in time to see Diane Dauria making her good-byes to a half-dozen people I didn't know. As she stepped through the door, I hurriedly handed my three-digit ticket to the young man in the tuxedo. He took longer than I would have liked to retrieve my trench coat; I didn't bother slipping it on until after I stepped outside. I couldn't see Diane, yet the debate was raging in my head—go to Rickie's so I could be with Nina at midnight as promised or follow her.

I moved quickly down the long driveway. I still hadn't made a decision until I saw Diane about fifty yards ahead, her back to me, her hands in her pockets. She was also moving quickly along the parked cars; I didn't know if it was the cold that propelled her forward or if she was late for an appointment. The fact that she was leaving the Szereto holiday party early made me wonder.

I decided to follow Diane. She's probably driving to the Hotdish gathering in New Brighton anyway, I told myself. That was practically on the way.

I had arrived at Mrs. Szereto's party before she did, so my Mustang was parked closer to the house. I was able to slip inside, start it up, and turn it around before Diane reached her own vehicle. I waited high on the driveway with my headlights off until she had a good head start and then began following at a discreet distance.

Diane led me along the narrow, twisting roads of Lake

Minnetonka, eventually catching Highway 12, which became I-394 as it approached Minneapolis. So far, so good, I thought, until she caught Highway 100 and drove south more or less in the opposite direction of New Brighton. Soon we found ourselves in Edina. I remembered Diane had informed me that she had moved to the upscale suburb soon after she had been promoted.

The woman's going home, I told myself, yet I kept following just the same. I glanced at the clock on my dashboard. Still plenty of time to get to Rickie's.

A couple of lazy turns later, we were on a tree-lined boulevard dotted with mini-mansions. Diane slowed and turned into the driveway of one of them. Lights on either side of the concrete apron flicked on automatically, and the large door of the attached garage opened. I kept driving straight until I reached an intersection. I managed to pull a U-turn just as Diane parked her car. I stopped on the street, powered down the driver's side window, and turned off the Mustang, extinguishing all of its lights. Diane emerged from her vehicle; the overhead garage light made it easy to spy on her as she headed toward the door leading to her fine house. A moment later the garage door closed.

There were lights already on in the house, two downstairs and one upstairs, as if that would fool your average working thief. Another light came on in the back of the house. I kept a pair of binoculars in my glove compartment for just such occasions. I was looking through them when the living room light came on. Diane had left her drapes opened, and I was able to see inside. She had unbuttoned her long, charcoal-colored wool coat, giving her ample breasts plenty of room to breathe, yet had not taken it off. She went to her window and looked out, glanced at her watch, and looked some more.

She's waiting for someone, my inner voice told me. *A date to take her to another party?*

Part of the question was answered when another vehicle turned onto the boulevard; its headlights reflected off my side and rearview mirrors. I scrunched down in my seat as the car passed me and pulled in to Diane's driveway. Diane left the window and disappeared from sight.

A woman emerged from the vehicle; I jotted down its license plate number. She was wearing a long winter coat similar to Diane's and a wide-brim felt hat, hunter green in color with a green and blue hatband that reminded me of the ribbon and bow on an elegantly wrapped gift. Because of the hat and the low light, I could see very little of her face. All I knew about her was that she was about five-six and white.

The woman followed the sidewalk to the front door. Diane opened it before she reached the stoop, yet did not turn on the overhead light. She held the storm door open, allowing the woman to slip past her inside the foyer. If they spoke I couldn't tell. Diane closed the storm door and turned to her guest. The two women embraced, and I thought, Maybe Stuart Mason is right, maybe Diane is a lesbian.

Not that there's anything wrong with that, my inner voice said.

The inside door was quickly closed, and I lost sight of both women. I glanced at my watch. If you want to get to Rickie's before midnight, I told myself, now's the time to leave.

I was distracted, though, when the two women appeared in the living room. Neither of them had removed her coat; the woman in the hat stood with her back to me. Diane folded her arms across her chest as they spoke and then unfolded them quickly, holding her hands up for her guest to see as if she were attempting to make a point. The other woman didn't move much at all except to reach inside the bag draped over her shoulder and retrieve a white six-by-eight envelope. She passed the envelope to Diane. Diane carelessly tossed it on the sofa behind her without bothering to look inside.

The two women hugged again, only there didn't seem to be anything sexual about it. Diane smiled, draped an arm around the woman's shoulder, and moved her out of sight. A few moments later the front door opened. The two women embraced once again, and the woman with the hat left the house and climbed into her car. Diane stood at the door until she drove away.

I glanced at my watch, told myself that if I disregarded the existing traffic laws—and was distracted yet again. This time a vehicle approached from the opposite direction, a black Toyota Camry. It also pulled in to Diane's driveway.

What the hell, my inner voice said. *Suddenly we're at the Union Depot?*

A man got out, slightly shorter than I was and thin. His coat was opened and his head was bare, and he moved to the front door as if he were tardy for a job interview. Again Diane opened the door without bothering to switch on the overhead light. Only by this time she had removed both her coat and her heels.

The man stepped inside, and they hugged.

The embrace was all sexual.

So, not a lesbian, my inner voice said.

His head was behind hers, so even with the foyer light I couldn't make out his face.

The door was closed, and I decided it was time to leave. Yet I couldn't resist one last peek through the binoculars when the couple appeared in the living room.

The man—and I use the term loosely—was Critter Meyer.

"Are you kidding me?" I said the words aloud, even though there was no one to hear. "Are you fucking kidding me?"

Diane slipped Critter's coat down off his arms and dropped it on the floor. They kissed as if they had done it before; their hands explored each other's bodies through their clothing as if they had done that before, too.

So, what are you upset about? my inner voice asked. *If it was an older man and a twenty-one-year-old woman, would you be so outraged?*

No, no, that's not it.

Well, then?

He's Katie's son and she's Katie's friend.

Probably nothing good will come of it, but it has nothing to do with you.

No, it doesn't.

Yet it pissed me off just the same, go figure.

The light was extinguished in the living room, and a few beats later I saw another, much dimmer light appear through the window of what I presumed was an upstairs bedroom.

I started the Mustang.

You know what? my inner voice said. *Recreational sex or true love, who are you to judge? After all, it's winter in Minnesota. It's cold out there.*

I put the car in gear and drove toward St. Paul.

I was fifteen minutes late by the time I arrived at Rickie's, and yes, I risked arrest getting there. I found Erica inside the front door at the hostess station. Her smartphone was pressed to her ear. I could hear her speaking as I approached.

"You say that, Robin," she said. "Except you're the one who decided to spend the holidays in Florida with your parents."

She saw me approach and said, "Hang on a sec." She wrapped her arms around my waist, and I wrapped mine around hers.

"Happy New Year, McKenzie," she said.

I kissed her cheek.

"Happy New Year to you, too, sweetie. Where's your mother?"

"In her office."

"Is she mad?"

"Probably."

I stood for a moment, listening to the jazz coming from the big room, debating what I was going to say. Behind me, Erica had resumed her conversation.

"That sounds like some Christmas present if you need to deliver it in person," she said. "I can send you yours in the mail."

I went to Nina's office, knocked on the door, and stepped inside without waiting for an answer. She was sitting behind her desk, staring at her computer, her cheaters balanced on her nose. Damn, she was beautiful.

"I am so sorry," I said. "I got caught up in what I was doing, and time just . . ."

Nina's response was to remove her glasses, rise from her chair, circle the desk and take me into her arms.

"As long as you come home at night in one piece," she said. "That's all I care about."

We kissed as if we were the only people in the world and preferred it that way.

ELEVEN

Noon New Year's Day found me doing one of the things I enjoyed most in the world—resting comfy-cozy against my large blue cushion with the Minnesota Twins logo beneath Nina's Steinway and listening to her play. She had earned a few bucks when she was a kid working happy hours and Sunday brunches, using the cash to help pay her way through college, yet had given it up when she became involved with the jerk that would soon become her ex-husband, gave birth to her daughter, and began building Rickie's. She started playing again about the time Erica went off to Tulane; I gave her the piano as a housewarming gift when we finally moved in together about a year ago. As far as our relationship went, it was the best investment I ever made.

Nina was working her way through "All the Things You Are" by Jerome Kern, improvising off the composer's main theme while asking, "What do you think of this?" and "Does this work?" She didn't expect an answer, which was fine, because I wasn't dumb enough to offer one.

From where I was lying, I was able to see Erica emerge from her room. Or rather I saw her sweatpants and fluffy slippers. She moved to the piano.

"McKenzie," she said. "Excuse me, Mom. McKenzie, I need your help."

Nina stopped playing. I slid out from beneath the piano and looked up at her. Erica's hair was badly in need of a brush, and her face had that I-just-woke-up look.

"Wut up?" I said.

"Wut up? Who talks like that?"

"What's wrong, honey?" Nina asked.

"Malcolm is missing. His mother just called." Erica held up her smartphone as evidence. "She's calling everyone he knows. She said Mal left a party last night and no one has seen him since. McKenzie, she's really upset."

"That doesn't mean he's missing."

"He hasn't been home. He doesn't answer his phone. What do you call it?"

"I call it—I really don't want to know the answer to this question, Erica, but have you ever gone missing overnight, not telling anyone where you were, not answering your phone?"

She was looking directly into Nina's eyes when she answered, "Why no, McKenzie, I haven't, but . . ."

"But what?"

"I know those who have."

"When did Malcolm leave the party?" I asked.

"His mom said around eleven o'clock. She didn't see him leave, so she wasn't sure."

"Was anyone with him?"

"She . . . she didn't say."

"Did he get a call or a text right before he left?"

"Do you think he went on a booty call? He's not like that."

"Are you sure?" Nina asked.

Erica didn't like that question coming from her mother.

"Are you telling me I don't know my friends?" she asked.

"Sometimes people can surprise us."

"Surprise you, maybe."

"Erica," I said. "We're just saying there are possibilities that Malcolm's mother might not have considered."

Erica kept staring at her own mother.

"He's not like that," she repeated.

"What time did you wake up?" I asked.

Erica glanced at the phone in her hand.

"Just now," she said. "Why?"

"Probably your friend had a few too many and he's still curled up on somebody's couch," I said. "It was New Year's Eve, after all. Give him a few hours."

Erica responded by retreating back to her room.

"I love her more than my life," Nina said. "But sometimes I want to strangle that girl."

"I'm sure she feels the same way."

"What do you know about it, McKenzie?"

I crawled back beneath the Steinway.

Nina was playing something by the Everly Brothers, giving it a five/four time signature.

"So many of these golden oldies have seeped into the American Songbook," she said, sitting next to Porter and Gershwin. Remember that time Sophia Shorai came to the club, did that cover of "I'm So Lonesome I Could Cry," the Hank Williams standard? Just her and the piano? I've always liked that."

To prove it, she started playing the song herself. Only I wasn't paying much attention. I was thinking of Malcolm Harris. His mother called everyone she knew when he went missing. Would she call them back once he was found? Probably not.

After an hour passed, I was tempted to knock on Erica's door and ask her to call Jayne and find out if the situation had changed. I don't know why I was so anxious about it. I didn't even like the kid. Before I could act, though, Erica came out of her bedroom and moved to the Steinway. Once again, all I could see was her sweats, her slippers, and the cell phone she carried in her hand.

"McKenzie?" she asked. Nina stopped playing. "It's Mrs. Harris."

I crawled out from beneath the piano. Erica gave me her phone.

"Jayne?" I said.

"McKenzie? I'm calling—I didn't know what else to do. I knew you were friends with Rickie, so I asked her if she could— McKenzie, Malcolm is missing . . ."

"I heard."

"I don't know who else to turn to. We don't think the police will help, and you're the only one I know who does—you do this, don't you, being a detective? You find people?"

"Sometimes." I tried not to sound unconcerned even though I was. "I'd hold off if I were you, though. Like I told Erica, your son is probably just curled up on someone's sofa sleeping it off— you don't want to embarrass him. I know you're anxious because of, well, your family history, but it's a little early to start worrying. Malcolm's a big boy now, and . . ."

"I know, McKenzie. I know all that but, but—his car, the car he was driving . . ."

"What about it?"

"They found it in the Long Lake Regional Park two blocks away."

I told Jayne I would be right over and hung up. I returned Erica's cell phone to her. She asked if there was anything she could do.

"Make a list of everyone that you know that Malcolm knows, especially the girls," I said.

This time she didn't even pretend to argue for her friend's virtue.

While I went to the closet for my coat and gloves, Nina rose from the piano bench and put an arm around her daughter's shoulder. Erica curled until her head was resting between her mother's chin and chest.

"This is probably nothing," I said.

"I don't believe you," Erica replied.

A moment later I was out the door and heading toward the elevator.

There were several cars parked in front of the Harris house, so I was forced to find a spot down the street. I knocked on the door, was let inside, and immediately found all the owners in the living room. Katie Meyer, Diane Dauria, and a woman who was introduced to me as Annette Geddings had gathered to offer support. They began talking at once, and I flashed on what Annabelle Ridlon had told me the night before, about how part of her job was making people feel calm and relaxed. I should have asked for a few pointers.

"This is probably nothing," I said.

The four women didn't believe me any more than Erica had.

"When did you decide Malcolm was missing?" I asked.

"This morning," Jayne said. She was sitting on the sofa. Annette was sitting beside her and holding her hand. Katie sat on a chair near the fireplace. Her face was devoid of all the effervescent charm I had seen there the day before, although her eyes were wide and shiny behind her black-rimmed glasses. Diane hovered near the doorway that led from the living room to the kitchen. She looked even more serious than usual.

"I went to his room to see if he wanted breakfast," Jayne said. "His bed was neatly made. He didn't sleep in his bed, McKenzie."

"Tell me about last night."

"We went to the party at the same time, only we drove separately."

"Why? Did he tell you he planned to duck out early, perhaps meet someone, go to a different party?"

"No. It was me. I thought I might want to leave early."

That raised a few questions, only I didn't give them voice. Concentrate on Malcolm for now, I told myself.

"He wasn't here when I got home," Jayne said. "That was about twelve thirty. I thought I might wait up for him, but I was too tired. I went to bed at one."

"Did you call the police?"

"What can they do?" Diane asked. "Issue an Amber Alert? It's not like he was taken. He left the party of his own free will."

"Are you sure of that? Did you see him leave?"

"I wasn't there," she said. "I was in Edina."

"Yes, I know," I said—and immediately regretted it. Knowledge was power, and I had just squandered some needlessly. Diane knew it, too. She understood in that instant that I must have followed her, and she was furious, yet determined not to show it. I spun away from her.

"What about the rest of you?" I had settled my gaze on Katie. She was next to the fireplace; the mantel came to her chin. She was examining the photographs arrayed there. "Did anyone actually see him leave?"

There was no verbal answer, just a lot of head shaking.

"Did he tell any of you that he was leaving? Mrs. Harris?"

"No."

"Nobody knows if he received a call or a text, someone asking to meet him?"

"I thought he might have gone to see that girl. The one he's always talking about, who's been teasing him since he was a freshman?"

"What girl?"

"Rickie Truhler."

She spoke the name like an accusation. I resisted speaking out loud—"You mean the girl who asked me to help him, that Rickie Truhler?" I refrained from saying a few other things as well. Your kid goes missing, I cut you some slack. But only so much. I told myself that if she said something disparaging about Erica again I'd explain it to her.

"Is there anyone else he might have left the party to see?" I asked.

No one could think of a name.

"What about the other Hotdishers?" I said. "The kids he played ball with?" I returned to Diane. "Your daughter?"

"Sloane never made it to the party," she said. "She told me that halfway there she decided to meet up with some of her friends from St. Kate's instead, stay closer to home."

Katie said, "I asked the other boys. They said they didn't notice when Malcolm left. Critter said he was pretty sure Malcolm was still there, though, when he took off to go to a party thrown by some college friends across town. That was about ten forty-five."

I did the math in my head while regarding Diane. New Brighton to Edina, arriving there at eleven thirty. Yeah, that worked. Diane didn't like me watching her and stepped into the kitchen. She returned a few beats later with a coffeepot and asked the other women if they wanted refills. No one did.

"I understand, McKenzie, what you're saying," Jayne said. "Malcolm probably left the party to meet someone. That's what I thought when I couldn't find him at midnight to give him a kiss. Except he's been gone for so long now, and he doesn't answer his phone; and his car . . ."

"Tell me about his car."

Annette Geddings spoke for the first time.

"My son found it," she said. "Steven. He went for a run in

the park and there it was. He knew Jayne was anxious about Malcolm, so he called me on his cell, and I called Jayne."

"McKenzie, the same park," Jayne said. "It's the same park where . . ."

She couldn't get the rest of the words out. Katie crossed the room and rested a hand on Jayne's shoulder. Jayne covered the hand with her own hand. Her entire body shuddered.

"Where is Steven now?" I asked.

"Probably at home," Annette told me. "Although he wasn't there when I left to come over here."

"I'll want to talk to him later."

"Why? He doesn't know where Malcolm went."

"Where exactly is Malcolm's car?" I asked.

It wasn't Malcolm's car. It was actually Jayne's car that her son drove when he was home. She had an extra key that she gave to me. I put it in my pocket and walked the two blocks to the Long Lake Regional Park. I found the vehicle in the lot near the pavilion where Steven Geddings told his mother it was parked. Asphalt sidewalks surrounded the lot. I presumed Geddings had been running on one of them when he saw the car, but I would ask him later to be sure.

There was nothing odd about how the car was parked; it could have been there last night, it could have been left an hour ago. Nor, while slowly circling it, did I detect any bullet holes or smashed windows. The doors were locked, and I needed the key to open it. The interior was remarkably clean. I say remarkably because I knew that Erica used her car like a backpack. I took a deep breath before popping the trunk and exhaled slowly when I saw that it was empty.

I slid behind the steering wheel. I was wearing my winter gloves, yet was careful anyway when I checked the glove compartment and armrest for fear of smudging fingerprints. Nothing screamed at me "This is important." I riffled through Malcolm's CDs. There were nine; I didn't recognize a single artist.

You need to get out more, my inner voice told me.

I slipped the key into the ignition and gave it a turn. The car started immediately and ran smoothly. I turned it off and returned the key to my pocket, trading it for my smartphone. I tapped the icon next to the contact information for Detective Downing. He must have had caller ID because he answered with my name.

"McKenzie, dammit, what?" he said. "It's my day off."

"I wouldn't bother you if it wasn't important."

"Define important."

"Malcolm Harris is missing."

"The son of our murder victim?"

"Yeah."

"Now define missing."

"He left a party thrown by the New Brighton Hotdish sometime after ten forty-five last night. No one has seen him since, and he doesn't answer his phone. Something else. They found his car in the parking lot of the Long Lake Regional Park. I'm guessing it's been here all night."

"Jesus, not again."

Long Lake Regional Park was tucked between Long Lake and Rush Lake and had a pavilion, a picnic shelter, thirty-two picnic tables, two playgrounds, two volleyball courts, a boat launch, a fishing pier, and in the summer a beach with a lifeguard. It also had three miles of paved trails that I began walking as soon as Downing hung up. God help me, I was looking for Malcolm's body, thinking he might have ended up in a ditch like his old man.

The light dusting of snow a couple of days earlier allowed me to detect those places where someone had left the trail. I followed footprints into the woods and marshlands and found nothing—thank you, Lord. 'Course, all that meant was that Malcolm's body hadn't been dumped in plain sight. If Downing and his superiors could think of a good enough reason to justify the expense, they would send in an army of cops, volunteers, and cadaver dogs to give the place a more thorough search.

Along the way, I met a surprising number of folks wandering about—at least I was surprised. It was twenty-eight degrees on the first day of January. If I had my way, I'd still be resting under Nina's Steinway in our toasty-warm condo.

I didn't have a pic of Malcolm to show, so I was forced to provide a vague description when I asked if anyone had seen him; I didn't even know what he was wearing.

Careless, my inner voice kept telling me. *You should have asked.*

Because of the incomplete description, half the people I met were sure they saw the kid just a few minutes ago walking over there or jogging along the lake or sitting near the shelter. The other half shrugged with confusion, occasionally tossing in a "nope" or "uh-uh." An older man out walking a golden retriever gave me a long, hard stare.

He said, "The last time anyone asked me a question like that, it was about this time a year ago. The police wanted to know if I saw anything suspicious. Is this the same deal? Has someone else been killed in the park?"

"Let's hope not."

"That would make three people, you know. Three people killed in the park and another fella over to the ball fields."

"You keep track?"

He squatted down to give his dog a pet.

"What a world," he said.

"It does have its moments."

"The man who was killed last year, he was a neighbor of mine."

"Did you know him—Frank Harris?"

"No, but"—he threw a thumb in the general direction of the north side of the park—"He lived a block away from me. Something like this happens, you wonder—could it have been you?"

"Very few murders are committed at random."

"Did they ever catch the guy who killed Harris?"

"Not yet."

"So you don't know for sure, do you?"

"No, I don't."

"Ain't none of us safe. What a world."

Detective Downing was in the parking lot when I returned. His hands were cupped against the glass of the driver's side window, and he was peering into Malcolm's car.

"I have the key," I told him.

"Were you inside? Did you find anything?"

"There isn't a pool of blood on the seat if that's what you're asking. Your forensics people will be able to take a closer look."

"We don't have those kinds of facilities. Probably we'd hand it over to Ramsey County or the BCA, except—McKenzie, I don't even have a good enough reason to impound the damn car, much less search it."

"It's parked illegally. At least it will be by ten tonight. If you can convince Mrs. Harris to file a missing persons—"

"Who did you say found the car?"

I explained it all again, this time in greater detail than I had over the phone. He nodded a lot but didn't take any notes.

"I'll need to interview all these people myself," Downing said.

"Can I watch?"

"You want to see how a skilled investigator elicits information from a witness that the witness might not even know he has?"

"There's a trick to it, then?"

"The trick is the badge, McKenzie, and you know it. Most people are afraid to lie to the police. So, yeah, why don't you tag along? We'll see if anyone tells me a story different from the ones they told you."

"Where do you want to start?"

Annette Geddings opened the door to her house; it was also on the north side of the Long Lake Regional Park, near the border with Mounds View. Downing stood directly in front of her, holding his badge and ID up for her to see, yet she was looking at me.

"What are you doing here?" she asked.

"We'd like to speak to your son, Steven," Downing said.

"What about?"

"Is he home?"

Downing was right about the badge. If it had just been me, Annette might have slammed the door. With a police officer standing there, though, she hesitated, uncertainty etched on her face as she considered what to do. Downing tried to help her out.

"This is simply routine," he said. "We just want to ask him about the car."

"He found it. What else do you need to know?"

"Is Steven home? May we come in and speak to him?"

Annette thought about it some more before stepping away from the door.

Downing said, "Thank you."

I didn't say a word, mostly because the detective had made me promise to keep my mouth shut.

He and I slipped past her into the house. It had been decorated for the holidays as if Annette were competing for a prize.

"Steve," Mrs. Geddings shouted. "Steven."

"Is your husband home?" Downing asked.

"He went ice fishing at Mille Lacs early this morning with Katie Meyer's husband. We don't expect to see either of them until Sunday night. Steven?"

Steven rounded a corner and halted like a kid playing a game of Red Light, Green Light. He looked first at me and then at Downing before glancing over his shoulder as if he were thinking of making a run for it. Downing flashed his badge and ID at him.

"I'm Detective Clark Downing of the New Brighton Police Division," he said. "I'd like to ask you a few questions."

"I didn't do anything," Steven said.

Downing gave me a quick glance. I was sure he was thinking the exact same thing I was—only people with a guilty conscious claim that.

"We'd like to ask you about Malcolm Harris's car," Downing said.

"I found it in the park," Steven said.

"When?"

"This morning."

"When?"

"You want to know the exact time? It was . . . I left here about noon, so it was . . . okay, it wasn't this morning. It was about twelve forty-five, one o'clock, somewhere in there."

"What were you doing?"

"I was jogging."

"Do you jog often?"

"He runs every day," Annette said.

"Mom . . ."

"Mrs. Geddings, please," Downing said. "This is your home and you're welcome to listen in, but if you keep interrupting, I'll need to ask your son to accompany me to police headquarters."

"You can't do that," Annette said.

"Ma'am, with all due respect, you son is not a minor. He's an adult."

"Hear that, Mom?" Steven said. "Just leave me alone."

"Do you jog often?" Downing asked.

"Yes, but not *every* day. I'm not a fanatic. I jog three, four times a week just to keep in shape. So I can run in a few 5- and 10Ks during the summer with my friends."

"Did you ever run with Malcolm Harris?"

"No, Malcolm—I doubt he could run across the street without gasping for breath."

"Do you usually run in the park?"

"About, I don't know, a third of the time, maybe? I have a couple of different routes mapped out. Three miles, five miles, it depends on how I'm feeling that day."

"You ran in the park today?"

"The paths are always plowed down to the asphalt, you know? So it's dry. You're not slipping on the ice and falling on your ass."

"How did you find Malcolm's car?"

"I was running and I looked and there it was."

"You're familiar with the car?"

"I've seen it before, sure."

"It's easily recognizable?"

"Well, I mean, if you have twenty of the same model lined up I doubt I could tell them apart."

"But you recognized his just running by."

"No, I mean . . ."

"What do you mean?"

"You're deliberately trying to confuse him," Annette said.

"Mrs. Geddings," Downing said.

"Mom, I'm not confused," Steven said. "I'm just trying to say . . . Detective Downing, what happened—Mrs. Harris called earlier. She was looking for Malcolm because he didn't come home last night. She was pretty upset, but I was thinking, maybe he got lucky last night because, you know . . . Anyway, I was running and I saw the car and I thought, Hey, that looks like Malcolm's car, and as I got closer to it, I thought, Hey, that *is* Malcolm's car. I can't recite the license plate or anything, but it was like, I knew it was his. So I called my mom and told her, and she called Mrs. Harris."

"Why didn't you call her?"

"I don't know, it's just—she and my mom are pretty tight, so . . ."

"Did you see Malcolm Harris last night?"

"Yeah."

"At the New Year's Eve party at Mrs. Meyer's home?"

"Yeah, yeah."

"Did you speak to him?"

"Well, yeah. It was a party."

"Weren't you involved in a fight with Malcolm just a couple of days ago?"

"Not me."

"At the Bru House coffeehouse?"

"No, no, no, that was Critter."

"Critter?"

"Christopher Meyer. They were the ones fighting."

"What were they fighting about?"

"I don't know."

"You were there."

"Yeah, but—"

"He said he wasn't involved in the fight," Annette said.

"Mom, stop it," Steven told her. "I got this. Detective, I didn't do anything. I was just standing there watching and this girl sucker-punches me, this friend of Malcolm's. Minding my own business and wham, she just whacks me. You want to ask questions, you talk to her. Ask her what the fight was about. Or Critter. Or Malcolm. Cuz I was just standing there."

"You and Malcolm didn't talk about the fight at the party?"

"Why would we? We weren't the ones fighting."

"Did Christopher Meyer and Malcolm talk about the fight?"

"Dang if I know."

"Did they seem to get along at the party?"

"I guess. They weren't yelling or anything. No one was throwing punches."

"Did you see Malcolm leave the party?"

"No. Like I told Mrs. Harris, I didn't even know he was gone until she came looking for him at midnight."

"You have no idea where he went?"

"N'-uh."

"If he received a text or phone call?"

"Like I said, n'-uh."

"You said that maybe Malcolm got lucky last night. What did you mean by that?"

"What I meant—I don't know—he stays out all night . . ."

Steven turned his head so that his mother couldn't see his face and gestured with it as if he wanted Downing to join in a conspiracy. "You know," he repeated.

"No, I don't know," Downing said. "Are you saying that Malcolm was with a woman?"

Steven gestured with his head more emphatically. "I don't know," he said.

"What woman?" Downing asked.

"I don't know, geezus."

"Don't know or won't say?"

"Mal and I have known each other for years, but it's not like we tell each other our deepest, darkest secrets, okay?"

"What deep, dark secrets?"

"Ah, geez."

"Steven, if you have information—"

"He said he doesn't know," Annette said.

"I'm just saying, if a guy leaves a party and he doesn't go home it's usually because he's going to another party is all," Steven said.

"But you have no idea what party?" Downing said.

Steven thought about it for a few beats and shook his head.

"What about Christopher Meyer?" Downing asked. "Did you see him leave?"

"Yeah, he said good-bye at—I wanna say ten thirty, ten forty-five, thereabouts."

"Right before Malcolm left?"

"Yeah, well, it must have been."

"Was he waiting for Malcolm when he left?"

"What? No. I don't know. Crittter said he was going to a party. He said the Hotdish thing was dead and he was going to a party crosstown thrown by a couple of guys he knew from college."

"Did you believe him?" I asked.

Steven, his mother, and Downing all turned to look at me at the same time. I think they forgot I was in the room.

"Whaddya mean?" Steven asked.

"Do you believe that's where Critter went?" I said.

Steven's casual shrug and vacant stare convinced me that Critter must have kept his rendezvous with Diane Dauria a secret.

How chivalrous of him, my inner voice said.

Downing gave me a look. It asked "Are you finished?"—and not in a nice way. I wasn't.

"Why were you following me?" I said.

"I wasn't," Steven said.

"Are you saying that you didn't follow me to the Bru House yesterday?"

"That was just a coincidence."

"The day before, when you followed me from the Szereto Corporation, was that a coincidence, too?"

"I didn't follow you, geezus."

Whatever Downing must have thought about the exchange, he decided to follow my lead.

"We have video from traffic cameras showing your car," he said.

Steven's mouth hung open as if he were wondering how that was possible. 'Course, there was no actual traffic footage, although if we jumped through enough hoops we could probably get our hands on it.

"I don't know what to say," he told us.

His mother did, though.

"That wasn't Steven," she said. "That was me. The Acura belongs to me; Steven just drives it sometimes."

"You were following me?" I asked. "Why?"

"It's not important."

"I beg to differ."

"It has nothing to do with Malcolm running away from home or whatever he did."

"Mrs. Geddings," Downing said.

"It doesn't."

"Please. Tell me the truth and we'll be on our way."

"McKenzie was making everyone unhappy with his questions about Frank Harris. He actually accused Jayne of killing her own husband, did he tell you that? What he said to Diane, practically accusing her, too . . . I thought—we thought—we should keep an eye on him."

"Who's we?"

"The members of Hotdish, some of the members. Okay, it was a mistake. We appreciate that. We stopped when McKenzie attacked my son in the parking lot at—what are you going to do about that? He attacked my son, dragged him from his car. Shouldn't you arrest him for that?"

Downing turned toward Steven.

"Are you willing to press charges?" he asked.

Wait. What?

"Charges?" Steven asked.

"For assault."

C'mon . . .

"You'd need to come down to police headquarters and swear out a complaint, sign a statement, provide evidence to the county attorney's office, eventually testify before a judge . . ."

Okay, my inner voice said. *He's looking out for you; making it seem as if the kid would be the one in trouble.*

"No, no," he said.

"But Steven," his mother said.

"Mom, nothing happened. There wasn't any assault. Gee-zuz."

Annette was clearly disappointed to hear it.

True to his word, Detective Downing ended the interview. A few moments later we were on the sidewalk and moving toward his car.

"That was interesting," he said.

"Which part?"

"The part where the New Brighton Hotdish was so concerned about the questions you were asking that they put a tail on you—such as it was."

"I've been wondering about that myself."

"Although you did promise to keep your mouth shut."

"I lied," I said.

"I noticed."

"What next?"

"Let's go chat with Critter Meyer."

"Works for me."

"I expect you to keep quiet this time."

"I promise."

TWELVE

Critter wasn't home. Or at least he didn't answer when Detective Downing rang the bell and knocked on the door. I told Downing that the last time I saw Critter's mother—Katherine Meyer—she was at Jayne Harris's house. We decided to drive over there. Jayne must have seen us get out of the car and move up the sidewalk, because she pulled open her front door before we reached it. I knew she recognized Downing because she called him by name before he flashed his ID.

"Detective Downing," she said. "McKenzie must have called you. Good."

"I'm sorry for your troubles."

"Thank you. Please come in. Please. McKenzie. Have you learned anything?"

Annette Geddings had departed, of course, but Katie Meyer and Diane Dauria were still there, looking even more somber than before.

"We took a look at your car at Long Lake Regional Park," Downing said. "There's no sign of an accident or . . . anything out of the ordinary. I'd like your permission to impound it and have our forensics people take a closer look."

"Do you think that's necessary?" Jayne asked.

"Honestly, I don't know. What has me curious is the fact that it was parked so close to your home. Why not *at* your home if Malcolm went off with someone of his own free will?"

The words made Jayne wince. I gave her the car key. She squeezed it in her palm before handing it off to Downing.

"Whatever you think is best," Jayne said. "People keep telling me that I'm overreacting, and probably I am, except I remember what happened before."

Downing rested a hand on her shoulder.

"You have no idea how sorry I am that I haven't been able to give you any answers concerning your husband's case," he said.

"Thank you."

"Technically, it's still a little early to involve the police in a missing persons investigation without evidence of, well . . ."

"Foul play," Jayne said. "Are those the words you're trying hard not to say?"

"Mrs. Harris, I'd like a list of Malcolm's friends and acquaintances."

"We've been calling all day," Diane said.

"I appreciate that, ma'am. My experience, though, a young man's friends are often more likely to confide in me than in the young man's family. No disrespect, Mrs. Harris. Usually kids are less afraid of getting their friends in trouble with the police than they are with their mothers."

"I understand."

"I would especially like to speak to . . . Do you know someone called Critter?"

"My son." Katie spoke in a soft voice that contained none of the breathless exuberance I heard when we conversed the day before. "His name is Christopher. Christopher Meyer. Why do you want to talk to him?"

Diane's face colored, although no one seemed to notice except me. She moved against the far wall.

"Where can I find him?" Downing asked.

Katie spun in her seat and angled her body so she could look through the door leading to the kitchen.

"Christopher," she said. "Chris, honey?"

Critter stepped through the door. He was drying his hands with a dish towel. The swelling around his nose had disappeared, and the bruising around his lip had turned from purple to a dull yellow.

"What can I get you?" he asked. "Do you want more coffee?"

He stilled himself when his eyes found me and then shifted to Downing. The detective pulled out his badge and ID and gave Critter a good look at both.

"Critter Meyer?" he said.

"Critter," Katie said. "This is Mr. Downing."

"Detective Clark Downing of the New Brighton Police Division. I'd like to ask you a few questions—"

"About Malcolm," Katie added.

Downing was clearly annoyed at Katie for interrupting him. He was even more irritated when I said, "In private," but went along with it.

"Can we use your kitchen, Mrs. Harris?" he asked.

"Of course."

Downing used his bulk to bully Critter back through the door. I followed behind. Diane seemed to be holding her breath. I whispered to her as I passed, "I'll try to keep your secret." I wasn't seeking to protect her as much as my personal knowledge of how she spent New Year's Eve and the muscle it might give me later. Sometimes I can be a sonuvabitch.

There was a table with chairs. Critter sat in one, and Downing sat in another close enough so that their knees nearly touched. I found a counter to lean against.

"Tell me about the fight," Downing said.

"What fight?" Critter asked.

"You decide. There were two of them, weren't there?"

"No, there was only the one at—it wasn't really a fight. At the Bru House. We were just . . . discussing something."

"Punches were thrown. Customers inside the coffeehouse had to break it up, didn't they?"

"I guess."

"You guess?"

"What I mean is—it wasn't that big a deal."

"What was the fight about?"

"I—I don't know."

"Damn, I'm tired of hearing that from you Hotdishers." Downing switched to full-blown bad-cop mode. "Am I stupid? Do you think I'm stupid, Critter?"

"No, I—"

"You have a fight with a man in a public place in front of thirty witnesses and you tell me that you don't know what it was about? It sounds like you think I'm stupid. Why else would you say such a foolish thing?"

"I don't—"

"Don't want to get into trouble? Is that why you're lying, because you don't want to get into trouble? Because guess what? You're in trouble."

"I'm not lying."

"Then tell me what the fight was about."

"It wasn't about anything."

"Did you hear that, McKenzie? Kid must think we're stupid."

I remembered my promise and shrugged.

"Do you want to know what I think?" Downing added. "I think the fight didn't end at the Bru House and he doesn't want to say. Isn't that right, Critter? Critter—what kind of name is that? Do your parents think you're a tiny animal? A rodent?"

"It's because my little brother couldn't pronounce—"

"No one cares, Critter."

"I don't like it when—"

"When you saw Malcolm at the party last night, what did you think? Did you think it was time to finish this thing, this fight that wasn't about anything? Did you and Malcolm decide to take it outside?"

"No."

"I think that's exactly what you did. The two of you went to the park last night to finish your fight. Either that or you waited outside for him to leave and jumped him. Is that what happened?"

"No."

"What did you do to Malcolm?"

"Nothing. I never touched him."

"What did you do when you left the house?"

"I went to a different New Year's Eve party with some friends from college."

"Are you lying to me?"

"No."

"I think you're lying to me."

"I'm not."

"Whose party did you go to?"

"I didn't know the host. My friends invited me—"

"Give me an address."

"I don't have—"

"The friends you say you went with—give me a name."

"I can't."

"You're lying, kid. I don't like it when people lie to me. It tells me that you think I'm stupid. What do you think, McKenzie?"

I shrugged some more.

"I think we should arrest him," Downing said. "I think we should take him to jail."

"Jail?" Critter was clearly panicked. "Why?"

"Let me tell you how it works, kid. I can bring you in; I don't even need a reason. The law lets me hold you for a minimum of thirty-six hours without a charge. Because it's the holiday, because it'll be hard to scare up a judge to listen to your whining, I bet I can keep you in jail until Monday morning. Is that where you want to spend the next three days? Do you really want to do that to your mother?"

"But I didn't do anything."

"Public brawling."

"It wasn't a brawl. It was—"

"It was what?"

"I don't know."

"Where did you go last night?"

"I don't know."

"Your choice, kid. If you want to spend the weekend in jail, it's all right with me. Stand up."

"No."

Downing rose to his feet and fished a pair of handcuffs from his pocket. Critter stared at them as if they were the scariest things he had ever seen.

"Stand up," Downing repeated.

"Please," Critter said.

"Critter," I said. "Answer the first question and you won't have to answer the second question."

Downing spun to face me. From the expression on his face, he wasn't so much angry at me for interfering as he was confused.

"Critter," I said. "Tell us what the fight was about and we'll end this. Everyone can go home."

"I can't."

"Just remember, this is all on you, kid," Downing said. He took hold of Critter's arm and pulled him out of the chair. Critter kept staring at the handcuffs, and I wondered, Was Downing really going to use them? Knowing what I knew, was I going to let him?

"He was with me," Diane said.

We turned toward the entrance to the kitchen. Diane was standing in the doorway; Katie and Jayne were crowded behind her. So much for privacy.

"Last night," Diane said. "Christopher was with me at my house. McKenzie knows."

"Diane," Critter said.

"With you at your house?" Katie said. "I don't understand. I thought—Chris, I thought you went to a party."

Diane stepped deeper into the kitchen.

"Chris spent the night with me," she said. "He was there from eleven thirty until two thirty this morning."

"What are you saying?" Katie asked.

"I've been sleeping with your son. I'm sorry."

"No. No, no, no, that's—that's not possible. Chris is—"

"He's an adult now. Twenty-one . . ."

"He's my child."

"Katie . . ."

I was astonished by how fast she moved. Katie's hand came up from her hip and slapped Diane's face with such speed, the force of the blow sent her hard against the wall. It reminded me of a gunfighter in one of those classic Western movies— Gregory Peck outdrawing Richard Jaeckel.

"How could you, Diane?" she asked. "He's my son."

"I'm sorry, I'm sorry."

"What is wrong with you? How could you do this?"

"Mom," Critter said.

"You were my friend."

"Stop it, Mother," Critter said. "Don't you dare talk to my woman that way."

He attempted to push past Katie to Diane's side, but his mother stopped him.

"Your woman? Listen to yourself. Your woman? She's older than I am."

"Age is just a number."

"Christopher, no," Diane said. "Don't, don't . . ."

"Do you think I'm going to let her treat you like this? I love you."

"Oh no—no, no. What have I done?" I don't think Diane was talking to us as much as she was to herself. "How could I let this happen? Katie, I'm so sorry."

"Don't talk to her," Critter said. "Talk to me. And don't be sorry. Mom, why are you behaving like this? You're ruining everything."

"Oh. My. God," Katie said.

"We're both adults. What's the big deal?"

"Oh my God."

From the living room came a voice—"I'm home"—followed by "What's going on?"

Jayne shrieked his name—"Malcolm"—and ran toward him. She wrapped her son in her arms. He nearly lost his balance and had to flail his own arms to keep upright, which was difficult because he was holding what looked like a quart-size Tupperware container.

"What the heck, Mom?" he said.

"You're all right, you're all right, you're all right," Jayne chanted. "I was so scared . . ."

Malcolm saw the rest of us filing out of the kitchen.

"What is this?" he asked.

Jayne grabbed both of her son's arms and pushed him back so she could get a good look at him. Her face went from happy to angry just like that.

"Where were you?" Jayne asked. "I was worried sick."

"I'm sorry. I crashed on a friend's couch."

"Why didn't you answer your phone?"

"I dropped it into a sink filled with water and it quit on me." Malcolm opened the Tupperware. It contained white rice and a smartphone. "I was told the rice would absorb the moisture and dry it out. I hope so. I'd hate to have to buy a new one."

"Where's your car?" Downing asked.

"In the driveway. I know you. You're the detective who investigated my father's—who came over when my father died."

"We were so worried," Jayne said. "We called everyone we knew. We even called the police."

"I'm so sorry, Mom. I didn't mean to worry you. I just—I had too much to drink so I . . . I should have called. I'm sorry."

"You're hurt."

Jayne's hand went to Malcolm's neck just below his ear. There was a bruise there, and from the look of it, recently acquired. Malcolm took his mother's hand and pushed it down.

"I'm okay, really," he said. "I ran into something."

Like a lover's bite? my inner voice said. *Because it sure looks like a hickey to me.*

"Ran into something?" Jayne asked. She seemed skeptical, too. "Who were you with?"

Malcolm was gazing across the room at where we all stood in a loose knot. His eyes seemed to fall on Diane, but that could have just been my imagination. In any case, he either didn't notice or didn't care that Critter attempted to slide his arm around her waist. Diane shrugged it away with a hiss.

"Can I tell you later, Mom?" Malcolm said. "I'll tell you all about it later, okay?"

Downing took my elbow and led me across the room toward the door.

"I'm glad it all worked out," he said.

"Thank you," Jayne said. She did something then that surprised Downing and me both. She hugged us each in turn. "Thank you for caring."

"Least I could do," Downing said. He gave up the key to Malcolm's car.

"I have a question," I told Malcolm. "Why did you leave your car in the park last night?"

Again he gazed at Diane while he answered.

"That's where I met my friend," he said.

"Why there?"

"It was convenient."

That way you could get together without anyone actually seeing you together, my inner voice said. *I get it.*

"Mr. McKenzie," Malcolm said. He leaned in and lowered his voice, although I thought everyone in the room could hear him just fine. "I want to thank you for—I know you've been trying to help me, and I'm grateful. I think, though, that we should forget the whole thing. What happened to my father, it's just something I'm going to have to live with, isn't it? Besides, it's not like he was a nice guy or anything."

"Mal," Jayne said. "He was a good father to you."

"He was a lying sonuvabitch who abused my mother. Bastard got what he deserved."

"Mal," Jayne said.

"Mom, I just don't want to think about him anymore. You're the one who's important. You're the one I should be thinking about."

"I would still like to know why you and Critter were fighting over at the Bru House the other day," Downing said.

The question seemed to throw him. Malcolm looked everywhere except at Downing before he said, "Like I keep telling McKenzie, that had nothing to do with my father."

"Nonetheless."

"My mother should never have called you. I'm sorry she did."

Downing didn't like the answer any more than I did, but what was he going to do?

I patted Malcolm's arm as I moved past him toward the front door.

"Call Erica," I said. "She's worried."

My own car was still parked up the street, so we walked first to Downing's vehicle. When we reached it, he said, "What the hell just happened in there?"

"I'm not entirely sure, but I think the New Brighton Hotdish suffered a serious setback."

"Is that on us?"

"I followed Diane Dauria to her home last night. I knew she was with Critter."

"That's why you told him if he answered one question he wouldn't need to answer the other. You were trying to spare him the embarrassment."

"No. I was trying to spare her. He wasn't embarrassed at all."

"If I was twenty-one years old, I wouldn't have been embarrassed, either. She's a looker."

"She is that."

"Critter was willing to go to jail before admitting where he was. That tells me something, though, protecting Dauria's reputation like that."

"Was he protecting Dauria's rep or—now that the affair is out in the open, now that his mother is onto them, I don't think Dauria will be inviting him to her bed anytime soon, and Critter probably knows it, so . . ."

"Who was he protecting by refusing to reveal what his fight with Malcolm was about? Who is Malcolm protecting? Do you think it's Dauria?"

"I don't know."

"Meanwhile, Malcolm shows up out of the blue safe and sound with a hickey on his neck."

"You saw that, too, huh?"

"He told you to quit the investigation."

"Makes me go 'Hmm.' How 'bout you?"

"What do you mean?"

"Yesterday Malcolm was desperate to find out who killed his father. He disappears overnight and suddenly he no longer cares? Something happened. Either someone talked him out of it—or he learned the truth and doesn't want to share."

"What are you going to do?"

"I haven't decided yet."

"Whatever it is, leave me out of it."

Detective Downing climbed into his car and started it up. I waited for him to drive off. Before he did, he lowered his passenger side window and called to me.

"On second thought," he said, "don't leave me out of it."

I drifted to the Mustang. By the time I reached it, the front door of Jayne Harris's home opened and Diane Dauria stepped out as if she were in a hurry. She was carrying her coat and bag. She set the bag on the stoop, quickly pulled on the coat, retrieved the bag, and buttoned up as she walked briskly along the sidewalk. She slowed when she saw me waiting. There were tears in her eyes and on her cheeks, yet none in her voice.

"Are you happy now?" she asked.

"I am so, so sorry."

"What? No smartass remarks? No accusations? No denouncements? Aren't you going to call me a cougar?"

"No."

"Why not? It's true, isn't it?"

"If you had asked me yesterday, I would have said yes. Now that I've had time to think about it—what have you done that guys haven't been doing for ten thousand years?"

"Katie was my friend. That's the difference. This is all on me, McKenzie. How could I have been so foolish? You, though. You were actually trying to help me back there, weren't you?"

"A little bit," I said, although, let's face it, I was trying to help myself, too.

"If I knew more men like you I wouldn't be spending time with boys like Christopher. Tell me—why did you follow me last night? Tell me that."

"Curiosity; the fact that you left Mrs. Szereto's party so early. To be honest, I thought you were leading me to the Hotdish party."

"I don't expect to be invited to many of those in the future. Poor Sloane, she's going to be—she'll never talk to me again. Never."

"Does she need to know?"

"Do you think there's any chance these people will keep it a secret?"

"They're your friends."

"Were my friends. I doubt I'll forgive me, why should they? McKenzie, what exactly did you see last night?"

The girl in the hat, my inner voice screamed at me. *That's why Dauria is being so expansive all of a sudden. She wants to know what you know.*

Oh, she's good, I told myself, even as I answered, "I saw Critter drive up—"

"God, I hate that name. I can't believe Katie actually thinks it's cute."

"I saw the two of you embrace in your foyer. When you shut the front door, I left."

"Before that?"

"Did something happen before that?"

She regarded me in silence for a moment. Her lips formed a thin smile.

"What I said earlier—if I knew more men like you I wouldn't be spending time with boys like Chris? I was kidding. It's guys like you that drive me to younger men. They're so much less complicated."

"They have more stamina, too. Three hours he was with you last night? Wow."

The fire in her eyes, this time it wasn't volcanic so much as smoldering. I had the distinct feeling that we would never be friends.

"I'm so tired," Diane said. "I need to go home. Good night, McKenzie. I hope never to see you again."

"Don't say that. We're just starting to have fun."

I waited until Diane was unlocking her car door and slipping inside before I drew my smartphone out of my pocket. At the same time, Critter Meyer emerged from Jayne Harris's house. He searched up and down the street, saw Diane's car, and started running toward it while waving his arms.

"Diane," he called. "Diane, Diane . . ."

Diane must have heard him, seen him in her rearview mirror, yet she put the vehicle in gear and drove off anyway, leaving him panting on the sidewalk in front of me.

"Diane, please," he said.

"Trouble in paradise?" I asked.

The look in his eyes, the expression of pain on his face—for a moment they made me feel sympathy for him.

"This is all your fault," he said.

"It's called growing up in a hurry," I said.

"Fuck you."

I recalled my conversation with Vanessa Szereto about recreational sex and the need for both parties to be on the same page, only I decided it wasn't something Critter wanted to hear.

"Believe it or not, I'm sorry for you," I said.

"Fuck you."

"Yeah. Listen—I noticed that you never did answer the question about the fight with Malcolm. What was that all about, anyway?"

His response was to give me a good look at the middle finger of both his hands before he stomped off.

I returned to the smartphone. Detective Downing answered on the fourth ring; traffic sounds told me he was driving.

"Now what?" he asked.

"I'm sorry to bug you."

"Yet you keep doing it."

"I need you to run another license plate for me."

"Why?"

"It belongs to a woman who visited Diane Dauria at her home last night just before Critter arrived."

"This is important because . . . ?"

"Remember what I said before about grasping at straws?"

"Monday. I intend to spend an uninterrupted weekend with my family. Send me a text and I'll look into it Monday."

"Thank you," I said. "Happy New Year."

Downing responded by turning off his phone.

The holidays were so hectic for them both that Nina and Erica had been unable to make time for a tradition that stretched back to when Erica was five years old, a tradition that they were happily engaged in when I returned to the condo—making Christmas cookies. I watched mother and daughter from the door and reflected on their relationship: all of the disagreements they'd had; the arguments over rules, some clearly stated, others implied, that were set and broken and rewritten; the unspoken disappointment of one in the other when expectations went unmet; the promises, some made in haste, some unspoken, some shattered, some that would last until the end of time between two women living together, one growing up, the other growing old, bound in a way I probably would never know or understand—it all confused me. Except in moments like this when it was obvious that despite the quarrels they loved each other immensely. More than that, they genuinely liked each other, reveled in each other's company. Respected each other. Wanted sometimes to be each other. It made me happy.

"You know what you two need?" I said. "Someone to manage quality control. But never fear. I'll be happy to taste-test all those cookies for you."

"Listen to this," Nina said.

"You can only have a couple of the coconut macaroons," Erica said. "I'm going to freeze the rest and take them back to Tulane with me."

"They don't have coconut macaroons in New Orleans?" I asked.

"Not the way Mom makes them, dipped in chocolate. Try one." I did. Delicious.

"What else do we have here?" I surveyed the counters where the cookies were set to cool. "Peanut butter blossoms, snickerdoodles, gingerbread, cinnamon pinwheels, walnut balls—hey? Where are the sugar cookies?"

"In the oven, you philistine," Nina said.

"Want me to put sprinkles on them for you?" Erica asked.

"Wouldja? But no frosting. I hate it when they're frosted."

Nina rolled her eyes.

"I spoke to Malcolm," Erica said. "He called right before you got home. He said that he told you to drop the investigation; said it like I was supposed to make sure that you did. I'm sorry about all this, McKenzie."

"Don't worry about it. These are different." I pointed at small, round chocolate cookies topped with chocolate glaze and white sprinkles. "What are these?"

"Mostaccioli," Nina said. "New recipe. Try one."

I did. Both mother and daughter watched while I chewed.

"These are amazing," I said.

"You can't go by him," Erica said. "He likes everything you do."

"It's such a pain," Nina said.

"I don't know how you put up with it."

"What can I say? It's the burden I carry."

"You see me standing here, right?" I said.

"McKenzie, what happened with Malcolm last night?" Erica asked. "Do you know?"

"No. I take it he didn't tell you."

"He refused to talk about it. I made out a list like you asked of all the people I know that Malcolm knows. The only names I could think of are my friends that I introduced him to or people at Tulane. It didn't occur to me until now that he's never introduced me to any of his friends from around here, which is odd. Most of the men I've known, they like to show me off."

Nina's head came up. "Beware of men like that," she said.

"You say that the same way you tell me to drive carefully when it rains and wear a hat when it's cold."

"We lose most of our body heat through the top of the head. Everyone knows that."

"You are such a mom." Erica hugged Nina playfully and kissed the tip of her nose. "You're cute, too. Isn't she cute, McKenzie?"

"Yep," I said.

The ringtone on my cell phone is the opening to "West End Blues," a fifteen-second trumpet cadenza during which Louis Armstrong altered the course of American music. Erica heard it and said, "Haven't you changed that yet?"

And they call me a philistine.

Caller ID said that the caller's name had been blocked, never a good sign. I answered the phone anyway.

"McKenzie," I said.

A male voice spoke with as much menace as it could muster. "You don't know me but I know you," it said. "I know where you live."

I forced myself to sigh heavily. I had been threatened over the phone before and figured I was about to be threatened again.

I found the prospect unnerving, so I did what I nearly always did when someone shoved me out of my comfort zone—I shifted into smartass mode.

"Okay, but make it good," I said.

"What?"

"Your threat. Pretend that you're on *America's Got Talent* and you really want to wow the judges. Ready? Go."

There was a long pause.

"Are you still there?" I asked.

"You're not a policeman. No one is going to care if something happens to you."

"And . . ."

"Keep your nose out of what is none of your business and you won't get hurt."

"Could you be more specific? I have my nose in so many different things these days that are none of my business."

"You've been warned."

"Nope, nope, sorry. Just not a convincing performance. My advice—get more practice, clarify your message, come back and try again."

The phone went dead.

"Hello?" I said. "Hello?"

I slipped the cell back into my pocket.

"Did someone just threaten you?" Nina asked.

"Yeah, but it was a weak attempt."

"Why?" Erica asked. "Why did they threaten you? Was it because of Malcolm and his father?"

"I honestly don't know. Maybe they'll tell me next time."

"Next time? You think they'll call again?"

Nina hugged her daughter with the same playfulness with which Erica had hugged her.

"You act like this is something new," she said. "Believe me, it happens all the time."

THIRTEEN

It was quiet. Too quiet. I preferred noise, even at 9:00 A.M. I thought of putting on some music, one of the vinyl records recorded by New Orleans jazz bands that Erica gave me for Christmas—along with a Preservation Hall Jazz Band T-shirt—and cranking the volume all the way to eleven; I had speakers hidden in nooks and crannies throughout the condo. Only Erica was still in bed because she was a college kid home for the holidays and never roused herself before noon, and Nina was still in bed because she owned a high-class saloon and often didn't return home until the wee hours of the morning. You're thinking, There is such a thing as headphones. Nina bought me a set a long time ago, except I hardly ever use them. Music just doesn't sound the same coming through headphones or earbuds, I don't know why.

So I sat, uncomfortable in the silence, staring at my landline, wondering if I should call Detective Clark Downing of the New Brighton Police Division or wait for him to contact me. I had sent him a text containing the license plate number I wanted him to check. He said he'd get back to me on Monday. Well, it was Monday.

I reached for the phone, removed it from the cradle, and heard a ping. My first thought—when did the phone start pinging? My second—my PC was announcing that I had received an e-mail. I hung up the phone and checked my account. Sure enough, it was from Downing. The subject line read: *license plate number.* The body copy read: *I got nothing. How about* you?

I opened the attachment. It told me that the license plate belonged to Rebecca Denise Crawford and listed her address in St. Louis Park. Date of birth: 02-07-1989. Sex: F. Eyes: BRN. Height: 5'6". Weight: 125. She was listed as an organ donor. She had no criminal record, not as much as a parking ticket.

I ran the name through various search engines on my computer to learn what I could about her and came up empty. There were a surprising number of Rebecca, Becky, and Becca Crawfords out there—at least I was surprised—yet none with the middle name Denise *and* a Minnesota address. She didn't have an account with Facebook, Pinterest, Twitter, Instagram, or any other social media outlet that I could find; nor was she affiliated with business sites such as LinkedIn. She had not uploaded a résumé on any of the more prominent job sites; nor was she listed in the alumni directory of any of Minnesota's forty-four colleges and universities. After a while I became so frustrated that I broke down and processed her name and address through a few of the for-profit people-finder Web sites and discovered that they were no more efficient than I was.

This is a woman who values her privacy, my inner voice told me.

I did a property tax search through the Hennepin County Web site to assure myself that Crawford, Rebecca D. did, in fact, own property at the address in St. Louis Park with an estimated market value of $284,000.

The *D* gave me an idea. I searched again, this time looking for R. D. Crawford. Most of the hits were for addresses found on a dozen different Crawford Roads scattered throughout the

country or for roads located in the various towns named Crawford. I kept at it, though, and found several Roberts, one Ro-
berta, a couple of Richards, and a dress store in Atlanta that
didn't explain what its initials stood for. I was about to lose
heart when I came across the Web site of a graphic design company in Chicago that promoted itself by displaying the work it
had produced for its better-known paying clients—including
last year's annual report for Barek Cosmetics, Inc. Among the
sample pages it displayed was the report's table of contents, with
these lines.

Photographer: Montgomery Leddy
Writers: Sarah Carrell, Charles Martin
Contributors: Renee Bennett, R. D. Crawford, Peter Sisco

I had to let that sink in for a moment.
Is this the same person? my inner voice asked.
I went to the official Barek Cosmetics Web site. It provided
a ton of information about its products—there were quite a few
of them—and the stores across the country where they could be
purchased, yet nothing about the parent company itself; not
even its location. There was a Wikipedia page, except it only
told me that Barek was founded in 1974 and its headquarters
was in Minneapolis. It did provide a link, however, labeled "corporate inquiries." I clicked on it and was directed to a page
that offered additional links for distributor and affiliate information as well as employment information. The page also listed
the company's address and an 800 number. I dialed it. A metallic voice told me that if I knew my party's extension I should
input it now or otherwise wait for an operator. I waited. Barek
apparently didn't like the song "The Girl from Ipanema,"
because it played the absolute worst cover of it that the company could find. Eventually, an operator came on and asked for
the name of my party.

"Rebecca Crawford," I told her.

A moment later, the operator told me she did not have a listing for Rebecca, but there was an R. D. Crawford in the Department for Research and Development.

"Yes." I tried hard to contain my excitement. "Rebecca Denise Crawford."

"Please hold."

A moment later a woman said, "This is Rebecca." Before I could say anything, she added, "I'm unable to answer the phone right now . . ."

I hung up without listening to the rest of the message.

At some point during all of this, Nina had materialized in the kitchen area and poured herself a cup of coffee. She was watching me from the island. I don't know if it was my smile or the way I did a little dance behind my desk, but she asked, "What?"

"I love detective work," I told her.

What do we know? my inner voice asked.

We know that Rebecca Denise Crawford works R&D for Barek Cosmetics.

We know that she and Diane Dauria are passing notes during late-night meetings.

We know that Barek Cosmetics has accused the Szereto Corporation of stealing trade secrets.

We know that Diane is anxious that we know.

How is this going to help us find out who killed Frank Harris or Jonny Szereto?

That we don't know.

What do we know?

You keep asking that.

Well?

We know that Malcolm was keen on finding out what

happened to his father until he met someone on New Year's Eve who gave him a hickey.

Who?

He won't tell me. Or Detective Downing. Or Erica, for that matter.

Who would he tell?

I thought about that long and hard before I came up with an answer—his mother.

Now the big question—why do you still care?

Good question. I felt a little like a historian working a Rubik's Cube, twisting the sides this way and that until it gave me a clear picture of what happened at such and such a time in such and such a place—but to what purpose? Usually with my cases— I didn't know what else to call them—I had a goal in mind, a specific outcome. But with Malcolm quitting on me, who was I helping? Who was I protecting? Who was I punishing? What good was I doing?

Well, you did promise Evelyn Szereto, sorta.

I went to the closet for a hat and coat, telling Nina that there were a few things that needed doing. She told me that she and her daughter had reservations for an English high tea complete with finger sandwiches and pastries at a shop in Anoka.

Nina raised her voice. "Assuming Erica ever gets up."

Erica replied from her bedroom. "You don't love me."

"It should take most of the afternoon, so we might not be here when you get back."

"Save a scone for me," I told her.

I had no idea what kind of reception I would receive when I rang Jayne Harris's bell. I steeled myself against the possibility she would tell me to get lost and slam the door in my face. Instead, she seemed delighted to see me, even gave me another hug.

"I didn't thank you properly for what you did last Friday," Jayne told me. "Dropping everything to help the way you did. It was so generous."

"I was relieved beyond words that it all worked out as well as it did."

Laying it on a little thick, aren't you, pal? my inner voice said.

"Come in, come in," Jayne said. "It's so gray today. They say there's a twenty percent chance of rain. Rain. Do you believe that? Not snow. Rain—in Minnesota—in January."

She didn't really care about the weather, I decided. It was just something that women in Minnesota often use as an ice-breaker before engaging in an important conversation. With men it's usually how badly they expect the Vikings to suck.

"How is Malcolm?" I asked.

"He seems fine. Happier than he's been . . . well, for a long time. It's like a weight's been lifted from his shoulders."

"I wonder why."

"He won't tell me. When I ask, he giggles. Twenty-one years old, for God's sake, and he giggles like a girl. Is that the reason you came over today, McKenzie? Because you want to know why?"

"Don't you?"

"No." Jayne took a deep breath and closed her eyes. They snapped open with her exhale. "Yes. For a long time I didn't care. I saw how not knowing affected Malcolm, and I still didn't care. Now he seems at peace with what happened to Frank, and I realize that I never have been; that I was just pretending. I don't know what to do about it."

"Where is Malcolm?"

Jayne waved absently at the door. "Out," she said.

"Did he tell you where he was New Year's Eve?'"

"Does it matter?"

"It might matter immensely."

"He said he was with Sloane—Sloane Dauria. She arrived just as he was leaving. He told her that he was tired of the party and was going home. She said she didn't want to be surrounded by a lot of people either and invited him to her apartment. He accepted. Wouldn't you?"

"At his age? Probably."

"They rendezvoused at the park and then drove to St. Paul together. McKenzie, you should have seen his body, the hickeys on his chest and—the girl marked her territory. She's worse than her mother. No, that's not fair. Sloane's just—we say 'red-blooded American boy.' Well, Sloane is a 'red-blooded American girl.' Maybe that's why Mal is so happy all of a sudden, because he spent the night with her. What do they call it? Emotionally focused therapy?"

"Among other things."

"Maybe I should get out there myself; find someone to take care of me like he did. Like Diane did. Diane—what a mess."

"How bad is it?"

"Bad."

"How's Katie taking it?"

"Hard to say. The woman is incapable of hate. She gets as angry as anyone, only it never lasts for long because she can't bring herself to hate the thing she's angry at. If it was me, if Diane had slept with Malcolm—McKenzie, you don't still believe I killed my husband, do you?"

I couldn't eliminate her as a suspect. Not yet, anyway. But her name was so far down on my list that I was able to say no and make her believe it.

"Malcolm doesn't seem to care anymore. Either that or he's put up a façade like the one I've been hiding behind for the past year. I care, though. It's time I admitted it. McKenzie, if you could find out what happened to Frank for me . . ."

"I'll do my best."

I don't take money from the people I do favors for. Still, I told myself, it was nice to actually have "a client." Made me think I was doing all of this for someone's good and not just to satisfy my own morbid curiosity.

Jayne had given me Sloane Dauria's address, and I drove into St. Paul looking for it. The search took me to Merriam Park, where I grew up. There was the house where I lived with my father after Mom died, the Church of St. Mark where the funeral services were held and its companion elementary school, the corner where the Burger Chef used to be, the library now New! and Improved!, St. Thomas University, the Merriam Park Recreational Center, and across the street the house where Bobby Dunston lived with Shelby and their two girls; the house where he grew up, where I often sought refuge from my loneliness.

I thought of stopping in. They plus Nina and Erica made up the extent of my family. Without them, I would feel outnumbered.

First things first, though.

I found the apartment building where Sloane lived on an active bus route. It was an old building. Its security system consisted of an intercom with the names of the apartment dwellers. I pressed the one marked S. DAURIA. A moment later her voice asked, "Who is it?"

"McKenzie."

There was a short pause followed by a buzzing sound and a metallic click. I opened the inner door and the buzzing stopped. I walked up two flights of stairs and searched the corridor for her door. I knocked. The door was pulled open. Sloane said, "Hello."

I said, "What happened to you?"

Sloane was wearing a tank top and gym shorts, and I could see bruising on her shoulders, collarbone, thigh, and calf muscle.

"Now you know why I wore that ugly dress on New Year's Eve," she said.

"Sloane . . ."

"Come in, come in. What can I do for you?"

The door was closed. Sloane turned and led me into her living room as if she were used to going first while the rest of the world followed along. She turned again and stood flat-footed, feet apart, hands at her side in front of me, giving me a good look at her body. Along with the bruises there was swelling and a few red blotches.

"Sloane," I said again.

"I've been fighting."

"I can see that."

"Don't tell Mom."

"She can't figure it out for herself?"

"I've been hiding the bruises until I get better. I don't want her to freak."

"Sloane, what the hell?"

"I wanted to learn to fight, so I've been working out at Gracie's Power Academy."

"In Frogtown?"

"You know it?"

"The owner, Dave Gracie—he's taught me a thing or two over the years. 'Course, that's when it was called Gracie's Gym."

"He's a sweetheart."

"The times I've worked out with him—I hadn't noticed that."

"They have a program now for training women to compete in mixed martial arts."

"Sloane, don't, don't, don't go there."

"I'm not. I can't compete with those girls. I learned that the first week. But they have a kind of introductory course that will teach you how to get by."

"Get by where? Syria?"

"McKenzie." Her voice became hard and unyielding. "No one

will ever do to me what they did to Jayne Harris or Katie Meyer. No one. Not without a fight."

"What did they do to Katie Meyer?"

Sloane turned and walked slowly to a chair where there was a gray sweatshirt with the name ST. KATE'S WILDCATS stenciled across the front. She put it on and fluffed her red hair over the collar.

"Mom always says not to speak when you're angry," she said. "At least she's said it enough that you'd think I'd catch on by now."

"Are you angry?"

"McKenzie, I spoke out of turn. Whatever happened to Katie belongs to Katie. If you have questions, you need to speak to her."

She has a lot of self-control; you have to give her that, I told myself. And a competent way of handling herself that you usually don't find in someone so young. Add that to the arrogance of invulnerability most people her age seemed to possess . . .

"Sloane, you're going to get hurt," I said.

"Just a few bruises until I learn to protect myself."

"That's not what I meant, but never mind."

"Why are you here, McKenzie?"

"I have questions I hope you can answer."

"About what? Malcolm?"

"Yes."

"He's kind of a romantic, isn't he?"

"He refuses to believe that his father abused his mother."

"That's what I mean."

"When Erica brought him to me—"

"Erica." She spoke the name as if she found it exasperating. "Another romantic."

"Have you met?"

"No, but Malcolm told me about her. Rickie. Another one who believes in fairy tales."

"I take it you don't."

Sloane made a fist and tapped it against the palm of her other hand. "I want to," she said. "I wish I could."

"When I met him, Malcolm was desperate to find out what happened to his father. He spent one night with you and suddenly he couldn't care less."

"You don't approve of Malcolm and me, do you? Us sleeping together."

"Hard to judge when all you're doing is pretty much the same thing I did when I was your age."

"Talk to my mom. She doesn't see it that way."

"She's your mother. What do you expect?"

"I expect . . . It doesn't matter. Anyway, you want to know what I told Mal."

"Yes."

"I reminded him that he has a mother who loves him more than anything. And he should love her at least as much."

"Could you possibly be more ambiguous?"

Sloane laughed at me.

"I don't mean to be," she said. "But McKenzie, it's the same thing. If you want answers about Malcolm, you need to talk to Malcolm."

"According to his mother, he's been pretty incoherent since he spent the evening with you."

"Like I said, he's a romantic."

"What's with all the hickeys?"

"He made fun of my bruises, so I gave him a few that I could make fun of. I didn't hear any complaints at the time."

"His cell phone?"

"That was something we made up to pacify Jayne. 'Course, we didn't know the cops were looking for him."

Sloane spoke so straightforwardly about her tryst with Malcolm that it set me back. I had been trying to figure out who she was since we met and failing, possibly because she was in the process of doing the same thing and was just as baffled as I was. I took a chance.

"Critter Meyer," I said. "You're the one who gave him the fat lip, aren't you?"

"He said something about my mother that I didn't like. I made him take it back."

"Do you want to talk about it?"

"Not particularly."

"Okay."

"Oh, why not? You know about Mom anyway, don't you? Her and Critter?"

"Yes."

"Of course you do. You want to know how I feel about it, too, I'll bet. I honestly don't know yet. Katie came over yesterday; we talked for hours. She's so concerned that I don't blame my mother. Actually, she doesn't care if I blame her or not, she just doesn't want me to stop loving my mother. Can you believe that? Is she incredible or what?"

"Seems to be."

"As for Mom—I've been riding that roller coaster all weekend. She keeps calling and I keep swiping left. I don't want to talk to her until I know what I'm going to say. Right now—if you look at it objectively, you have a gullible, dreamy college boy who meets a beautiful, lonely MILF—"

"I've never liked that acronym."

"Romance blooms, at least on his side. On her side, what? Companionship? Someone warm to cling to on a cold winter's night? A fuck toy? Goddammit, Mother."

I rested what I thought was a reassuring hand on her shoulder. Sloane might have had the look of someone who was hard to jolt, but that jolted her. She tensed and backed away quickly until she was out of reach.

"Excuse me," I said.

"No. Excuse me. It often takes a long time before I feel at ease with people."

"I'm much the same way."

"What would you tell my mother, McKenzie? If she were standing in front of you right this minute, what would you say?"

"Never do anything you wouldn't want your daughter to know about."

Sloane laughed at that.

"And never do anything you wouldn't want your mother to know about," she said. "I've been so concerned over what I'm going to tell her about Critter that it didn't occur to me until just now that she might have a few choice words to say about Malcolm."

Sloane smiled, stepped forward, and shook my hand.

"I'm sorry I couldn't answer your questions, McKenzie," she said. "If Mal won't tell you, I guess you're out of luck. Now you'll have to excuse me. I need to call my mom."

And I thought, Sloane really is a fighter, a ring girl who could take a shot that lands her facedown, but who pushes the canvas away at the three count, comes to one knee at six, stands at nine and, grinning foolishly, brings her gloves up and moves forward.

I'd wager that her mother was the same way.

I sat in the Mustang outside of Sloane's apartment building, listening to Wes Montgomery on the radio and checking my mirrors. A small tingling sensation told me that I was being watched. But by whom? Sloane's apartment was on the far side of the building; she wouldn't have been able to see me from her window.

I started the car and drove off, accelerating and slowing, making random turns through the neighborhood I knew so well. I couldn't pick anyone up. I felt disappointed. I realized that I wanted something to happen. I needed a new puzzle piece to work with because the ones I had just didn't fit together; they gave me no sense of the picture they were supposed to display.

Why was it important that I discover the reason Malcolm and Critter were fighting outside the Bru House? Why did it bother me that the kid no longer wanted to know who killed his father? Why should I care that Diane Dauria and R. D. Crawford met New Year's Eve? Why did it matter that Vanessa owned the Szereto Corporation instead of Evelyn?

I believed in momentum. I believed that if you keep moving, peeking under beds, peeping over fences, turning over rocks, there's a better chance of accidents happening, some good, some bad; of the fortuitous unearthing of the odd puzzle piece in the most unlikely nook or cranny. Except I was stalled. I had no idea what to do next. Where to go. Whom to talk to.

Driving back to the condo, I got caught by a light. While I waited, I heard Louis Armstrong's trumpet solo playing from my cell phone. The caller ID told me that it was Diane Dauria.

"Diane," I said.

"No. This is Evelyn Szereto. I'm using Diane's office. I'm calling from her phone."

"Good afternoon, Evelyn."

"We were supposed to talk New Year's Eve. Jack told you."

"Yes, sorry 'bout that. You retired upstairs, and I didn't want to disturb you."

"Nonsense. I saw you standing on the staircase watching us. If you had waited ten minutes . . ."

"Here I thought I was being a gentleman."

"It wasn't necessary."

"Nonetheless."

"Have you eaten?"

"No."

"Come to the corporate offices. We'll have a late lunch in the employee cafeteria, and I'll tell you what's on my mind."

"I'll be there in twenty minutes."

I parked in the visitor's section of the sprawling lot and walked toward the entrance. As I approached, a woman stepped outside the building that housed the Szereto corporate offices. She was five-six, 125 pounds, with brown hair and brown eyes, but all that registered later. What I noticed first, what made me stop and stare, was her hunter green felt hat with a wide brim and a festive green and blue hatband.

I blocked her path. For a moment we engaged in that little dance people do when they're caught in an aisle at a supermarket or department store until she realized I kept sliding in front of her on purpose. She looked me hard in the eye.

"May I help you?" she said.

"I like your hat."

"Thank you. Now, if you'll excuse me . . ."

"R. D. Crawford, right?"

"Do I know you?"

"Rebecca Denise Crawford."

"Who are you?" she asked.

I recited her address in St. Louis Park. I meant to panic the woman. Instead, she tilted her head prettily as she assessed the weight of my words. A thin smile formed on her lips.

"McKenzie," she said.

"Yes."

Rebecca reached out and set a hand on my arm.

"Diane Dauria warned me that you might have seen us the other night," she said. "I must say, honey, you're taller than I'd thought you'd be."

"Oh?"

"Considering some of the words she used in describing you— sniveling toady, busybody night crawler . . ."

"Ahh."

"Peeping Tom, scandalmonger . . ."

"Yeah, I get it."

"How do you know my address?"

"I ran your license plate."

"How resourceful of you, baby." Rebecca rubbed my forearm a bit just to remind me that her hand was still there. "What else do you know about me?"

"Very little. You don't leave a large footprint. I presume it's on purpose."

She seemed pleased by my admission. Let her be, I told myself. In the meantime, I'd keep Barek Cosmetics in my pocket. Knowledge really is power, and I didn't want to repeat the mistake I had made with Diane, giving up too much of it too soon.

"You work for Mrs. Szereto, don't you?" Rebecca asked.

"You could say that."

"Then we're both on the same side."

"Quite possibly."

"Would you like to have a drink with me?"

"I'd like that very much."

Rebecca rubbed my arm some more and suggested a family restaurant-slash-bar just off the freeway and provided directions before we broke for our separate cars. I had the number for Evelyn's landline, but I knew she wasn't home. My cell had captured Diane Dauria's phone number, though, and I called that. Someone must have been using it, however, because I was sent immediately to voice mail.

"Diane, this is McKenzie," I said. "Please convey my apologies to Mrs. Szereto." I told her where I was going. "Something came up involving one of your employees. I'll try to call her at home first chance I get, or she can contact me. Thank you."

I was smiling when I hung up. This was what I meant by momentum.

FOURTEEN

It was one of those national chains where the waitstaff wore garish shirts and relentless smiles and where there were weekly, daily, and hourly specials on just about everything. The hostess tried to seat us at a tall table near the bar, but Rebecca lobbied for a booth against the wall. My first thought—she wanted privacy. That opinion changed when she claimed the far seat, the one that gave her an unobstructed view of the entrance.

Rebecca folded her charcoal coat and set it on the seat next to her, dropping her flashy hat on top. She positioned her cell phone, screen up, on the table in front of her. I left mine in my jacket pocket. A moment later, the waitress enticed us with all manner of food choices from appetizers to desserts. Rebecca declined them all, though, so I did the same. She ordered a vodka gimlet. I thought about a Summit Ale but went with a Maker's Mark on the rocks because I thought it made me look tougher. Despite her near-constant smile, Rebecca struck me as a woman who liked tough.

I paid for the drinks as soon as they were served.

"How well do you know Mrs. Szereto, sweetie?" Rebecca asked.

"I've been to her house."

"That's nothing, honey. Everyone who works for Szereto has been there—for her party, if nothing else."

"Have you been to her party?"

"A couple of times."

How is that possible? my inner voice asked.

"In my case, it was a private affair," I said aloud.

She leaned across the table to rest her fingertips on my hand. Her voice was soft, just above a whisper.

"*Private affair*—aren't you the mysterious one," she said.

"Me?" I said. "You're the one engaged in mysterious late-night meetings."

"But baby, you're the one spying on them from parked cars— that was your Mustang in front of Diane's house, wasn't it? I should have known. It's illegal in that neighborhood to park on the street at night."

Do not underestimate this woman, my inner voice warned. *Do not, do not . . .*

My cell played for me. I pulled my hand away, fetched the phone from my pocket, glanced at the caller ID—it was Mrs. Szereto—and swiped left, before turning off the ringtone and dropping it screen down on top of my coat.

"Louis Armstrong," Rebecca said. She reached for my hand again, and I let her. "I'm impressed, honey."

"What was in the envelope you gave Diane?" I asked.

Again I meant to panic her, yet my question didn't seem to joggle Rebecca one damned bit.

"A belated Christmas card," she said.

"That you delivered at 11:30 P.M. on New Year's Eve?"

"I was in the neighborhood."

"You didn't stay long."

"Oh, sweetie, it was late. I needed my beauty sleep."

"Don't we all?"

"Why were you following Diane?" she asked.

"Curiosity."

"What do they say—curiosity killed the cat?"

"But satisfaction brought him back."

"Are you really that guy?"

"I am. And while we're at it—can I ask what school you went to?"

"Why do you ask, baby?"

"You're using a lot of names that end in *y,* and you keep touching me when you speak with that breathless voice of yours. Straight-up Seduction 101. Just wondering where you took your degree."

"The school of hard knocks."

"Not actually a thing, but okay."

Rebecca withdrew her hand, and her voice became harder, colder; yet I still found it pleasant to listen to.

"You know nothing about me," she said.

"How long have you been working for the Szereto Corporation?"

"On and off for five years."

On and off?

"Do you like it there?" I asked.

"It's okay. The benefits are nice."

"Plus, there's the profit sharing."

"Mrs. Szereto is very generous."

"Seems not everyone is happy about that."

Rebecca tilted her head and paused as if she were wondering what to make of my remark before deciding she didn't care.

"McKenzie, I want you to leave me alone," she said. "I want you to leave Diane Dauria alone. I want you to go far, far away and never come back."

"Yeah, I get that a lot."

"Please. I'm serious. It'll be better for all of us. You included. I mean it. Bullshit aside. We can still be friends. We can have a few drinks, get something to eat, and later if you want I'll take you home and screw your brains out—if you will just promise to walk away."

"Helluvan offer, I have to admit."

"But you're going to turn me down."

" 'Fraid so."

Rebecca glanced at her smartphone and back at the door.

"Yeah, I figured you would," she said. "But there's no harm in trying, is there? Tell me, though, just out of curiosity—would you have accepted the offer if Diane had made it?"

"No."

"Seriously?"

"Why do you ask?"

"I was just wondering if you preferred her over me. The woman looks good in black even if she is older." She glanced at her cell again. "McKenzie, I know what you're doing for Mrs. Szereto."

Diane must have told her, my inner voice said. *So why is she telling you?*

She's killing time, I told myself.

"It has nothing to do with me, I promise you," Rebecca said. "I am not involved in any of that. Neither was Diana. We had nothing to do with what happened to Jonny Szereto. Not a thing. I'm trying to be honest here."

"What are you involved in?"

Rebecca exhaled dramatically and shrugged as if to say, "I tried," then began gathering up her belongings.

"You're cute," she said. "I didn't expect that, either, what with the names Diane called you. I'd hate like hell to see someone mess up your pretty face."

It was the most blatant threat I had ever heard from a woman—and you have to remember, I live with two girls who have threatened to kill me on numerous occasions. The fact Rebecca mentioned damage to my face made me assume it was something that she feared and figured I would fear as well.

"It is a pretty face," I said. "Some people say I look like Bradley Cooper."

Rebecca slipped her phone into her bag and stood.

"Not that pretty." She looked toward the entrance. "Gotta go."

I spun in my seat to look at the door, too. There was no one there. By the time I turned back, Rebecca was buttoning her coat. She put on her hat, positioning it just so.

"I wasn't kidding before," I said. "I really like the hat."

"Thank you. I found it in a consignment shop. Ten bucks. Crazy. Good-bye, McKenzie."

Rebecca headed for the door. I gave her a head start and followed.

The restaurant-slash-bar actually had two doors, inside and outside, separated by a small foyer. A large man opened the outside door just as Rebecca opened the inside door. He held it for her as she passed through the foyer and went outside. The man let the door close behind him just as I stepped into the foyer. He set a beefy hand against my chest. I stopped. He was bigger than I was but not by so much that I was anxious about it. The inside door closed behind me, leaving us alone inside the foyer with no one to hear him say "You're Rushmore McKenzie" except me.

The man continued speaking with a voice that suggested he was used to getting his way, reciting in surprising detail the facts of my life: my name and exact address in Minneapolis down to the number on my condo door, the year and color of my Mustang and its license plate number, where I went to college, what I used to do for a living. He didn't pause a moment for me to reply. Apparently he expected me to shut up and listen, so I did.

"You're an ex-cop who sold his badge to collect a reward on a felon everyone was chasing," he said. "You grew the reward with some very smart investments that someone else made for you, and now you have a net worth of about five million, all of it in low-risk, low-yield mutual funds. You live with Nina Truhler, who owns a club called Rickie's on Cathedral Hill in St. Paul. She has short black hair and silver-blue eyes. She drives a Lexus that she parks on the far side of the lot so her customers can park closer to the door. It's not unusual for her to be the last one to leave after the place closes. She has a twenty-year-old daughter named Erica who attends Tulane University in New Orleans, although she's staying with you for the holidays. She was state champion in fencing her senior year of high school, it was épée, I believe. Honor student. Should I tell you what dorm she lives in on campus? Her roommate's name? It's Caroline. I can reach out and swat either one of them anytime I like."

His words were meant to terrify, and they probably would have if I hadn't used the same ploy myself; if I hadn't tried it on Rebecca Crawford just an hour earlier. A complete stranger stopping you on the street, telling you stuff about yourself that he shouldn't know, of course it would make you feel exposed and vulnerable; make you believe that he actually could hurt you or someone you love anytime he wanted, and there would be nothing you would be able to do about it.

I have to admit, it did give me a twinge, except—the intelligence he had gathered was superficial, the kind of thing you might learn by running someone's license plate number or reading someone's Facebook page, just as I had attempted to do with Rebecca. He didn't mention, for example, that I had friends in the St. Paul and Minneapolis police departments as well as the BCA, FBI, and ATF; or that an assistant U.S. attorney named Finnegan owed me a huge favor that I had been hoarding like a rare bottle of wine that could only go up in value. Nor did he list the names of the people I've killed or mention that fourteen months ago I was in the newspapers for shooting a man who hurt someone I cared for a lot less than I cared for Nina and Erica.

"Do not concern yourself with things that are none of your business," he said.

"Do I look concerned?"

My response seemed to catch him by surprise. His response was to double down. He shoved a finger in my face.

"Stay away from Szereto," he said. "Do you understand?"

I didn't say.

He leaned in close. His breath smelled of the lunch he ate that day.

"Do you understand?" he repeated.

I nodded my head.

"Thank the boss you're getting this warning," he said. "If it was up to me, I'd kill you right now."

He turned, opened the outside door, and left the foyer. I gave him a slow five count and started following; I was going to count to ten, but he was moving too fast. He was halfway across the parking lot before he noticed me. He stopped. I stopped. He stared at me. I stared at him. His coat was zippered tight, and his pockets were flat; he was wearing thick gloves. If he was carrying, I would have plenty of time to decide what to do before he could turn a gun.

He started walking again. I followed. I slowed a little bit when he reached into his pocket, but sped up when I realized that he had pulled out a black key fob. He aimed it at an SUV. Its lights flashed, and I heard a distinct click.

He stopped again. I did the same.

"What do you think you're doing?" he asked.

"I'm following you, can't you tell? Is this your car?"

I pulled my cell from my pocket and took a pic of the rear of the SUV.

"What the fuck?" he said.

"Say cheese," I said.

I made a production of taking his pic.

"Stop it," he said, adding "asshole" for dramatic effect.

He took a step forward.

"Have you forgotten what I told you already?" he asked.

I took a step backward while slipping the cell back into my pocket.

"Yeah, yeah, yeah, you know where I live," I said. "You told me last Friday over the phone."

He took another forward step.

"What the fuck are you talking about?" he said. "I never called you."

I took another backward step.

"Whatever."

He moved toward me. I stopped and went into my stance—shoulders sideways, feet at 45-degree angles and a shoulder's width apart, knees slightly bent, left hand up so my left fist was chin high and my right fist was even with my rib cage.

"Are you fucking kidding me?" he asked.

I spoke slowly and succinctly. "Pricks like you get away with your bullshit because you refuse to play by the rules, but you expect everyone else to. I'm not that guy. You dare threaten the people I care about? You should have done better research."

To prove it, I raised my rear leg high into the chamber, and snapped it up and out so that my heel hit him square in the face. The force of the blow sent him backward against the SUV.

I bet he didn't know I could do that, I told myself, although in all honesty, I hadn't practiced in nearly six months—which is probably why he was able to peel himself off the car, shake his head, and, despite the cut that had opened up above his eyebrow, move forward in a boxer's crouch, both hands up.

I did a little hop and kicked him again. Only this time I brought my front knee up until my foot was in the blade position and then struck down as hard as I could against his knee. I heard a satisfying crunch. He screamed and crumbled to the ground as if he had been hit with an air-to-surface missile.

While he was rolling around on the asphalt, holding his knee with both hands, I searched him until I found his wallet in his back pocket. He screamed some more, adding a few poorly chosen obscenities, while I pulled out his driver's license. I read it aloud, starting with his name—"Ronald Cardiff"—and threw the wallet in his face.

"I'm going to keep this," I said. "I'm going to show it to all my friends. If any of them tell me they saw someone who looks even remotely like you, I will find you. It will not be a fair fight. You will not see me coming. Do *you* understand?"

He didn't answer, so I nudged his smashed knee with my toe.

"Yeah, yeah," he said.

"Tell Crawford she and I are going to have words."

"Who?"

I heard footsteps coming fast behind me. Probably some good Samaritan rushing to the rescue, I told myself.

I turned to look.

A man raised a short section of pipe high in the air and swung it down hard toward my head.

I dropped the driver's license and brought my left arm up to ward off the blow.

The pipe hit the bone above my wrist.

I knew it was fractured before I felt the pain.

I also knew that if I stopped to assess the damage, the next blow might kill me. One of the things Dave Gracie taught—you never stop fighting.

The thug raised the pipe again. I noticed the white athletic tape wrapped around the end he was holding. Apparently he had used the weapon before, probably with considerable success.

Instead of attempting to block it, though, I pivoted out of the way.

The pipe caught nothing but air; the man who was wielding it nearly lost his balance.

I dodged around him, holding my left arm close to my body.

This is on you, my inner voice said. *You should have made sure Ronald was alone.*

Yeah, but he took so long coming forward, I told myself. What was I supposed to do?

Careless, careless, careless.

The thug swung the pipe again, this time sideways as if he were attempting to cave in my ribs.

I danced away, then steadied myself.

He lifted the pipe high again and came toward me.

I knew I couldn't outpunch him with a broken arm.

This is going to hurt, I told myself.

As soon as he was in range, I jumped up and fired my left foot into his solar plexus.

The blow staggered him. He dropped the pipe, but he didn't fall; I thought I hurt myself more than I did him, the way the pain in my wrist reached my spine.

I braced my arm against my body some more and kicked him in the groin just as hard as I could.

He howled in pain, yet still did not fall.

I kicked him again.

He cupped his groin and fell sideways almost in slow motion; it was like a scene in a Sam Peckinpah movie.

By then Ronald was standing. Most of his weight was on his undamaged leg while he leaned against the SUV; blood poured down his face from the cut above his eyebrow. He had an oddly quizzical expression. It was if he were watching something he had never seen before and couldn't quite make sense of it.

I bent with my knees and scooped up his driver's license, making a big deal of stuffing it into my pocket. I turned and walked away, letting my left arm swing freely at my side despite the pain the movement caused, because I didn't want them to know that I had been hurt.

———

I went to the North Memorial Health Care Clinic near the Ridgedale shopping center because the voice on my onboard computer told me it was closest. It wasn't easy getting there because I was too damn old-school to own a Ford Mustang with an automatic transmission. Oh, no—I had to drive a stick. Try managing a stick shift with one hand someday.

Everyone there was nice to me, though, even if they did seem to take their own sweet time fixing me up—two hours and twenty-seven minutes by my watch. As it turned out, x-rays revealed I had suffered a simple fracture of the ulna bone just above the wrist. There was plenty of tenderness, inflammation, and bruising over the fracture site, yet no sign of nerve or vascular damage. They gave me a couple of pills for the pain, put me in a cast, and said it would take six to eight weeks to heal but that I should go in for additional x-rays in a couple of weeks to make sure the bone was knitting properly.

I was quizzed a number of times about what had happened. I invented a simple lie consisting of ice and a metal railing. I suppose I could have told the truth and called the cops, called Detective Sergeant Margaret Utley of the St. Louis Park Police Department, except—I hit Cardiff first, as I recalled, so . . .

Neither of my dance partners turned up at the clinic. Either they weren't badly hurt, which would have been disappointing, or else they had gone elsewhere for treatment. Or maybe they died from the fright I gave them.

What a moron, my inner voice told me. *You could have handled that so much better.*

Who was I to argue?

While I was being treated, I checked my cell phone. The log told me that Evelyn Szereto had called three times. I took a deep breath and called her back.

Her first words—"What happened to you? I waited for half an hour."

"Didn't Diane Dauria tell you?"

"I haven't spoken to Diane."

"I left a message on her phone."

"I never received it."

"Sorry about that."

"I called and called. Where are you?"

"The hospital."

"The hospital?"

"Specifically, the North Memorial Clinic. Nice people here. You'd like them. They'd like you."

"McKenzie, are you all right?"

"I've been better."

"What happened?"

"It's a long story. I may or may not tell you about it, depending on how things go from here on in."

"What's that supposed to mean?"

"Where are you?"

"At my home on Lake Minnetonka."

"I might come by and see you in a little bit. I'll let you know. In the meantime . . ."

"What?"

"Tell me about Rebecca Denise Crawford."

"I don't know who that is."

"Sometimes goes by the name R. D. Crawford."

"I don't think I know her."

"You don't think or you don't know?"

"McKenzie . . ."

"Because she knows you. She says she's been to your house."

"If she came to one of my parties—McKenzie, I don't know the name of every one of our employees."

"Fair enough. I want you to call Annabelle Ridlon. She's your human resources—"

"I know who she is."

"Tell her that I have questions that *you* expect her to answer."

"What questions?"

"Just tell her."

"It's getting late in the day . . ."

I glanced at the time displayed on my cell phone: 4:46 P.M.

"Tell her to wait for me," I said.

"I will. McKenzie, are you all right?"

This time she actually sounded concerned.

"To be honest, Evelyn, I'm a little pissed off," I said. "You might want to tell Annabelle that, too."

I don't know who called whom or what was said, but it was Candy Groot who met me when I stepped off the elevator at the Szereto corporate offices twenty minutes later.

She pointed at the cast and said, "You're hurt."

"Was hurt. I'm healing now. Did Evelyn tell you to keep an eye on me?"

"She wants to see you as soon as you're done here."

"What does Diane Dauria want?"

"I don't know what you mean."

"I hope that's true. I'm here to see Annabelle Ridlon."

"I know."

"Would you care to lead the way?"

"Of course."

I walked into the office without knocking, Candy trailing behind. Annabelle was sitting with her feet up on her desk and a keyboard in her lap while she stared at a computer screen. By then I had removed my winter coat, so my cast was on full display. Her eyes found the cast and settled back on the screen.

"I lost track of you Friday night," Annabelle said. "I was going to make you dance with me."

"What would your husband have said?"

"He wouldn't have liked it at all, which is why I wanted to do it. I see you broke your arm."

"Just a few hours ago. Want to be the first to sign my cast?"

"Tell me you weren't injured on Szereto property or while on Szereto business."

" 'Fraid I'll sue? Hire an attorney who knows how to get rich by accident?" I saw tiny muscles tugging at the corners of Annabelle's lips as if she felt insulted by my remark but didn't want me to know. I was afraid she'd think less of me than she already did, so I quickly added, "It was explained to me that an HR director's job is to serve the interests of the employer, not the employees."

"Sometimes I forget. What do you want, McKenzie? And was it necessary to have Mrs. Szereto threaten my life if I didn't cooperate?"

"Sorry 'bout that."

"I bet you are."

"Annabelle, I need help."

"Psychiatric or otherwise?"

"Psychiatric goes without saying. But I'm here for the otherwise."

"If I can help you I will."

The *if* impressed me. Even with Mrs. Szereto throwing her weight at her, it meant that Annabelle had drawn a line in the sand and she wasn't going to step over it. Period. And I thought, I really do like tall women.

"Pretend that I'm an employer calling to verify a job candidate's credentials," I said.

"Okay."

"Tell me the employment history of Rebecca Denise Crawford."

"I'm not familiar with the name."

I spread my hands wide as if I hadn't expected her to be.

Annabelle's feet came off her desk and the keyboard went on top. She started typing, moved her mouse and right-clicked a few times, typed some more.

"Crawford, Rebecca D.," she said. "The woman was hired to work in our Department of Research and Development five years ago. She resigned without explanation thirty-three months later."

Annabelle's eyes found mine and grimaced. I'm sure she was thinking the same thing that I was—that Crawford quit at about the same time that Jonny Szereto was running amok. I glanced at Candy Groot. Her expression gave me nothing at all.

"Crawford, Rebecca D.," Annabelle continued, "was rehired to work in R&D on a contract basis a little over a year ago. This can't be right."

"Why not?"

"We use independent contractors in marketing, freelance writers, graphic designers, that sort of thing, but never in R&D because of the sensitive nature of their work. The amount of money she's being paid seems awfully high, too."

I turned toward Candy Groot.

"Have you met her?" I asked.

Her head shake was so imperceptible that I nearly missed it.

"I thought you knew everybody."

She shook her head again.

"I met Crawford walking out of this building only a few hours ago."

She shook her head some more.

I was staring at Candy but speaking to Annabelle. "How 'bout Ronald Cardiff?"

This time Candy didn't even bother to shake her head.

"Who?" Annabelle said.

"Ronald Cardiff." I spelled it for her.

"No. We have no employees by that name."

"Can you tell me who hired Crawford five years ago?"

Annabelle hit a few more keys.

"That would have been—Diane Dauria was in charge of research and development back then," she said.

"Who rehired her last year?"

"I don't know, but—Frank Harris checked off on it."

That turned my head. Annabelle was grimacing again.

"This can't be right," she repeated.

"Who's head of R&D now?" I asked.

"He's not in the office," Candy said. "He left an hour ago."

"Diane, then."

"I haven't seen her."

"I'm going to look into this," Annabelle said.

"No. Annabelle, don't. Please. Let me handle it."

"What are you talking about?"

I told Candy, "Let's go have a chat with Diane."

"McKenzie . . ." Annabelle said.

I folded the fingers of my left hand over the edge of my cast and squeezed. She caught the gesture, but if it meant anything to her, she didn't show it.

"Don't make me call Mrs. Szereto again," I said.

"If you don't, I will," Annabelle said.

I let it go at that.

Candy and I took the stairs one flight up and walked the meandering corridors in silence until we reached Diane Dauria's corner office. The lights were on, but there was nobody home. Candy moved to the elaborate telephone system on Diane's desk and punched a couple of numbers. Diane's voice was clear enough you'd think she was still in the same room.

"Ms. Groot," it said. "I'm leaving early. Girls' night out with my daughter."

Good for them, my inner voice said. *Not so much for you.*

"Don't forget," Diane's voice continued. "I'll be in Owatonna tomorrow morning lighting a fire under manufacturing. They'll probably keep me for lunch, so we should reschedule both my one and one thirty. I expect to be back by two, though."

A moment later, Diane was replaced by a metallic voice that said, "End of message. To delete message press seven."

Candy hit a button and the voice said, "Message deleted. To reclaim message press nine."

Instead, Candy hit yet another button and the phone was silenced.

"It's starting to be a long day," I said.

"I'm going home," Candy said.

"Sounds like a plan."

"What about Mrs. Szereto?"

"I'll talk to her tomorrow."

"But she said—"

"What do you care what she said?"

Candy didn't answer. Instead she gathered up her belongings and headed to the elevators. I followed. When we reached the front entrance of the building, we noticed for the first time that it was raining.

"How can this happen?" Candy wanted to know.

"The weather guy said there was a twenty percent chance."

"That's not the point. It's January. It should be snow."

Candy announced that she needed to return to her office for an umbrella. I told her it was only a short walk to the parking lot.

"I didn't drive," she said. "I live one-point-three-five miles from the office, and I like to get my steps in."

"Steps?"

She held up her wrist, and I noticed the black band with a digital display.

"I use a fitness tracker to measure the steps I take every day, the miles I walk, the calories I burn; it reminds me to exercise even if the exercise is only taking the stairs instead of the elevator. Sitting at my desk all day—you'd be surprised how many hours I spend without actually moving."

"I'd be happy to give you a ride."

Candy regarded her digital display while she thought it over.

"That's very kind of you," she said.

We made a dash for it. My Mustang was parked in the visitors section of the lot closest to the entrance. I opened the passenger door and held it until Candy slid inside. A moment later I was behind the steering wheel.

"It's been a long time since a man opened a car door for me," Candy said.

I didn't know what to say to that, so I didn't say anything. I started driving.

"I'm sorry you were hurt," Candy said.

"Thank you."

"What happened exactly, may I ask?"

"A couple of semipros were unhappy that I was looking into Rebecca Crawford's relationship with the Szereto Corporation."

"Are you sure?"

"Honestly? No. I dropped Crawford's name, but my assailant refused to pick it up. Could be he did that on purpose. Or it could be the entire episode had something to do with my investigation into Jonny Szereto's murder instead. Or both. I don't know. It's all very confused right now. I'll figure it out, though."

"Why? Why should you figure it out?"

"It's what I do."

"Then what?"

"We'll decide that when the time comes."

Candy gave me a few directions that I followed.

"It used to be so much fun," she said. "I remember when it all started back in the seventies, Mr. Szereto building the firm, breaking new ground in the beauty industry—it was so exciting; Mr. Szereto making a mockery of the old line that nice guys finish last. He was kind to everyone and yet a great business-man. We're told that you can't be both. Untrue. Those people who justify terrible behavior by saying it's not personal, it's just business—liars and hypocrites. They put entire communities out of work by relocating their factories or whatnot and then have the audacity to proclaim to the world what nice guys they are, what good businessmen. Mr. Szereto was never like that. He took personal responsibility for everything the company did. He was an honest man and a gentleman, and I miss him very much."

"What about Mrs. Szereto?" I asked.

"Evelyn—I was upset when they married, I can't tell you how much. She was so young and so beautiful, and I was so very, very jealous. It wasn't just me, either. Those of us who had been with Mr. Szereto from the beginning, we all thought that she was nothing more than a gold digger. She turned out all right, though. She was very protective of Mr. Szereto, both him and the company. We became allies, Evelyn and I, looking out for Mr. Szereto, doing silly things like making sure he bundled up in the winter, but also more important things like keeping track of his professional relationships. Mr. Szereto was smart and cunning, but he was also extremely kind and generous. We wanted, Evelyn and I, to make sure no one took advantage of him.

"When he died—we all saw it coming, but it was heartbreak-ing just the same. At his seventy-eighth birthday he was such a robust presence. By the time he reached eighty, his body had failed him, and then his mind and spirit. Evelyn and I ran the company, literally, those last years while he slowly slipped away. When I pass, McKenzie, I want to go all at once, not linger like he did. We can't choose how we die, though, can we?"

"When did Jonny take over the company?"

"Almost immediately after Mr. Szereto's will was probated."

"Was he any good at it?"

"No. He liked being in charge, enjoyed being the boss, reveled in it, yet he hated the work, the day-to-day grind. He left it for others to do, Evelyn and me, the executive staff. The company became—it was like a ship without a captain. That's not my metaphor. It's how Diane Dauria described it. Key personnel left and weren't replaced, poor performance went unchecked, sales goals were ignored, new product development was pushed back. The year after Jonny took over was the only year that the corporation failed to pay profit sharing since Mr. Szereto started the company. Employees were . . . I want to say outraged, but more than that I think they were shocked to the point where they were afraid for the future. Rumors began circulating that the company was for sale."

"How did Evelyn feel about all this?"

"As upset as I had ever seen her. Only there was nothing she could do. She was the chairperson of the board of directors, but that was Jonny's doing. It surprised me when I learned that she didn't own a single voting share."

"You have ten percent."

"Yes. Mr. Szereto was very generous to me in his will. I told you he was a good man."

"Could you have done anything?"

"No. Even if we had rallied all of the minority shareholders, Jonny still had a twelve-point advantage. There was talk of suing the corporation for malfeasance, forcing him out that way, except it might have taken years. Then there was the other thing . . ."

"I meant it when I said I was sorry for dredging up painful memories."

"They're never far away. That's my house."

I stopped in front of it. I told Candy that my odometer said we had traveled one-point-eight miles from her office.

"I take short cuts when I walk." She opened the car door. Then closed it again.

"What you said at Evelyn's house New Year's Eve," she said. "I've been thinking about it. Finding a beach somewhere. An island. Tahiti. Bali. Jamaica. Martinique. Why not? Just go away and start over. Pretend to be the person I want to be and hope that's the person I become. Put some distance between me and . . . and those painful memories. Do you think that's possible for a woman my age?"

"It's possible at any age."

"McKenzie, I don't want you to get the wrong idea, but I need to know—do you think I'm pretty?"

"Yes, I do."

"Sexy?"

"Yes."

"A woman my age?"

"Especially at your age. You look at the lines and creases and think you're old. I look at them and think, Here's a woman with character. Someone who's seen life and knows what it's about."

"If only that were true."

"Candy, it is. If I weren't happily involved with someone else, I'd be all over you like a cheap suit."

She was laughing when she said, "McKenzie, you are such a terrible, terrible liar."

"Who? Me?"

"Yes. You."

Candy opened the car door again.

"Thanks for the lift," she said.

She was smiling as she walked slowly to her front door in the rain. I was smiling, too.

By the time I reached my condominium, the rain had become a hard, wet snow that shattered tree branches and downed power lines. I watched it slowly blanket the Twin Cities on the Weather Channel, a practice Erica found amusing.

"If you find the weather so interesting, why don't you just look out the window?" she asked.

"You don't get the play-by-play," I told her.

At about 10:45 P.M., Nina arrived. I met her at the door with a quick kiss and a hug. She noticed the cast right off but said nothing. Instead she held a single finger in the air and said, "Give me a sec."

After discarding her coat and bag, she went to the kitchen area and poured herself a hard apple-and-pear cider from her personal stash. Hands off her Lilley's, imported at great expense and inconvenience from Somerset, England, was one of the few rules in our place. She sat on the sofa, wiggled around a little bit to get comfortable, took a long pull from her glass.

"Okay," Nina said. "I'm ready. Tell me what happened."

My first thought was to lie—so she wouldn't worry, I told myself. But of all the things I owed her, the truth was at the top of the list. Besides, she had to be used to it by now. Just a few days after we met, some questionable choices put me in Regions Hospital with an epidural hematoma that required the emergency room docs to drill two dime-size burr holes in my skull to drain the fluid. Nina came for a visit.

"I'm not going to get involved with you if you're going to make a habit of this," she told me at the time.

I promised her that I wouldn't, but I did.

She stayed with me anyway.

So I gave it to her straight, without spin or embellishment.

"Sounds like it was a close call," Nina said.

"You need to add a little color every once in a while. Otherwise, it'd be like a real job."

"Couldn't have that; punching a clock like the rest of us working stiffs, oh, no. Seems to me, though, you could have handled it better."

"You're right about that. You are very right. I was just so angry. I let it get the better of me."

"Because he threatened me and Rickie?"

"He was lucky I wasn't carrying."

Nina patted my knee.

"In that case, I'm glad you don't like guns as much as you used to. Where is Erica, by the way? Did she go out?"

"No, because of the snow. She's in her room Skyping or whatever it is that millennials do now instead of using the phone."

"Well, then, I think I'll quick slip into my jammies, get cozy in my big, warm bed, and catch up on my reading. Care to join me?"

"You know I don't like to read in bed."

"Oh, McKenzie." Nina started making "tsk, tsk tsk" noises as she walked toward the bedroom.

I'm not an idiot. It only took me a couple of minutes to figure it out.

I was heading to the bedroom at a brisk pace when my smartphone slowed me down. Once again the caller's ID was blocked.

"You were lucky today." The voice was the same one that made the call last Friday—but *not* the voice of the man I fought with in the parking lot. "Only a broken arm. Next time you won't be so lucky. Stay out of Szereto business."

I was going to award him points, tell him his performance had improved since last time, but he ended the call before I could say anything.

I spent a few beats staring at the phone.

"What is it?" Nina asked.

I spun toward her. She had a hanger in each hand, one holding a silver nightgown trimmed with white lace and the other holding a red nightgown with narrow straps.

"I just had a thought," I told her. "But you know what? It can keep till morning."

FIFTEEN

The snow had stopped falling around 2:00 A.M., which meant all the school kids—and a few adults—who had gone to sleep with visions of a snow day dancing in their heads woke up disappointed. Our snow removal system was so efficient that by 5:00 A.M. power had been restored to all those communities that had lost it; by six the main arteries had been plowed and traffic was moving normally. By eight, even most of the side streets had been cleared. At ten the sun was shining bright and the snow had already started to melt.

"I don't remember a winter like this," Erica said. She appeared in front of my desk dressed in a turtleneck sweater, jeans, long black boots, and a jacket that was meant to be worn during autumn football games. "Do you know it's going to be forty-three degrees today? I'm starting to wonder if this might not be the new normal because of climate change."

"Haven't you heard? Climate change is a hoax perpetrated by liberal scientists for financial gain."

"Yeah, right. Even someone with a nature as cynical and suspicious as yours has to know that's a load of crap."

"Speaking of which, you're up awfully early, aren't you?"

"It's ten o'clock."

"That's my point."

"If you must know, I'm going to brunch."

"On a Tuesday?"

"People have brunch on Tuesdays."

"They do?"

"Just because your idea of brunch is hanging at Mom's club on Sunday morning chugging mimosas and listening to jazz."

"You say that like it's a bad thing."

Erica asked about my wrist again. My impression, she thought I might have left something out when I told her the story the night before. I hadn't, but that was then. Now I had Ronald Cardiff's driver's license sitting face up on my desk. Unlike Rebecca Denise Crawford, he had been an easy research subject, appearing on all manner of Web sites. Turned out Cardiff had been a boxer back in the day, a middleweight who went by the name "Kid Cardiff," which explained his stance when he came at me in the parking lot. He had a twelve-and-twelve record, then became a sparring partner for Caleb Truax when Golden was coming up. Age forced him out of the game, Father Time being the one true undisputed champion, and he went on to tend bar in a couple of decent spots over on the East Side. His skirmishes with the law had all been of the public intoxication and disorderly conduct variety. His biggest jolt was a thousand-dollar fine for tuning up a couple of guys that had been unimpressed by his ring record in an exceedingly loud and challenging manner. What I couldn't do was connect him to Crawford or Szereto or anyone else I was investigating. I thought maybe his partner was the link and wished I had taken the time to learn his name.

"You're sure it had nothing to do with Malcolm," Erica said.

"Pretty sure."

"Well then, try to stay out of trouble. I'll see you later."

"Who are you going to brunch with—just in case your mother asks?"

"Malcolm."

"Ahh."

"Yeah."

"Have you seen him lately?"

"You mean have I seen his new body art? We're just friends, right? That's what I keep telling him, so if he wants to let some MMA pug mark him like that, what's it to me, right? I've got no right to complain, right? Doesn't mean we can't still be friends, does it? I'll be seeing him at Tulane, anyway; all the people we have in common down there . . . McKenzie, am I an idiot?"

"I never thought so."

"Sometimes I think so."

"Do me a favor. Ask Malcolm if he knows what happened to Katie Meyer."

"Who's Katie Meyer?"

"Friend of the family. Ask him and then tell me how he reacts."

"Is this going to cause a scene?"

"Possibly."

"Then I'll be sure to get a table in the center of the restaurant. McKenzie, men can be such—morons."

"Yeah."

"Women, too."

"Make sure he picks up the tab."

"Oh, I will."

An hour later, Jack McKasy led me into the Szereto house. We passed through the living room to a den that I had missed the last time I was there. It was a man's room—leather, wood, stone, and books, a cluttered desk, and a cabinet with rifles, shotguns, and a few handguns behind a glass front. There was a bar in the corner. On one wall, an elegantly dressed man of advanced middle age stood casually next to a straight-back chair; the king comfortable in his domain. On another was an equally huge oil painting of a beautiful young woman wearing an ivory gown and a knowing smile; Evelyn Szereto forty years ago. She seemed to be staring at the man and he at her across the expanse of time and space. Today's Evelyn stood waiting in the center of the room when we entered, her makeup and clothes model-perfect, a slight grin on her face that was very close to the one in the painting.

"I have to admire your audacity, McKenzie," she said. "Very few people would dare blow me off like you have the past couple of days."

"I assure you, Mrs. Szereto, I have nothing but your best interests at heart."

"Uh-huh. Thank you, Jack. You may go."

The dynamic had changed since I had seen the two of them together New Year's Eve. So much so that Jack's response to being dismissed was to hug Evelyn's shoulder and kiss her cheek. He was looking directly at me when he said, "I'll see you later, darling," before leaving the room.

Evelyn frowned and shook her head slightly as if the gesture had upset her yet she didn't know what to do about it. She decided to put it on me.

"This is what comes from your snooping around," she said.

"It's only snooping if you learn something you're not supposed to."

"Exactly."

"Then I apologize, although Jack seems happy that your relationship is no longer a secret."

"No longer a secret from you. I have no desire for the rest of the world to know my business."

"The rest of the world won't hear it from me."

"I'll hold you to that. Now that you do know about Jack and me, though, what do you think?"

"Do you care?"

"Yes, McKenzie, I do."

"You could do better."

"You don't know him."

"My experience, the best relationships are between equals."

"I have money and he doesn't, is that what you're thinking?"

"That's part of it."

"The other part—he's so much younger than me?"

"That factors into it as well."

"I'm surprised at you, discriminating because of age. McKenzie, you're a prude."

"Seems I'm becoming one as I get older, God help me. Except that's not what I meant. Older women and younger men—I've been seeing a lot of that lately, and I don't care. Just the other day I told a woman who's approximately your age that she ought to go out and get her groove on."

"I don't know what that means."

"Angela Bassett? *How Stella Got Her Groove Back*?"

"Oh, yeah. The movie. But if not that, McKenzie, what did you mean?"

"I have already been told today that I have a cynical and suspicious nature."

"You think Jack's only with me for my money? After all these years? What a terrible thing to say."

"I didn't actually say it. Besides, isn't that what you thought when Vanessa started seeing your son?" I gestured at the painting of the middle-aged man. "Isn't that what people thought when you became involved with Mr. Szereto? And so on and so forth?"

Evelyn gazed at the painting.

"I actually posed for my portrait," she said. "The artist

painted Jonathan from a photograph. The man never could sit still for very long. He was angry about the things some people said when we married, although he never showed it. There was nothing to gain by lashing out, he said. Time would change people's opinion of us. I told him that it was all right, I didn't mind; told him that the only opinion I cared about was his. Except I did mind. It hurt, the things people said about us. Or rather what they said about me. No one seemed to care that an older man married a much younger woman. It was the other way round they objected to. I've never forgiven the world for that bit of hypocrisy. Does that surprise you, McKenzie? That I would carry a grudge all these years?"

"Not especially."

"Surprises me, sometimes. Are you going to tell me about your arm?"

I did.

"Does this Crawford creature work for me?" Evelyn asked.

"On and off."

"What does that mean?"

"I don't know, but I'm going to find out."

"What can I do?"

"Tell me—was Jonny trying to sell the Szereto Corporation?"

"God no! Who would tell you such nonsense?"

"It seems to be common knowledge."

"It's common knowledge that buyers sometimes come sniffing around. The Europeans. Many companies that are successful but comparably small, like ours, generate that kind of interest. That's why it was so important to Jonathan that the family maintain two-thirds of the voting stock, so it would be easy to rebuff such rumors."

"Two-thirds with Candy Groot."

"She's been with us for so long now, she might as well be family."

"So when the Europeans made their offer, it was Jonny who turned them down."

"Yes."

"I was told that it was Vanessa who said no, after Jonny was killed."

"I don't know where you got your information, McKenzie, but you had better go back and get some more."

"Okay."

"What exactly are you implying, anyway?"

"Could someone have believed the rumors that the Szereto Corporation was up for sale? Someone outside the family? One of your shareholders, for example?"

"Like who?"

"Pamela Randall."

"She knows better."

"Some guy, I think his name is Neil."

"Tall man, dyes his temples gray?"

"Sounds right."

"Neil Lohn—one of those people who do nothing all day but look for things to complain about. He's made it clear on several occasions that he doesn't care for how we run the company, doesn't believe in profit sharing."

"If that's how he feels, why doesn't he sell his holdings?"

"Because we're making him money."

"How much money would he make if you sold Szereto?"

Evelyn paused.

"The short-term rewards would be enormous, but not as great as the long-term gains he'd receive if we didn't sell, though," she said.

"Yet he still would have been unhappy that Jonny refused to sell the company."

Evelyn paused some more.

"A lot of shareholders would prefer that we chase the quick

buck. But you know what? McKenzie—do you know who Ricky Nelson was?"

"Pop singer from the fifties, wasn't he? Fifties and sixties?"

"He had a great song late in his career, "Garden Party," where he sang *you can't please everyone, so you've got to please yourself.*"

"Words to live by."

"Especially if you're rich, like us."

Yeah, I'm sure that's what Ricky was thinking, my inner voice said.

"I've been doing a lot of talking since I arrived," I said. "Now it's your turn."

"What do you mean?"

"You called me, remember? You said you wanted to tell me what was on your mind."

"Oh, yes. It was nothing."

"Nothing?"

"I just wanted to check on your progress."

I didn't believe her. Evelyn had wanted to tell me something and then changed her mind. It had to be because of something I told her. I reviewed our conversation during the long drive from Lake Minnetonka back into downtown Minneapolis but couldn't think what it was. I thought Pamela Randall might have part of the answer, so I drove to her condominium about a mile from mine on the other side of the Mississippi. An earnest young man in a well-pressed blue suit passed me from the security station in the lobby to her door on the top floor. Pamela pulled open the door with a yip of welcome and the kind of seductive smile that Rebecca Crawford had tried for but had been unable to manage.

"Come in, dear, come in," she said.

Her hair was piled on her head, and she was wearing an

oversized man's blue dress shirt with a button-down collar, plenty of paint smudges, and nothing else that I could see except the single strand of pearls around her neck and the red polish on her toes. She took my hand the way Candy Groot had at the New Year's Eve party and led me through her condo; unlike Nina and me, she had plenty of rooms. Eventually we found ourselves in a corner studio bathed in natural light that was littered with paintings, many of them unframed. A floor easel had been set near the glass, along with a table covered with painting supplies and a stool. There was a half-finished canvas on the easel.

"My sanctuary," Pamela said.

"Nice."

"I have embarked on a career as an artist. This is my fourth, by the way. Careers, I mean."

"Nice," I said again.

"There's a poet named Jenny Joseph who wrote that when she's an old woman she'll wear purple. To hell with that. I'm not waiting till I'm old. I'm going to wear purple now. In fact, my panties are purple. Do you want to see?"

"I told myself when I woke up this morning that there wasn't enough sexual tension in my life."

Pamela thought that was awfully funny. Instead of lifting her shirt, though, she pulled me over to the easel. A combination of paint and pencil drawings revealed a picture of a fifteenth-century queen sitting on her throne, her legs pulled up under her gown, her head resting on her knees, and smiling at a young courtier who was doing his best to entertain her. Meanwhile, an older man, who was also wearing a crown, stood watching from a distance, stroking his beard as if he were wondering if there was something going on. It reminded me of a painting I had seen before. I couldn't remember its name, but I remembered the artist—Edmund Leighton.

"What do you think?" Pamela asked.

"You're channeling the Pre-Raphaelites."

"A little bit. I'm trying to give historical scenes, medieval and Regency, a modern sensibility. I'm impressed that you would know that."

"Don't tell anyone, but from time to time, I'll even read a book."

"Smartass."

"Yes, ma'am."

She released my hand and made herself comfortable on the stool, letting the tails of her shirt slide up her bare thighs. Standing in front of her I could see down her shirt, and sitting in the only empty chair in the room would let me see up it, so I found a spot on the wall that I could lean against and not see anything. Pamela seemed to enjoy my discomfort and added to it by running her fingertips gently over her pearls.

"What's the line?" she asked. "I know nothing about art, but I know what I like."

"Please don't do that."

"Do what, dear?"

"My ego appreciates the gesture, but I'm in a committed relationship."

"Does it matter?"

"Yes, it does."

"Good for you." Pamela folded her hands in her lap. "But committed relationship—not with Candy Groot?"

"No."

"Or the little princess?"

"No."

"Good. I don't think Nina Truhler would approve."

That raised an eyebrow.

"I said if you gave me a day I would learn everything there is to know about you," Pamela said. "You're a bit of a scoundrel, aren't you?"

"I've been called worse."

"According to the newspapers, you've been involved in a number of sordid incidents, yet you were never quoted directly. Why is that?"

"I'm anxious to keep a low profile."

"That makes you a rarity in today's YouTube world, doesn't it?" Pamela made a production out of crossing her legs. "It's with great pride that I tell you that most men *love* to talk to me."

"I can't imagine why."

She made a rueful face that quickly gave way to a practiced and charming smile.

"Obviously, you didn't come here to hit on me, more's the pity," Pamela said. "So tell me, dear, to what do I owe the pleasure?"

"What can you tell me about Jonathan Szereto Jr.?"

Pamela stared at me, her eyes slightly narrowed the way some people's do when they're trying to read something that's very small.

"Are you asking on Evelyn's behalf?" she said.

"You might say I'm looking for a less personal perspective."

"You're unsure Evelyn is telling you the truth, the whole truth, and nothing but the truth, is that it?"

"She's his mother."

"Mother to the boy king. He would never have turned me down like you did. Jonny was what my generation called a womanizer."

"He was married."

"So?"

"His wife was extraordinarily attractive."

"So? McKenzie, you should know, cheating isn't about what you have. It's about what you want, and men like Jonny want everything they can grab hold of all the time."

"He was that selfish?"

"He was that much of a narcissist. Exactly what do you want to know, anyway?"

"I overheard your conversation with the gray-haired gentlemen Friday night," I said.

"I know. I'm surprised they didn't hear Neil in Taylors Falls. What about it?"

"From what he said, I got the impression that the Szereto Corporation had been up for sale at one time."

"A lot of people thought that; the minority shareholders. Things were happening at the company—budgets were slashed, pay frozen, training ignored, travel moratoriums issued, more work being outsourced. Senior leaders started jumping ship and weren't replaced. Web site and marketing material wasn't being updated. Reviews and sales goals were pushed back. There was no buzz, no new initiatives, no future plans."

"I was told that was all a result of very poor management."

"Could well have been," Pamela said. "A lot of the shareholders, myself included, thought so at the time, which didn't make anyone happy, believe me. But then we heard that Jonny had approached the Europeans."

"They didn't come to him?"

"He went to them to gauge their interest."

"Evelyn denies it."

"Wouldn't you?"

"If Jonny was actually attempting to sell the company . . ."

"I wouldn't trust Evelyn as far as I could throw this building, but you might need to give her the benefit of a doubt on that one. News of an impending sale gets out; more often than not a company's value will rise. Jonny could have been attempting to goose our stock price."

"For what purpose, if he wasn't selling?"

"Improve the company's profile, make it easier to raise capital, convince vendors and customers to accept long-term contracts—a lot of reasons. Nothing came of it, though. I knew it wouldn't at the time. The family actually selling the Szereto Corporation? The old man would have rolled over in his grave."

"When was this?"

"What do you mean?"

"How long before Jonny was killed?" I asked.

"Let's see . . . I think I first began hearing the rumors . . . It was at Evelyn's New Year's Eve party. A very somber affair. It was the first time the company hadn't paid profit sharing ever. That kind of fed into the rumors. It didn't help that the economy was in the toilet at the time, either. Our customers losing all that disposable income; our high-end products in particular took a beating. That was what? Five months, six, before Jonny was killed?"

"Neil Lohn wanted the sale to go through, didn't he?"

"Neil is a small player with a big mouth."

"But he would have made money."

"A few bucks, sure."

"How 'bout you?"

"Oh, McKenzie, I would have been swimming in it."

"You wanted the sale to go through, too, then."

"It was never going to happen. The only way the corporation could be sold is if somehow the Szereto family lost control of the board."

"How would that happen?"

"I don't know, McKenzie. How would that happen?"

"I heard the term 'corporate malfeasance' bandied about."

"Neil Lohn and his big mouth again. Yes, that's the easy way. If it can be proven that a member of the board of directors is unfit to serve because of behavior that compromises the corporation's fiduciary credibility, she can be voted out."

"Even if she has a majority of stock?"

"If the board's existing fitness-to-serve protocols allow it, sure."

"Does the Szereto Corporation have such protocols in place?" I asked.

"The old man put them in decades ago when he made his

IPO. He wanted to make sure that he could remove directors who were . . . disruptive. Not only that, once a director is removed, he still retains his stock; there's nothing you can do about that. But he's no longer allowed to vote his stock; he no longer has any say in how the company conducts its business. That way the old man would avoid a potential coup from the disgruntled. 'Course, he never meant for the protocols to be used against his own family. Or maybe he did. Who knows?"

"Could these protocols have been used against a womanizing president like Jonny?"

"He wouldn't have been the first corporate officer to be dismissed over allegations of extramarital affairs and inappropriate personal relationships."

"So it's possible that he might have been attempting to sell the Szereto Corporation before someone took it away from him."

"Depends. Was he involved in activities that made him unfit to serve? I mean besides doing a lousy job as president?"

"Damned if I know," I said.

"In other words, you're not going to tell me."

"Honestly, Pamela . . ."

"I understand. You're a very good liar, McKenzie. But a liar nonetheless."

"Do you know many of the employees at Szereto?"

"The worker bees? Not many, no. I only socialize with the little people at Evelyn's year-end soirées."

"How 'bout Barek Cosmetics?"

"Hardly."

"So you don't bother to associate with those whose hard work actually produces the wealth you enjoy?"

"It would be unbecoming of you to rant against the one percent, McKenzie, especially considering that you're a member of the club."

"Have you ever met a woman named Rebecca Denise Crawford?"

"No. Who is she?"

Did you see it? my inner voice asked. *She hesitated just for an instant. Those appraising eyes of hers flicked away and returned; a pink tongue tip became visible in the corner of her mouth—just for an instant.*

"She's another scoundrel, like us," I said. "Pamela, let's say for argument's sake that I have a few bucks lying around in low-risk index funds gathering a nice, safe amount of interest. If I wanted to turn them into a lot of bucks in a hurry, where would you suggest that I invest them?"

Pamela studied me for what seemed like a long time, a frown of doubt on her face that slowly gave way to the comforting smile I had noticed before.

"Rule of thumb," she said. "There's always a predictable short-term effect on the stock prices of both companies when one buys another. The acquiring firm will lose value, while the target company will gain. But again, that's short-term. If the acquisition goes smoothly, it will also be very profitable in the long run for the acquiring company. That, after all, is why people buy and sell."

"So if I were to buy stock in both companies . . . ?"

"Win-win."

"You wouldn't know of two such companies that you'd be willing to recommend, would you?"

"Nothing off the top of my head. Why do you ask?"

"You accused me of being a member of the one-percent club, and I suppose I am. A junior member. But the thing about running with Evelyn and Vanessa, and you, too, for that matter—you start to wonder why you're standing still."

"Is that right?"

"Lately, I've been thinking how much fun it would be to own a minor-league hockey team."

"Give me a day or two and I'll see what I can come up with."

There was more chitchat after that, Pamela trying to determine if I might be of some use to her. I hoped I left her with the impression that anything was possible.

Fifteen minutes later, I walked to my car. I reached to open the door with my left hand before switching to my right, thinking the cast was going to be damned inconvenient over the next six weeks.

Wait, my inner voice told me. *Pamela—she didn't ask about your wrist.*

Why would she?

It's only natural. You see someone with a broken wrist, broken arm, broken leg, hobbling around on crutches, whatever, you ask "What happened to you?" Maybe not the first thing you say, but during a long conversation . . .

So why didn't she?

Because she already knew what happened.

How could she?

Someone told her.

I wonder who.

SIXTEEN

I was anxious to confront Diane Dauria about Rebecca Denise Crawford, but I knew she wouldn't return to her office for at least another ninety minutes, so I returned to my condominium with the idea of making lunch. I found Erica there. She was sitting at her mother's piano and slowly picking out a tune with one finger. She wasn't the player Nina was, but she was a lot better than that.

"Hey," I said from the door.

She waited until I was standing near her before she replied, "Katie Meyer was raped."

"No. No. C'mon."

"At the ballpark when Malcolm and the others were kids. They never found out who did it. That's what he told me, and I didn't ask for more."

"I don't believe it."

I didn't recognize the tune, but Erica kept picking at it even as she spoke to me.

"Somewhere in America, a woman is raped every two minutes," she said. "One out of five women will be sexually assaulted in their lifetimes. My chances are one in four because I'm in college. You act surprised that you actually know someone it's happened to."

"I know more than one."

"So do I."

"I'm sorry," I said. And I meant it. Erica didn't seem to care one way or another. She kept picking at the song. It followed me across the condominium to my desk. I finally recognized it, surprised that I hadn't earlier since it was one of my favorites: "What a Wonderful World."

Detective Clark Downing seemed happy to hear from me.

"Still working at it, huh McKenzie?" he said. "Atta boy."

"I need a favor."

"Another one?"

"Katherine Meyer was raped. From what I heard, it was probably at the baseball fields in New Brighton about seven or eight years ago. What can you tell me about it?"

"I don't know anything. Seven years ago was before I came on. We're talking about Critter's mom, right? Slight woman with glasses and a sexy librarian vibe?"

I winced at Downing's description of her, but that's what I had thought, too, wasn't it?

"Yeah," I said.

"I'll get back to you."

Downing called ten minutes later.

"Meet me," he said.

"Where?"

"Same place as before."

This time Downing was drinking vodka, never mind that it was in the middle of his workday. I joined him, ordering bourbon, forget the ice.

"The incident report, the supplementals—they were so thin as to be almost invisible," Downing told me. "Just the facts, ma'am."

"Not everything the responding investigator knows or thinks he knows goes into his reports."

"Except this time—the man did the bare minimum, McKenzie. The rape kit wasn't even processed."

"Why not? Was it because of the backlog?"

It was discovered recently that there were thousands of untested rape kits gathering dust in Minnesota police and crime lab evidence rooms. They piled up because some crime labs were financially crunched—it costs about a thousand dollars to test a kit—or because the suspect confessed to the crime or the victim decided not to proceed.

Downing shook his head sadly. "The investigator didn't follow through," he said.

"Why the hell not?"

"He was short, man, just putting in the time before he got his thirty."

"C'mon."

"I don't know how else to explain it."

"Do you still have the rape kit? Is it viable?"

"Yes, but it doesn't matter."

"Why not?"

"The statute of limitations—"

"No."

"Expired last year. The suspect could confess tomorrow; there's nothing we could do about it."

"Do you have a suspect?"

Downing shook his head some more and took a sip of his drink.

"What happened," he said. "Katie—Ms. Meyer arrived early at Veterans Park, something she often did, getting to the ballpark before the players. She went to use one of those portapotties near the picnic pavilion. Suspect forced her inside, took her from behind. She did everything we ask of a rape victim. Reported the crime immediately. Went through the sexual assault exam. Consented to multiple interviews; and you know how that can go, the personal questions that are asked. Studied mug shots. We did nothing for her in return."

"Who was the investigator?"

"I spoke to the man maybe a dozen times, mostly about old cases. He was gone before I arrived; it was his slot that I filled."

"Who?"

Downing told me.

"McKenzie," he said. "I know what you're thinking because I'm thinking the same thing. But you can't go over there and punch him out. I'll arrest you if you do."

"Do you know what's wrong with the law?"

"Give me twenty minutes and I'll make you a fucking list."

I found Timothy Olson roasting marshmallows over a fire that he had built in a large metal saucer set on an iron stand in his backyard. There was a small TV table at his elbow stacked with a bag of marshmallows, graham crackers, and Hershey's chocolate candy bars. There were half a dozen preschool kids dressed in snowsuits running around, and he called to them.

"Who wants another?"

"Me." One of the kids broke away from the group and ran to his side. "Me, me."

Olson carefully scraped the marshmallow on top of a graham cracker, and topped it with a slab of chocolate and another graham cracker.

"Don't drop this one," he said.

The kid promised he wouldn't and ran off to roll around in the snow with his pals.

That's when Olson saw me.

"Help ya?" he asked.

"Detective Tim Olson?"

"Not for a long time now."

"My name is McKenzie. Detective Downing said you might be able to help me out."

"Clark?"

"It's about a case you caught right before you retired."

He waved his hand at the kids like a magician showing off a trick.

"I'm doin' the grandfather thing," he said. "If you don't mind talkin' out here . . ."

"That'd be great."

"You want to ask about the homicide?"

"No. A rape at Veterans Park."

Olson stared into the fire for a moment.

"Hey, you want a s'more?" he asked.

"No, I'm good."

"How is Clark doin' over there, anyway?"

"Pretty well, as far as I know."

"I used to drop by the shop once in a while during the first couple of years after I retired. Just to say hello, you know how it is. Now I stay away. You think when you retire you're going on to a better life. One where you ain't likely to get shot in the face during a traffic stop or knifed in the back while tryin' t' break up a domestic. But you miss it. The action. The camaraderie. You know, I still have my old uniforms hanging in my closet."

"So do I."

"You serve?"

"Almost twelve years with the St. Paul PD."

"Yeah, yeah, now I remember. McKenzie. You retired about

the same time I did, I think. Took the reward after catching some embezzler, was that it? Yeah. Everybody was talkin' about it back then. I remember thinkin' at the time, Damn, that would've been somethin' to go out on. How'd that work out for you, anyway?"

"Not too bad, except—what is it they say? You don't actually retire from the cops, you just leave active duty."

"I know what you mean. So you workin' private now?"

"Little bit."

"Clark thinks I can help you?"

"The rape . . ."

"Katherine Meyer. Pretty little thing as I recall. Said she couldn't ID her assailant, except that he was big and white. Found that hard to believe."

"You did?" I asked. "Why?"

"The portapotty. Awful small space. She said he took her from behind, shoved a rag or something into her mouth t' keep her from screaming. But she couldn't turn her head to take a look? Made me think something else was goin' on."

"Like what?"

"Like maybe it was consensual and her partner got a little rough and marked her, tore the buttons on her shirt, and she needed a story to tell the husband and kids? Just a feelin' I had at the time. The woman was so cooperative. You don't usually get that, the vic bein' so cooperative."

I had suppressed most of my rage during the drive over there, but now it was bubbling toward the surface. I couldn't allow that, not while I still needed Olson's cooperation. I turned to the TV table.

"May I?" I asked.

"Help yourself."

I popped a rectangle of graham cracker into my mouth and chewed slowly while I watched the kids making a competition out of snow angels. I spoke around the remains.

"What you just told me, none of that was in your supplementary report," I said.

"No, no, man, of course not. You don't write that down. Besides, maybe Meyer was tellin' the truth. You don't know."

"What did you do?"

"Not much I could do. No witnesses. No physical evidence. I had her act it out for me, you know; go through the motions. She was pretty good about that. Then she spent a couple days going through the mug shots on the computer. Nothin' came of it, though."

"What about the rape kit?" I asked.

"They take forever, you know how goes. I get so pissed off at those TV cop shows where the evidence is analyzed on the spot; people thinkin' that's how it's done. It's civil service work, man. The rape kit, it was going to be like three weeks before anyone could get around to testing it. By the time it was sent in—"

"It was never sent in."

"The hell you say?"

"Downing found it in the evidence room."

"No kidding? Well, goddamn, that's on me. I was going to send it to Ramsey County. Can't remember why I didn't. Musta forgot cuz by then I was into somethin' more important."

"More important?"

"Raymond Bosh. Worked for the Park and Rec Department. Someone caved his skull with an aluminum baseball bat. That was going to be the cherry on my sundae, you know? Solve a homicide my last case; go out in a blaze of glory. Can't always get what we want, though, can we."

"No, we can't."

"Thought I might've had 'im, too. The person or persons unknown. The call, 911 got the call must have been moments after it happened, some of Bosh's drug buddies or gamblin' partners givin' it to him. Some black kid. What was his name, now? African name. Jalen. Jalen Phillips. That's it."

Wait, my inner voice said. *What?*

"Friends called 'im Philly," Olson said. "Philly called it in, claimed he saw a guy get it over the head with a ball bat. We had it on tape. Everything you say to 911 is on tape, you know that. When the operator asked for his name, though, the kid refused to identify himself and hung up. Except the 911 operator, she thought he mighta been in danger, the way he hung up so quick. What she did, she called him back. She captured his phone number, right? But the kid didn't answer. Instead the call was transferred to the voice mail on his cell phone, and the voice mail message said, 'Jalen Phillips can't come to the phone right now,' somethin' like that.

"Eventually I got all this intel from the communications center, and I tracked the kid to his house. But I was a cop, see, and a white one to boot, and African kids today, they're taught from the get-go not to talk to the po-lice. 'Course, it mighta had somethin' to do with the ol' man, too; a twice-convicted felon named Dwayne, standin' right there. You don't interview minors without a parent present, you know that. Jalen not only wouldn't tell me what he saw, he wouldn't even admit that he made the 911 call in the first place, and we had his voice on tape."

"What did Dwayne Phillips do time for?" I asked.

"Drugs. Manslaughter."

"Were you able to connect him to Bosh?"

"Nah, the old man was clean. From what I could tell, he'd been a law-abiding citizen from the time the kid Jalen was born. Saw the light, I guess. He was very polite, too. Called me 'Officer.' But you could tell, he wasn't on our side."

I thought that might have been because six percent of the population in Minnesota is African American, except in our prisons, where it's thirty-six percent—but didn't say so.

"I'm not tryin' to make excuses, 'kay, McKenzie?" Olson said. "Slippin' up on the rape kit, there's no excuse for that. But Meyer, Katherine Meyer, you have to remember—today New

Brighton has three detectives, but in my time there were just the two of us, and we only had the time and resources to work those cases we thought we had the best chance of solving. Ninety-seven percent of the assholes who commit rape in this country, they get away with it. What are you going to do?"

Try harder, my inner voice said.

I walked back to my Mustang thinking, Downing must have come across the names of Jalen and Dwayne Phillips when he took a hard look at the Bosh case last summer. But he didn't connect them to the New Brighton Hotdish. Why would he have? They were both long gone to New Ulm when he caught the Frank Harris homicide. They weren't among the members of the club that he interviewed.

Even so, there was no reason to believe that what Jalen might or might not have seen in Veterans Park that day had anything at all to do with Frank Harris being stabbed in the head and left to die in the snow six years later.

Why would it?

On the other hand, what did Detective Sergeant Margaret Utley of the St. Louis Park Police Department tell me—*My experience, someone that kills and gets away with it, often feels empowered to do it again.*

I wondered how many African Americans named Jalen and Dwayne Phillips could be found in New Ulm.

Not many, I bet.

SEVENTEEN

I told the receptionist that I knew the way and promised I wouldn't wander. She insisted on having someone walk me to Candy Groot's office anyway. Apparently the Szereto Corporation had rules.

Candy was sitting behind her desk. She smiled when I arrived and came to me. I thought she might actually give me a hug, but instead she gripped my arm above the cast and said, "Good to see you," as if we were old friends too long apart.

You should flirt with older women more often, my inner voice told me.

Candy dismissed my escort and said, "No one's signed your cast yet."

"You could be the first."

She led me deeper into the office. "I'd like that, except—you didn't come here to see me, did you?"

"No, that's just a pleasant bonus."

"Ms. Dauria hasn't returned from Owatonna yet. I expect her at any time, though. You're welcome to wait."

"Wait for what?" Diane said. She swept through the door, her long winter coat flying open and a heavy bag hanging from her shoulder. I wasn't at all surprised that she stopped, pressed her fists against her hips, lowered her head, and sighed dramatically when she saw me standing there. But when she lifted her head and said, "McKenzie, what happened to your arm?"—that made me wonder.

"It's a long story," I said.

"I'd like to hear it."

"I'd like to tell it."

Candy helped her remove her coat and carried it to a rack near the door. Diane kept hold of her bag.

"No calls, Ms. Groot, except—"

"I know," Candy said.

"Thank you."

Diane motioned me into her office. I was surprised yet again when she closed the door behind us.

She dropped her bag next to her desk and sat in the swivel chair behind it. As usual, the desk was empty of everything except a laptop, a telephone system, and a pen. Diane picked up the pen and started rolling it in her fingers. I sat in the chair in front of her.

"Well?" she said.

"I don't have much time. I need to get to New Ulm."

"What's in New Ulm?"

"Besides the August Schell Brewing Company? Not much."

"McKenzie . . ."

"Rebecca Denise Crawford."

"You saw her giving me a Christmas card at my home on New Year's Eve. Big deal. Are you going to start spreading rumors that I'm gay, too?"

"I don't care if you're gay or not, although Critter Meyer might."

"Dammit, McKenzie."

"Tell me about Rebecca."

"Why should I?"

I held up my cast for Diane to see.

"All right," I said. "Let me tell you a story about Rebecca."

Diane stared at me for a good three beats after I finished.

"That doesn't make sense," she said. "Why would Becky want to scare you? Why would she want to harm you?"

Now it was my turn to stare.

Is it possible she doesn't know? my inner voice asked. *She asked about your cast. If she and Rebecca were in cahoots . . .*

"McKenzie?" Diane asked.

"She works here," I said.

"Yes."

"Tell me about that."

"I have no idea what you already know and what you don't."

"About Jonny Szereto?"

"Then you do know. Okay. Rebecca was one of the women that he . . . approached. She quit rather than let him touch her. She didn't tell me this, though; not at the time. I had hired her out of grad school. I suppose you could say she was a protégé of mine. It bothered me a lot that she left without an explanation. Later, after Jonny was killed and the police started asking questions, I figured it out. I contacted her soon after I was named president, tried to make it up to her. Rebecca was working for Barek Cosmetics at the time, and she said she hated it but that she had a noncompete clause in her employment agreement and couldn't move. A year later, though, she called back and said the agreement had expired and she would love to return to Szereto, but only on a contract basis, meaning she could set her own hours, come and go as she pleased—at least to start with. She was still upset because of her experiences with Jonny. It was against our usual business practices, but I agreed. I felt I owed her."

"You honestly don't know—that's what you're telling me?"

"Know what?"

"Rebecca is still working for Barek Cosmetics."

"That's not possible."

"I don't know how it's possible, but it is. If you don't believe me, call her."

"All right, I will."

Diane reached for her heavy bag.

"No," I said. "Don't call her cell. Call the corporate offices. Ask the operator to connect you to R. D. Crawford in research and development."

Diane reached for her desk phone. Her hand hovered above the receiver. I had seen her burn through a lot of different emotions in the brief time since we met, but the one that etched her face and scoured her eyes startled me. She was afraid.

"What are you telling me?" she asked.

"Rebecca is selling Barek's corporate secrets to you."

"No. No, McKenzie. Absolutely not. She would never do that. I would never do that. Besides, it's not even possible. We have security systems in place that prevent just that kind of thing. Protocols."

Protocols, my inner voice repeated.

"Rebecca never handed you a thumb drive with Barek's trade secrets on it?" I asked.

"Never."

"Are you trying to tell me, Diane, that you're not using Rebecca to conduct a little corporate espionage on Szereto's chief rival?"

"How dare you?"

"Well, then, if she's not selling Barek's secrets to you, she's selling your formulas to Barek."

"No, no, no. McKenzie, formulas, end products, are of limited value. What's important is the means of production, the research and development, the know-how. What helps you cut down on development costs and aids in long-term production; what helps get your product to the market first."

"You mean like what a trusted employee might be able to pass on to a competitor?"

"You can't be right about this."

Protocols, my inner voice said again.

"When I met Rebecca coming out of the building yesterday, I tried to contact Mrs. Szereto. I didn't have her number, but I had yours. I left a message for her on your voice mail."

"I never received it. The time you called, the time you say you called, I was on the phone talking to Sloane. After I finished, I left the office to go to her apartment."

"You're saying you didn't send those thugs to rough me up?"

"I didn't."

"If it wasn't you, it had to be Rebecca."

"No, McKenzie. No."

"I don't think she's working two full-time jobs simultaneously for corporate rivals just to pocket an extra paycheck. Do you?"

"I don't know what to think."

"I believe you."

"I don't give a damn."

"Yes, you do."

"McKenzie . . ."

"Diane, do you meet with Rebecca very often?"

"Not often. Just from time to time."

"Not here, though. Not at Szereto; in the employee cafeteria, for example."

"No. We meet . . ."

"At out of the way places. A coffeehouse. A bar. Just the two of you. Usually at night. And when you meet, she always gives you something. A card. A small gift. An appreciation from a protégé to her mentor."

"What are you telling me, McKenzie? What's going on?"

"I think I get it now."

"Get what?"

"Protocols."

"I don't understand."

"I need a favor, Diane. A big one. Perhaps the biggest favor you've ever done for anyone in your entire life."

"What?"

"I need you to trust me."

Except she didn't. I could see it in those volcanic eyes of hers. She was *this*close to telling me where to go when Candy Groot's voice cut in.

"Sorry to interrupt, Ms. Dauria," she said. "Call on line one."

Diane lowered her head and spoke sharply into the speaker-microphone.

"I don't want to accept any calls from anyone unless it's my daughter," she said.

"It's Katherine Meyer."

"Oh. All right. Thank you."

Diane snatched the receiver off the cradle and spun in her chair until her back was to me.

"Katie," she said. "Are you okay?"

I could hear only Diane's side of the conversation.

"Yes, I'm fine, but you shouldn't be worried about me . . . Sloane and I spent hours and hours talking last night. God, that girl can eat . . . I wish I were as thin as you say. Did you know she was involved in, what do they call it . . . ? Yes, mixed martial arts . . . She didn't tell me until I saw the bruises . . . Every woman in the world should know how to fight . . . I didn't mean it like that . . . How can you be so kind to me after what I've done . . . ? No, it wasn't a mistake. It was worse than that. It was . . . Katie . . . I haven't spoken to Critter. He probably hates me, too . . . Well, you should . . . I can't . . . I can't . . . McKenzie?"

Diane spun back in her chair until she was facing me.

"Yes, I know how to reach him. Katie, just a second. I'm going to put you on speakerphone."

Before she did, though, she put a finger to her lips—the universal sign that I should keep my mouth shut.

"What about McKenzie?" Diane asked.

"Just tell him to give me a call," Katie replied in her usual bright and breezy voice.

"May I ask what it's about?"

"I think he's entitled to know the truth."

"He's not entitled to shit."

"Oh my God, Diane, listen to you being all protective of me. And the kids, too, giving the poor man the runaround. I have such great friends. I'm including you, Diane. I mean it. And something else since I have you on the phone, it's not my turn, but I'm going to host the next Hotdish and everyone is going to come, especially you."

"Katie—"

"I don't want to hear it. I. Do. Not. Want. Oh, you know what you should do? You should make those mini-eggrolls like you did that one time. With the mushrooms and shrimp? I know it's a lot of work, but those were the best things. Everybody loved those. And don't worry, for God's sake. Can't we all just get along? I mean, we've been together so many years now, and oh, you know what I just found out? Maybe Sloane already told you. She's the one that hit Critter in the mouth. Oh my God. Do you believe that? Everyone thought it was Malcolm—"

"Katie, I'm so sorry."

"Don't be sorry. Sloane punching him, I would have loved to have seen that. You go, girl. He deserved it, too. What he said, if Critter had said those things while I was standing there, I would have hit him, too. Slapped him right up the side of his head. Train these kids while they're young, that's what you need to do. Okay, okay, I gotta go. So have McKenzie call me."

"Does he have your number?'

"Yes, he does."

"If he has your number, how come you don't have his?"

"I do."

"Then why did you call me?"

"Just an excuse to say hi. Okay, I gotta go. Remember, mini-eggrolls. Okay. See you later, alligator."

"Good-bye, Katie."

"Oh my God, Diane. See you later, alligator."

Diane paused, a mystified expression on her face. Katie spoke again.

"See you. Later. Alligator?"

"After a while, crocodile?"

"You're a work in progress, Diane, but I love you so much."

And Katie hung up.

And Diane hit the button that ended the call on her end.

And she spoke in a halting voice, the fire in her eyes doused by the tears.

"Katie wants you to call her," she said.

"I will."

"She's the best person I've ever known, and because she trusts you, I will, too."

"Thank you."

"What do you want me to do?"

"Call Rebecca. Arrange to meet her."

"When?"

"Tonight. Tell her you spoke to me and you're concerned about something I said. Don't tell her what. Let her pick the location so she feels comfortable. I'll be coming with you, of course, but don't tell her that, either. You need to set the meeting for later tonight, sometime after ten because there's something I need to do first."

"You're not going to hurt her?"

"I wouldn't think so."

"What are we going to do, then?"

"Buy her affections."

"What?"

"I'm going to offer her a bribe."

The first thing you see when you drive Highway 14 south across the Minnesota River into New Ulm is the baseball field, Johnson Park, home of the Brewers. Behind it is a town that Nina might have labeled quaint, although there are only three buildings older than 1862. The rest were burned to the ground by the Dakota for all the reasons you might expect Native Americans to rise up against the white government, forcing the entire population of the town to flee to Mankato, about thirty miles away.

Among the buildings that were destroyed was Turner Hall. It was rebuilt on the original site, though, after peace had been restored by force of arms and the largest mass execution in U.S. history, thirty-eight Dakota men. In the basement of the hall is the Rathskeller, which the natives claim is the oldest bar in Minnesota. It's also quaint, the walls adorned with 150-year-old murals that had been restored through a grant from the Minnesota Historical Society.

I sat at the bar. ESPN was on the TV in the corner near the ceiling, and a collection of bottles of alcohol, labels facing out, was stacked in front of the mirror. I ordered a Snowstorm, a product of Schell's brewery, one of the few places in New Ulm left untouched during the war. Apparently the owners had treated the Dakota with respect and consideration before hostilities broke out. As they say, no good deed goes unpunished. Dwayne Phillips now worked for the brewery in some sort of management capacity.

The bartender was a pleasant middle-aged woman who treated me the same as the regulars who assembled one and two at a time around the bar starting at about 5:00 P.M. until there were enough to field a baseball team. They were drinking Grain Belt, an iconic Minnesota brand once brewed in Minneapolis but now made by Schell's, and complaining about the Vikings' quick exit from the playoffs. Yet despite their disappointment, to a man they predicted a Super Bowl appearance the following season. Which made me grimace. One of them must have noticed.

"What?" he asked. "You're not a believer?"

"Let's just say I've had my heart broken before."

"You can't live without hope, son."

"Here we go," the bartender said.

"You can last forty days without food. You can go four days without water; four minutes without oxygen. But you can't last four seconds without hope."

"Where have I heard that before?" one of his partners asked.

"You believe that, son, don't you?"

"Not when it comes to the Vikings, no," I said. "I appreciate the sentiment, though. Let me buy you guys a beer."

I had never seen so many men drain so many glasses so quickly.

"Grain Belts all around," one of them said.

The bartender started pouring them even as she glanced at her watch.

"Goin' somewhere?" one of the regulars asked.

"I gotta date," she said. "Need to go home and get ready."

The announcement caused a commotion among the regulars, most of them wondering who the lucky man was.

"It is a man, right?" one of them asked.

The bartender asked if he knew any.

Another hoped that her leaving didn't mean the Rathskeller was going to close early because he certainly didn't want to go home early.

The bartender assured him that Philly would soon be there to sub for her, which caused another commotion among the regulars, most of them wondering how the young man had been doing since leaving for the big city, specifically Chicago and Northwestern University. The news made me smile, too. It meant my research hadn't all been in vain.

I waved the bartender over.

"Why don't you let me settle my tab before your replacement arrives," I said. "So you get the tip."

She made sure the regulars saw her pointing at me.

"This is what we've been missing around here," she announced. "Class."

I paid in cash, leaving her a twenty-five percent tip, which made her smile.

"Who's Philly?" I asked after we became friends.

"Jalen Phillips. He's the local fair-haired boy, although he really isn't fair-haired." She chuckled at her own joke. "Great baseball player for the Legion teams, and just the nicest young man. Him and his father. He works as a part-time bartender for us summers and when he's back from school. You'll meet him."

I did, about ten minutes later. The regulars shouted his name like they did Norm's in the classic *Cheers* TV show. He seemed to remember all of their names as well. He gave the bartender a hug and she kissed his cheek and then she left, leaving him in charge. First thing he did was make sure everyone's glass was filled with the beverage of their choice. I ordered another Snowstorm.

"Be careful of that one," a regular warned. "The way he was talking before, I'm pretty sure he's a Green Bay Packer backer."

"Hey," I said. "Do I call you names?"

"You know where they hate the Packers even more than we do?" Philly asked. "Chicago."

"About the only good thing you can say about Chicago," another regular said.

"Man, that's my home away from home you're dissin'."

That launched a discussion about the many different places one might choose to live, with the general consensus being that the number of assholes one encountered rose dramatically the farther away one traveled from New Ulm.

Eventually Philly returned to make sure I was happy with my beer.

"Where are you from?" he asked.

"New Brighton."

"Hey, I'm from . . ."

And the smile ran away from his face.

"Shit," he said.

The night began to drag. More customers arrived, yet the energy that had been in the Rathskeller earlier seemed to dissipate. Or maybe it was just me. For a while, Philly was quite busy, although he did take time to make a call on his cell phone from a corner of the bar where no one could hear his voice. Eventually the crowd began to thin out, along with the regulars.

"Supper's on the table," one of them said.

I was nursing my fourth beer when Philly said, "There's always a lull about this time on weekdays. It'll get busier again after people have had their dinner, about the time the Wild game starts."

To emphasize his point, he aimed a remote at the HDTV in the corner and switched the channel to Fox Sports North. The Wild hockey pregame show was just starting.

"Need another beer?" he asked.

"I'm good."

"Bar menu?"

"No."

He stepped away and busied himself with some glasses. He was waiting for something. I didn't know what until the black man entered the bar and sat one stool down from me. Philly smiled at him, and the man smiled back.

I said, "Mr. Phillips, I presume."

"Dwayne. Who you?"

"McKenzie."

"You police?"

"No."

"What you want with my boy?"

Since he got to the point so quickly, I decided it would be better if I did the same.

"I want to know what your son saw that day," I said.

"What day?"

"Mr. Phillips . . ."

"That was seven years ago."

"Yes, it was."

"Why anybody care all this time?"

"Do you remember Frank Harris?"

"Yeah, I remember him."

"Malcolm's old man," Philly said.

"Prick," Dwayne said.

"Yes, he was," I said.

"Was?" Philly said.

"Someone stabbed him in the head with a knife and left him to die in the snow."

"No way."

"When this happen?" Dwayne asked.

"Year ago last Christmas," I said.

"Who did it?" Philly said.

"No one knows."

"What's this got to do with my boy?" Dwayne asked.

"Probably nothing."

"Then what you want here?"

"Jayne Harris asked me to find out what happened to her husband. Malcolm, too."

"She's a nice lady," Philly said. "Malcolm's kind of a jerk like his old man, but he played a solid second base."

"This don't answer my question," Dwayne said.

"Neither of them cares if anyone goes to jail. They just want to know the truth."

"People say that like it's something you can hold in your hand; carry it in your pocket and take it out once in a while to look at. Don't work like that."

"I never said it did."

"McKenzie," Philly said, "do you believe that the person who killed that man in the park is the same one that stabbed Mr. Harris?"

"I honestly don't know. That's why I'm here."

"I know how things work," Dwayne said. "Citizen ain't under no legal obligation to report a crime, and you can't make him testify if he don't want to."

"That's true."

"Anything anyone says to you is hearsay; can't repeat it in no court."

"That's true, too."

"You ain't no cop, anyway."

"No."

Dwayne was speaking to his son when he said, "What you want to do?"

"What happened before is one thing," Philly said. "But if it's happened again, that's something else, man."

"She's your friend. You decide."

"If it makes it any easier," I said, "whatever you tell me in New Ulm stays in New Ulm."

Philly hesitated for such a long time that for a moment I thought I had lost him. Finally he aimed the remote at the TV to increase the volume, leaned in close, and started speaking, his voice just above a whisper as if he were desperate that only his father and I would be able to hear him.

"What you need to understand is that I didn't actually see anything," Philly said. "It was after school, and I was cutting across the park. We had a lot of rain the last couple of days and we couldn't get on the field, so the coach, he wanted everyone to get to the ballpark early for infield and BP. I'm crossing the park and I look up and I see Katie—"

"Katie Meyer?" I asked.

"Mrs. Meyer, uh-huh, and she was walking toward this shed. I called to her because Mrs. Meyer, she was so nice to me. And to Sloane. Sloane Dauria. She was like—I didn't have a mother growing up, McKenzie, because of what the drugs did to her, but if I had, I would have wanted to her to be like Mrs. Meyer. It's important that you know that because . . . I called to her, but she didn't hear or see me. So I ran toward her, toward the shed. By the time I got there she was already walking back to the field. That's when I noticed that she was carrying a bat, one of Critter Meyer's baseball bats. And then I saw the guy . . ."

Philly paused as if he were seeing him again. I knew I was.

Are you frickin' kidding me? my inner voice said. *Katie Meyer beating someone to death with a baseball bat? How is that even possible?*

"I called the emergency number," Philly said. "I told the operator what I found. She asked for my name. While she was asking, I could see Mrs. Meyer. She had already returned to the baseball field and she was setting the bat against the backstop, and I decided there was no way. I didn't even try to reason it out. I wasn't going to give her up. I just wasn't. You know, that woman hugged me every time I saw her. Even my old man didn't hug me that much."

Dwayne shrugged as if to say, "What do you expect?"

"I hung up and turned off my cell phone," Philly said. "I went to the field, and she must have seen that I was agitated because suddenly she was worried about me and wondering if there was anything she could do. She hugged me—again—and I could smell the scent of her shampoo in her hair and I vowed right then and there that I was going to protect her no matter what. I went five-for-five that game, too; two dingers and six RBIs. That's how upset I was about my decision. Anyway, I thought that would be the end of it until this fat cop from New Brighton showed up at the house and started acting, well, that doesn't matter. I denied calling 911, and he left me alone after that."

"Did you know that Katie had been raped?" I asked. I needed that to be the reason why Katie killed Raymond Bosh.

"Yeah. We all did. It wasn't a secret. It happened right before one of our games, and when I got to the field, the cops were already there investigating. Only it wasn't anything we ever talked about. Man, we were thirteen, fourteen years old at the time. We didn't *want* to talk about it. Mrs. Meyer didn't want us to talk about it, either. She kept telling us it had nothing to do with us; that we should forget about it and play baseball. She didn't want the season to be about her, you see? That's the kind of person she was."

"Did you think that one thing might have been connected to the other?"

"Not at first, but later it occurred to me. Why else would she have done it? That wonderful, caring woman? It had to be because he was the one who raped her. The police hadn't done anything about it; it was like three, four weeks later, and that fat cop—honestly, it made me feel better about it all. Like justice was being served. But now . . . If she also killed Malcolm's old man . . ."

"She didn't," I said. I remembered Detective Downing's supplemental reports. Among the fourteen New Brighton Hotdishers who were prepared to testify that Jayne Harris was with them when Frank was killed—Katherine Meyer.

"Are you sure?" Philly asked.

"I am absolutely sure. Tell me—does anyone else know what happened?"

"Who d'you mean?"

"I know you refused to talk to the police. What about the Hotdishers?"

"The parents? Hell, no. Are you kidding?"

"The other ballplayers?"

That slowed him down.

"It's important," I said.

"Critter," Philly said. "He was really upset about what happened to his mother, never seemed to get past it, the fact that the man who hurt her never got caught, and going into the championship game he was in tears even, so, what I did—I told him that he shouldn't worry about it, tried to make him feel better. Sloane and Malcolm were there, too, and I tried to tell them what happened without actually telling them what happened; dropping hints, you know, until they sorta figured it out on their own, and then we vowed, the four of us, we promised to never speak of it again. I kept my promise. Did they?"

"Yes, they did," I said.

"What happens now?" Dwayne asked.

"I leave New Ulm and pretend that we never met."

"You're not going to mess with Katie?" Philly said.

"Why would I do that?"

"So you put us to a lot of bother for no reason," Dwayne said.

"Good-bye, Mr. Phillips."

Only it wasn't good-bye. After I settled my tab, Dwayne followed me to my Mustang.

"Nice ride," he said.

"Thanks."

"You say you're not a cop, but I know the look."

"I used to be, in St. Paul. Not anymore."

"St. Paul, you say. That's where I'm from." He named an intersection. "You know it?"

"I know it," I said.

"I was standing on the corner when I was twelve years old and a guy drove by and shot me. Shot me twice. To this day I don't know why. Did he mistake me for someone else? Did he just not like the way I looked? I spent four months in the hospital. Not once during that time did anyone come to visit me. That's my childhood, McKenzie. The way I grew up. Five years later, I was standing on the exact same corner with a man owed me money over some coke he was 'spose to be movin' for me. I shot him twice. Killed him. They put me inside for that. I had just turned seventeen, but it was adult time. Got out, went straight back to the life. Did another jolt for possession with intent. Got out. Went back to the life. Goin' nowhere fast. Woman I was with, strung-out bitch got pregnant. Jalen born premature. You have kids, McKenzie?"

I thought about Erica and said no anyway.

"It changes a man—if he is a man," Dwayne said. "I got outta the life. Tried to take my woman with me. She didn't want to go. OD'd a few months later. Took Jalen to New Brighton. Don't seem like that far, only twenty minutes by car from that corner. But it was a lifetime away. Tried to raise him right. Give him a chance. He took it, too. Scholarship at Northwestern University, man. He's gonna be a fucking economist. Then this thing happened with Katie Meyer. All I could think about was that goddamned street corner. Right before school start, I got an opportunity to move to New Ulm and work for the brewery. Took it, man. Took it and ran. Now you show up, dragging the past with you."

"Mr. Phillips, the past is in St. Paul and New Brighton. Not here."

"You say that."

"I told this to someone just a couple days ago and I meant it—you're known by your children. I met your son. You're a good man, Mr. Phillips. Neither of you will ever have a problem with me. My word."

"You say that."

"Maybe in twenty years when nothing happens, you'll believe me."

EIGHTEEN

Rebecca Crawford had chosen a bar on the east side of St. Paul, a neighborhood not known for its geniality. The bar itself was nice, though—carpeted floor, padded chairs, rounded booths, lighted candles on the tables. Nonthreatening music was piped in, the volume low; no TVs, no jukebox. The waitstaff wore red shirts and black vests; the clientele seemed to conform to a self-imposed dress code that embraced sweaters and dark blazers and eschewed hats and anything with holes. It was the kind of place where you went before or after the theater, although I couldn't think of any theaters located on the East Side. It made me miss the Rathskeller.

We found Rebecca at a table with three empty chairs at about a quarter to eleven. Her expression went from impatient to alarm when she saw me enter behind Diane Dauria, yet she did nothing drastic about it like draw a gun or run for cover.

"Diane?" she asked.

"Sorry we're so late," Diane said. "I think you know McKenzie."

"What's going on?"

"You tell me."

We sat without being asked, me across from Rebecca, and Diane at her elbow. Rebecca was drinking a dark cherry-colored liquid with ice from a squat glass that she slowly rotated a quarter turn at a time on the table in front of her.

"So what do you want to talk about?" she asked.

"Let's start with McKenzie's broken wrist," Diane said.

"How did that happen?"

"Your friends didn't tell you?" I said.

"Hmm? Friends?"

I decided to take a page from Dwayne Phillips's playbook and get right to the point.

"We didn't come here to threaten you," I said. "No one is going to call the police. No one is going to sue for employee fraud."

"Why did you come here?"

"To make you a better offer."

"I'm listening."

"First, tell me—how much is Pamela Randall paying you to set up Diane?"

"Why? Do you want to cut yourself in, too?"

Too? my inner voice asked.

"I just want to know where to start the bidding," I said.

Rebecca didn't say.

Diane leaned in close.

"Becs?" she said. "I don't understand any of this."

"It isn't personal," Rebecca said. "It's just business."

"What is?" I asked.

"I thought you had it all figured out."

"I do. But Pamela doesn't. She made a huge mistake. I'm just trying to contain the damage to keep innocent people from getting hurt."

"Innocent people? Name one."

"Your mentor."

Rebecca flashed her eyes at Diane. "You knew what Jonny Szereto was doing and you didn't help me," she said.

"I didn't know," Diane said.

"You were the smartest person in the building. Don't tell me you didn't know."

"I didn't. Not until after he was killed. Not until the police started asking questions."

"I don't believe you."

"Becs, why didn't you come to me when it happened? Why didn't you say something?"

"Why didn't you quit when you found out?"

"I was trying to fix the company. Make it better."

"You and Evelyn Szereto?"

"Yes."

"You actually believe that Evelyn didn't know?"

"Does it matter now? Jonny's dead, Becs. Evelyn's son is dead."

"That's not enough."

"What do you want?"

"Ask McKenzie. He claims to have it all figured out."

I caught an expression in Rebecca's eyes at that moment of absolute and total indifference, which was gone the moment I saw it, and I realized that I had met her many times before. She wasn't a mystery woman after all. In fact, she was quite predictable and kind of dumb in that I'm-the-smartest-person-in-the-room way some people have that disregards everything someone might have to say except "I agree."

Rebecca finished her drink in one long gulp and excused herself to the restroom.

"Order me another Manhattan," she said.

I turned in her chair and gestured to the waitress. She came to the table quickly, took our orders, and left. Not much was said while we waited for Rebecca to return. When she did,

Diane asked, "I've never been to the East Side; do you live here now?"

"I live in the same house that I bought when I was working for you," Rebecca said.

"I remember."

The drinks were served. The waitress asked if we wanted to close our tab because she was going off duty; the bartender would be there to serve us, she said. I noticed then that the bar was empty. Late Tuesday night in St. Paul. I paid for the drinks. The waitress left. I sipped mine. Diane sipped hers. Rebecca stared at us both.

"What offer?" she said. "You said you were going to make a better offer."

"First, you need to understand, Pamela Randall's plan isn't going to work."

"Why not?"

"You might get Diane fired, maybe arrested; ruin her career over allegations that she's paying you to commit corporate espionage. Isn't that why you gave her all those little gifts? So people would remember seeing you pass Barek's trade secrets? But the endgame—the Szereto Corporation isn't going anywhere."

"Why not?" Rebecca repeated.

"I don't feel well," Diane said.

I turned my attention to her. She seemed pale. Her eyes were heavy. Her breathing was labored.

"McKenzie, I . . ."

Her eyes closed and she slipped out of her chair.

I tried to catch her.

We both ended up on the floor.

I wrapped my arms around Diane's shoulders and cradled her head.

I called her name.

Someone called mine. There was an echo-chamber quality to it.

I found Crawford. She was looking at me, an expression of curiosity on her face.

I closed my eyes tightly and opened them again.

She was still staring.

The room tilted sharply.

"Well, dammit," I said.

For a long time I couldn't tell if I was awake or asleep. I could move my head, but that was all. Someone was talking to me. Or was I talking to myself? I had a habit of doing that. The inner voice usually told me things that I already knew. This time it was telling me that I was too, too clever for my own good. Trying to turn Rebecca Crawford; pay her to join my side like any decent mercenary and give up her co-conspirators. It didn't occur to me that she might be angry at me for ruining a scheme that was at least a year in the making. Or that she might be frightened into doing something rash.

You're a shrewd one, the voice said. *Yes, you are.*

"You can shut up now," I told the voice. "I get it."

This is why you're not a real private eye. Who the hell would give you a license?

"I said I get it."

"McKenzie."

"I'll think of something. I always do."

"McKenzie. Wake up."

My eyes snapped open. I was staring at a white wall. The wall became a couple of walls, a floor, a ceiling, a closed door—no windows.

"McKenzie."

I turned my head. Diane Dauria—her arms and legs had

been fixed to a chair with duct tape. Her hair was disheveled. There was swelling and a deep redness between her ear and her chin.

"Are you awake?" she asked.

"What happened to your face?"

"He punched me. I woke up while he was carrying me into the office and tried to get away. I guess I drank less of my drink than you did."

"Office?"

"In the bar. He dragged us through the kitchen to this place."

"He?"

"Bartender. I guess a friend of Becs—Rebecca."

"He fixed our drinks."

Nothing gets past you.

"This bartender," I said. "Does he walk with a limp?"

"He's wearing a leg brace."

Just wonderful. You knew Kid Cardiff tended bar on the East Side.

"What are we going to do?"

"Give me a minute to think."

Think? You?

"Enough," I said.

"McKenzie," Diane said. "Are you here?"

"I'm here, I'm here."

It was a small office and crowded with a desk, file cabinets, and large cardboard boxes. One of the boxes was opened—paper napkins with the name of the bar imprinted on them. There were two chairs. Diane was in one and I was in the other. I struggled to get out of my chair. Whoever taped Diane down had done the same to me, and he did it well enough that I knew I would be unable to break through my bonds. I stopped struggling.

"We're in trouble," I said.

You think?

"What are we going to do?" Diane asked.

I regarded my cast. "How long was I out?"

"An hour. Maybe more."

The cast had been taped to the arm of the chair, I told myself, but not the wrist inside it. "What happened to Rebecca and Cardiff?"

"After they taped us to the chairs, Cardiff said he'd have to keep tending bar until closing so no one would wonder why the bar closed early. Rebecca said that was okay, she needed to make a call."

There was a clock on the wall—12:46. But did the bar close at one o'clock or two?

"Okay," I said aloud.

This is going to hurt, I told myself silently.

I straightened my fingers and tried to pull my arm out of the cast.

I was right, it did hurt.

Yet my wrist didn't move.

I tried to twist it out.

Which only caused it to hurt some more.

"McKenzie," Diane said.

"Shhhh."

I kept pulling and twisting even as the pain rippled up my arm into my spine. I noticed—my wrist didn't move, but the cast did. It slipped ever so slightly beneath the tape. That's when I realized it wasn't genuine duct tape. It was a cheap knock-off, and the dust from the plaster cast was starting to erode the adhesive. I kept twisting. My wrist kept hurting. The cast kept turning until it broke away from the adhesive.

The door opened.

"McKenzie," Diane said.

I stopped struggling against the tape and looked up. Ronald Cardiff stepped in front of me. There was a metal contraption protecting his right leg. He was balancing most of his weight on the left.

"Hey, Kid," I said. "How's the knee?"

"I owe you."

"About that—"

Cardiff hit me with a straight punch hard enough to loosen my teeth. The sound it made and the jolt of hard bone against his knuckles seemed to make him happy.

"At least you're hitting me and not a woman," I said.

He punched me again.

I didn't have anything to say after that.

Rebecca arrived. She didn't mind at all that Cardiff was slapping me around. She moved to the desk and leaned her butt against it. Suddenly it was very crowded in there.

I said, "How are you doin', Becs?"

"You should have taken my offer when you had the chance."

"The dinner and drinks sounded fine, but the sex part—ewwww."

"Who are you kidding?"

"Rebecca," Diane said, "this is insane."

"I knew you'd think that. That's why I didn't ask you to join us."

"Join you in what?"

"A chance to get rich and retire in a year."

"How many of you are involved?" I asked.

"Eight, including the Kid."

I glanced up at Cardiff. "What about your pal?" I asked.

"He's in the hospital."

"Too bad. So sad."

Cardiff looked as if he wanted to punch me again and then decided it wasn't worth the effort.

"He was just a hired hand," Diane said. "If he had been paying attention like he was supposed to, you would never have left that parking lot."

"The others—all minority shareholders of the Szereto Corporation?"

"Szereto and Barek both."

"Candy Groot, too?"

"No. Pamela didn't trust her to go along with the plan."

"What plan?" Diane asked.

"Didn't McKenzie tell you?"

"Rebecca intends to frame you for corporate espionage against Barek Cosmetics," I said. "Maybe the FBI will step in, maybe it won't. If it does, Rebecca will turn government informer and take a pass. You will be portrayed as the big bad boogie-woman; the heartless, greedy mentor manipulating the poor, naïve, starry-eyed protégé into making bad choices. In any case, Barek most certainly will take legal action, like when Starwood Hotel and Resorts sued Hilton or when GM sued Volkswagen over trade secrets. Once the scandal is percolating nicely, the Szereto Corporation board of directors, led no doubt by Pamela Randall, will use the company's unfit-to-serve protocols to remove Evelyn Szereto, accusing her of compromising the company's fiduciary credibility by fostering an atmosphere that allowed the scandal to take place or some such nonsense and, of course, for handpicking you to run the company.

"Next, the conspirators will make Szereto available for sale to Barek, thus eliminating a need for lengthy and expensive litigation. Evelyn won't be able to prevent it because when they remove her from the board for conduct detrimental to the company, they'll also remove her ability to vote her stock. She'll make a great deal of money, like everyone else who owns a piece of Szereto, but she'll lose her company. Meanwhile, having made a bundle by selling their stock to Barek, the conspirators will make more money still when the value of Barek's stock increases after the company absorbs the Szereto Corporation products, customers, brand name, and market share. That's the plan, anyway. Right?"

"You put it together nicely," Rebecca said.

"Only it's not going to work."

"Why won't it work?" Pamela Randall asked.

She was standing on the other side of the doorway looking in, the kitchen behind her. I smiled when I saw her.

"I knew you'd be along sooner or later," I said.

"How did you know that?" Rebecca asked.

"Because I didn't wake up dead. Obviously you were waiting for instructions."

"Instructions?" Pamela said the word as if it surprised her. She stepped into the office and saw Diane for the first time. "Oh. No."

"What?" Rebecca asked.

"What is Dauria doing here?"

"She came with McKenzie."

"What do you expect to do now?"

"That's what I wanted to ask you."

"You're missing the point. Dauria is the villain. The bad person who committed corporate espionage against a competing company. The one who blatantly stole a Barek product and introduced it to the marketplace on Valentine's Day."

"So?"

"You have her taped to a chair."

"So?"

"So what do you think is going to happen once you untape her?"

"Why should we untape her?" Cardiff asked.

Pamela practically screamed her answer. "Because we need a villain, not a victim. None of this works without a villain."

"Pamela," I said.

"What?"

"It's a moot point anyway."

"Why?"

"The entire plan hinges on you removing Evelyn from the board of directors in such a way that she would be unable to vote her stock against a sale."

"Yeah?"

"She doesn't own any stock. Not a single share."

"She's chairperson of the board."

"So Vanessa doesn't need to be."

"What are you saying?"

"Vanessa owns everything. She's letting Evelyn run the company while she raises her son. My bet? She'll vote against a sale. In fact, she was the one who killed the deal with the Europeans in the first place."

"No. No, no. I was there when the vote was taken. It was Evelyn."

"It was Vanessa. Evelyn was merely voting her proxy."

"She didn't say she was voting Vanessa's shares."

"That Evelyn," I said. "She surely loves being large and in charge, doesn't she?"

"What does this mean?" Rebecca wanted to know.

"Let me think," Pamela said.

"Are you telling me that everything I did was for nothing? I killed a man for you."

"Give me a second."

"Randall, I promise—if I go down for this, I'm not going alone."

Pamela stared at me for a moment.

"We need to talk," she said. "Outside."

She led Kid Cardiff and Rebecca out of the room and into the kitchen before firmly shutting the door behind them.

"I knew you were trouble the minute you walked into my office," Diane said. "Now what's going to happen?"

"You're a businesswoman. What would you do?"

I yanked at my cast until it slipped out from under the duct tape. I used my free hand to quickly untape the other, or rather I should say I used the fingertips that were uncovered by the cast, which made the task take an agonizingly long time.

Behind the door I heard voices raised in argument. I didn't

think the debate was going in our favor. At the end of the day, Pamela was a pragmatist. She'd vote to cut her losses. My only question—why was it taking them so long?

After I freed my hand I worked on the tape that secured my ankles to the chair legs. When that was done I crossed the small office to where Diane sat. I had managed to free one hand when the voices ceased. A moment later I heard someone at the door.

I dashed to the side with the hinges.

The door opened slowly. It not only hid me from view; it kept me from seeing the rest of the room.

Diane screamed.

I pushed hard against the door and hit something solid, knocking it off-kilter.

I came out from behind the door and found Kid Cardiff.

He had a gun in his hand and the same expression on his face as the time I fought him in the parking lot—as if he were unsure of what was happening.

Diane screamed again.

She wasn't frightened—no, that's unfair. I'm sure she was as scared as could be. But she was screaming to distract Cardiff.

I grabbed the hand that held the gun.

Cardiff attempted to pull it away.

I used my cast to hammer down hard on the inside of his elbow, causing his arm to fold. The gun was now pointing upward.

It went off. Debris from the ceiling rained down on us.

I forced the cast against Cardiff's arm to hold it in place while I wrestled for the gun with my good hand.

Rebecca was standing on the other side of the doorway, Pamela behind her.

She also had a gun.

She pointed it at me.

I pivoted so that Cardiff was in front of me.

She fired anyway.

The bullet hit Cardiff low in his left side.

He cried out in pain and fell backward against me. I was so wrapped up around him that his weight forced me down. He rolled on top of me. The gun slipped from his hand and rattled on the floor. It was just out of reach. I lunged for it, wrapped my fingers around the butt.

Rebecca moved against the doorframe and pointed her weapon at me. A nine-millimeter SIG Sauer P228—the same damn gun that I usually carry when I feel I need one.

Diane screamed at her, "Rebecca don't."

Rebecca hesitated for a single beat. It was enough time for me to bring Cardiff's gun up.

I swear to God, Rebecca fired first.

I have replayed the entire scene over and over and over again in my memory, and each time Rebecca fired first—her bullet tearing into the floor about a foot and a half from my head— before I shot her three times in the chest.

Diane screamed again. Only this time she meant it.

Pamela turned and ran. I shouted at her, "Where do you think you're going? Where do you think you can hide?"

I pushed and pulled my way out from under Cardiff. He was still alive. I checked his wound. If you have to get shot, the lower left side of the abdomen is the best place. There are no major organs to worry about. I didn't tell him that, though. I checked his bleeding. He didn't see me do it, but I also pulled my smart-phone out and set it on record.

Diane freed herself from the chair. She grabbed the office phone and called 911. She was weeping while she told the operator where she was and what happened.

We both tried to ignore Rebecca's body as best we could.

I leaned in close to Cardiff's face.

"You're dying, Kid," I said.

"No."

"It's true."

"The bitch shot me."

"She was looking out for herself."

"She always did."

"Kid. Kid, you don't have much time."

"I know."

"Tell me about Frank Harris."

"Frank?"

"Frank Harris. He came here a year ago last Christmas."

"The bum from Szereto?"

"Yes."

"How'd you know 'bout him?"

I didn't, I told myself. I was just taking a chance because of something that Rebecca had said earlier—*Do you want to cut yourself in, too?*—and what she said later—*I killed a man for you.*

"Rebecca said you did it," I told him.

"No, it was her. He found out she was working for Barek while pretending to work for Szereto."

He was the director of human resources, I reminded myself; was working the job when Diane hired Rebecca on a contract basis.

"He tried to blackmail her," Cardiff said. "Dumb fuck. Said he was tired of doing dirty work for the bosses. Said he was going to change his life; said if she took care of him he'd disappear, she'd never see him again. Becs said she'd be happy to give him a piece. Told him to follow her to the office. Fucker actually licked his lips. McKenzie, I don't want to die."

None of us do, I told myself. Aloud, I said, "What happened?"

"Becs took a knife from the kitchen and stabbed him in the head. Then she asked me to help get rid of the body. We made out like he was drunk and took him to his car. Becs thought it'd be funny to take him home, leave him in his driveway as a Christmas gift to his wife."

"But he wasn't dead."

"I know that. But I didn't. I thought he was dead. She had stabbed him in the head, man. Only he sat up while we were driving and started talking. Scared the shit out of me."

Cardiff had been pressing his hand against his wound. He held it up and took a hard look at it, covered with his own blood.

"Help me," he said.

"Paramedics are on their way."

"Will they be in time?'

"Kid, what happened next? Frank Harris was alive . . ."

"I freaked out and pulled into a parking lot near his place. Rebecca was following, wondering what I was doing. I told her. She didn't believe me. Then Frank let himself out of the car. Opened the door and started walking down the path. Damnedest thing. Rebecca said get him. I wasn't going to get him, Jesus Christ. We watched for a few minutes, wondering what to do, until he fell into a ditch and we left."

"Okay."

I silenced the record function on my smartphone.

"I'm going to die," Cardiff said.

"Eventually," I said. "Probably in prison."

I stood up and turned toward Diane.

"This could have been a lot worse," I said.

She punched me three times—two quick jabs and a right cross that sent me against the far wall.

I might have been angry about it, except you know what? I deserved it.

As soon as Commander Bobby Dunston of the St. Paul Police Department's Major Crimes and Investigations Division learned it involved me, he recused himself from the case and handed it off to Detective Jean Shipman. Jeannie didn't like me at all and, in fact, always became angry when I called her Jeannie. I was both relieved and comforted when she took my side with the assistant Ramsey County attorney and practically giddy when she said, "McKenzie, you're free to go."

Before that happened, though, both Diane and I were subjected to the bureaucratic nightmare that was a thorough homicide investigation. G. K. Bonalay, my intrepid attorney, was summoned. Diane Dauria didn't have a personal attorney, so she called Szereto's corporate lawyer, a man who seemed to materialize in an impeccably tailored Brioni navy and blue plaid suit at 3:10 A.M. at the James S. Griffin Building. Once Detective Shipman was done with me, he decided he wanted a piece, too.

I let him rant about my putting his client in danger and compromising the reputation of the Szereto Corporation for a while because, well, I deserved that, too. When he finished, I told both him and Diane a few things that they needed to hear. It didn't make either of them happy, especially when I invoked the name of Detective Sergeant Margaret Utley of the St. Louis Park Police Department.

"You need to do what I ask," I told them. "You need to do it now."

Afterward, the lawyer volunteered to take Diane home. No one offered me a ride. Before they left, though, I called out to Diane.

"Now what?" she asked.

I brandished a fist at her.

"Nice combination," I said.

"Every woman in the world should know how to fight," she said.

The sun was threatening to rise when I finally returned to my condominium. I was afraid of waking Nina, so instead of retiring to our bedroom, I perched myself on a stool at the kitchen island and drank bourbon straight. I wasn't looking to get drunk. I had learned a long time ago that it didn't do any good. I was just hoping to take some of the sting out of my aching mouth where Cardiff had slugged me and my wrist, which I had convinced myself needed to be reset.

I was working on my third shot of painkiller when I looked up. Nina was standing there in her silver and lace nightgown, and I remembered once when someone had asked me if I believed in God. I answered, "Yes, I do. I just don't have a lot of faith in him." Yet the most beautiful woman I had ever known was standing in front of me. How could that be possible if God didn't love me?

She said, "Come to bed."

I thought that was a very good idea, but really, I was only looking for someone to hold me tight while I explained how and why I shot a woman three times in the chest.

Eventually I fell asleep. My dreams were filled with dark skies and rain, the only light coming from the occasional flash of lightning.

NINETEEN

I convinced myself that Nina really did need to go to the club early; that she wasn't trying to escape the violent head case that she had agreed to move in with.

Eventually I left my bed. I didn't even bother to brush my teeth. Instead I dressed for the gym and drove to Dave Gracie's Power Academy. I wanted to take out my frustrations on someone, anyone, but because of the cast on my wrist Gracie wouldn't allow me into the ring to spar. I couldn't do exercises like speed rows, polymetric push-ups, medicine ball slams, or even dumbbell punches except with my right hand, so I spent most of my time practicing roundhouse kicks against a freestanding heavy bag until Gracie told me to go home before I hurt myself.

I half expected to see Sloane Dauria there, yet was happy that I didn't.

When I returned to the condo, I found Malcolm and Erica playing chess in front of the big fireplace that Nina and I loved but almost never used. I stared at the board for a moment before asking, "Whose turn is it?"

"Mine," Erica said.

"Bishop to queen four, checkmate."

Erica looked at me as if I had ruined the punch line to a good joke.

"I knew that," she said.

"You cared about your father." I was speaking to Malcolm, and he knew it. "You loved him. It made sense that you were desperate to find out what happened to him. What really bent you all out of shape, though, was the fear that one of your friends might have killed him. One of the Hotdishers. Katie, perhaps—yes, I know about Katie. That's why you came to me. Critter was upset when he heard about my investigation because he thought it might blow back on his mother. That was the reason for the fight outside the Bru House. Then Sloane stepped in to get you to quit the investigation, too—because she also thought it might have been Katie or one of the Hotdishers. Or even your mother."

Malcolm flinched just enough to convince me that I was right.

"That's when you finally had to make a choice, and you did it while lying in Sloane's bed. Mom or Dad? You chose Mom. Maybe she had something to do with your father's death, maybe she didn't. But you decided that she had been abused enough by the sonuvabitch. You all but said so when you told me to go away that day at her house.

"But you were wrong. All of you. It wasn't your mother. Or Katie. Or any of the other New Brighton Hotdishers. Your father was killed by a woman he was trying to blackmail. She's dead, by the way. I shot her late last night. I won't bother you with the details. They'll probably be in the paper. I'm not happy about it. You're Erica's guest, so it's not up to me to tell you what to do, but I wish you would leave now."

I retreated to my bedroom. By the time I emerged, both Malcolm and Erica were gone and my cell was ringing.

Detective Utley said, "Jesus Christ, McKenzie."

"Do you have anything you can work with?"

"Plenty, now that I know where to look."

"I bet you a nickel no one spends so much as a day in jail."

"We'll see."

The next call came from Szereto's corporate attorney.

He said, "You're wanted at the Szereto estate. Is one P.M. convenient?"

"Who's asking?"

"Mrs. Szereto."

"C'mon, man."

"Vanessa is asking—against my advice, I might add."

"I'll be there. How about you?"

"Not until later. There is much to do."

Jack McKasy met me at the door.

"I'm here to see Vanessa," I told him.

"I know. She wants to see me, too. Do you know why?"

"Haven't a clue."

Jack led me to a sunroom, a terrace protected from the snow and ice and freezing temperatures by three walls and a slanted ceiling all made of treated glass. There were plenty of plants in the room and wicker furniture painted white.

Jack left me. A few moments later he returned with Candace Groot in tow.

She said, "What's going on? Do you know, McKenzie? People going in and out of Diane's office all morning and then I get a call to come here?"

"I couldn't say," I told her.

Evelyn Szereto arrived.

"I don't have time for this," she announced.

"Make time," Vanessa Szereto said.

She stood in the doorway and surveyed the four of us. She looked like the tiredest person in Minnesota.

"Please keep your voices down," she added. "I don't want to wake my son."

"Nessa," Evelyn said, "what's wrong?"

"Everything."

Vanessa stepped into the center of the room. As she did, I noticed something odd—her posture became straighter, her eyes clearer, her voice stronger. She reminded me of one of those birds that puffs its chest and displays its colors when threatened; the greater the danger, the more imposing they become.

"I'm going to tell you a story the way it was related to me by Detective Margaret Utley of the St. Louis Park Police Department," Vanessa said. "And then I'm going to tell you what I'm doing about it. Or maybe . . . McKenzie? Do you want to tell the story?"

"No, you go 'head. I'd like to hear how it sounds coming from someone else."

"To begin at the beginning, then—never mind the disgusting crimes my husband committed against the female employees of the Szereto Corporation. As despicable as they were, that's not why the three of you conspired to kill him. You did it to keep him from selling the Szereto Corporation to a European conglomerate."

"That's not true," Evelyn said.

"Don't interrupt me again, Evelyn."

The sharpness of Vanessa's words actually caused the older woman to take a step backward.

"First, Evelyn discovered a handwritten codicil to Jonathan Szereto's will stating that ten percent of his shares were to be given to Candace Groot. She insisted at the time that Jonathan's last wishes be honored. Jonny, of course, vowed to resist them, only he didn't get the chance. Having spoken to Detective Utley, I now believe that it was payment for luring Jonny to her home."

"It wasn't like that," Candy said.

"What was it like?"

"Candy," Evelyn said.

"You're interrupting again," Vanessa said.

"Jonny was abusing his female employees," Candy said. "Not just in the office but in their homes. He—"

"Forced himself on you," Vanessa said.

"Yes."

"Evelyn paid off other employees to keep them from trashing the company over what Jonny did to them," I said. "Was the stock her payment to you?"

Candy didn't answer.

"Do you want to tell this story after all?" Vanessa asked.

"I'm good," I said.

"I don't believe the codicil was legitimate, whatever reason Evelyn gave it to you. What I believe, Candace, what Detective Utley believes, is that when Jonny came to your home that evening, you called here. Only Jack was available to answer the phone because Evelyn had arranged to take me to Club Versailles to celebrate my pregnancy. After he received the call, Jack helped himself to a nine-millimeter handgun from the gun cabinet in Jonathan's study. He drove his car—a black Toyota Camry—to Candy's house and waited. When Jonny left, Jack followed him until Jonny stopped his car at a red light. Jack drove up next to him and shot him twice. He came back here. He replaced the handgun and waited for Evelyn and me to return home. A week later, he sold the Camry."

"That's crazy," Jack said. "Why would I do any of the things you say?"

"Because Evelyn promised to marry you."

"None of this is true," Evelyn said. "It's all a product of McKenzie's feverish imagination."

"You might be right. I hope you are right. Just to be sure, though, I gave Detective Utley permission to seize all the guns in Jonathan's study and check them against the bullets that killed Jonny. I also gave her written permission to examine all of our phone records, including your cell phones since technically they're owned by the Szereto Corporation. And not just around the time Jonny was killed, but also during the past two weeks. You see, I believe that it was Jack who made the threatening calls to McKenzie on Candy's behalf. I have also ordered our corporate attorney to turn over the codicil to the police so a handwriting analysis can be performed to determine if it actually was written by Jonathan."

"You ordered?" Evelyn said.

"I have assumed the role of chairperson of the board of directors of the Szereto Corporation."

"You can't."

"I own fifty-seven-point-seventy-eight percent of the stock. How much do you own?"

"You're making a terrible mistake."

"I don't know how deeply you're involved in my husband's murder," Vanessa said. "It doesn't make sense to me that you would ask McKenzie to investigate if you were guilty. What I think must have happened . . . Early in the twelfth century, King Henry the Second of England and Thomas Becket, the Archbishop of Canterbury, were locked in a bitter conflict over the separation of church and state. They were good friends and had been for many years, but they couldn't find a way to get past their differences. Finally Henry said, 'Who will rid me of this troublesome priest?' Later, Henry insisted that he was speaking rhetorically. Yet whatever he meant, four of his knights interpreted it as a royal command to assassinate Becket. I like to think that's what happened here. I *want* to think that's what happened here. That you didn't actually plan it. But it's hard."

"Nessa."

"I want you out of my house. Leave now. You can contact me later and we'll arrange to have your belongings sent to you." Vanessa pointed at Jack. "Take him with you."

"Eve, now we can get married," Jack said.

"Shut up," Evelyn said.

"That might not be a bad idea," I said. "A spouse can't be compelled to testify against their husband or wife in a court of law."

Vanessa turned to face Candy.

"Ms. Groot," she said, "I haven't the words to express how terribly sorry I am for what my husband did to you. I can't even imagine how you must have suffered."

"Thank you."

"You're fired. Your personal items are being boxed up as we speak and will be sent to your home. If you go anywhere near the Szereto offices again, I will have you arrested for trespassing. The same with you, Evelyn."

"You can't do that," Candy said.

"You can sue us for unlawful termination," Vanessa said. "Put me on a witness stand and force me to explain myself. The decision is yours."

Vanessa stepped back into the center of the room. I liked what the bright sun did to her golden hair.

"Now, I want you all to leave," she said. "Do it now. Go someplace together and call me names."

There was much grumbling and gnashing of teeth after that, but Vanessa didn't budge an inch. I stayed to make sure the complaints were verbal and not physical. Eventually the room emptied except for Vanessa and me.

"I'm sorry about all this," I said.

"What happens next?"

"You tell me. You're the one who's in charge."

"I never wanted to be. How could this have happened?"

"Good people doing the wrong thing for the right reasons;

bad people doing the right thing for the wrong reasons—take your pick."

"No. I don't believe that. They could have called the police, any one of them, for what Jonny did to those women."

How did that work out for Katie Meyer? my inner voice asked.

"The company would have survived," Vanessa said. "The family would have survived. I would have survived."

"I'd bet serious money on that."

"I'm already wondering what I'm going to tell my son about why Grandma isn't around anymore. McKenzie, would it have been such a terrible thing if I had never learned the truth?"

"I don't know. Would it?"

"What more can we do to help the police?"

I like that she said *we*.

"I don't know," I said. "If they need anything they'll ask."

"What about you?"

"Me?"

"You've done so much for me, for Diane Dauria, for the Szereto Corporation. I know you don't accept money for the favors you do, only I have nothing else to offer in return except for my gratitude."

"I'll take it."

Vanessa gave me a smile that must have ached. She was still anxious, yet covered it up pretty well, I thought.

"All hell is going to break loose, isn't it?" she said.

"Depends on how the cops and prosecutors handle it. You could turn your PR people loose to cover up the damage. You have plenty of them working for you."

Vanessa gave me the wide-eyed stare of an innocent while she weighed my words and then said something that wasn't innocent at all.

"Fuck that."

Later I was sitting in a chair on the balcony of our condominium as far away from the railing as I could get and thinking about Katie Meyer.

Eventually Nina found me.

"What are you doing out here?" she asked.

"Just getting some fresh air."

"First, it's cold. Second, you're afraid of heights, remember?"

"It's okay as long as I don't look down."

Nina knew something was wrong beyond my lingering guilt over Rebecca Crawford; after all these years, of course she did. She didn't ask what, though. Instead she pulled the only other chair on the balcony next to mine and sat. She knew I'd tell her all about it in my own good time. Eventually I did.

"I don't know what to feel about this," I said. "After everything else that's happened, why should this bother me?"

"Because you don't really understand what it's like to be raped. What it means."

"Do you?"

"No."

"That's a good thing, right?"

"I worry about Erica."

"So do I."

"If it had been Erica, if it had been me, what would you have done?"

"I don't want to think about it."

"Think about it."

"I'd probably want to beat someone to death with an aluminum baseball bat, but you see, that's why we have laws. So people won't do that sort of thing."

Nina thought about it for a few beats and asked, "Why did you shoot the man who raped and murdered Reney Rogers?"

"Are you asking if this is the same thing?"

"You could have taken him prisoner. You could have turned him over to the police."

"He might have escaped. He might have . . ."

"Yes?"

"I needed to make sure that he got what he deserved."

"What does Katie Meyer deserve?"

"A long and happy life."

"Problem solved."

"Is it?"

"What would you have done if she had killed that man when he first attacked her?"

"Nothing."

"Nothing? You would have praised her courage, admired her strength. Heck, you would have thrown her a parade."

"You're rationalizing."

"Isn't that what you want me to do? McKenzie, you're not going to turn her in. You're not going to destroy Katie Meyer's life. Her family's. Her friends'. You decided that in New Ulm. You're just trying to find a way to reconcile your decision with your sense of justice, with the fact that you were a good cop for such a long time."

"Nina, it makes me afraid, a decision like this. Not physically afraid, or emotionally. I've felt that before and I know how to deal with it. But deep down where the soul lives."

"All those discussions we had before we moved in together about why you do the things that you do. One time you told me—I won't forget it—you said you wanted to make the world a better place, even if it was only a little bit better. Remember?"

"I remember."

"Will the world be a better place if Katie Meyer goes to prison?"

"No."

"Well, then?"

"First do no harm."

Nina kissed my cheek and hugged my arm.

"This is an easy decision," she said.

It wasn't, but I made it and vowed to stick with it.

JUST SO YOU KNOW

Randall "Kid" Cardiff was the only one who went to jail, and that was because they found him on the office floor surrounded by guns and dead bodies and a digital recording of him explaining his part in the murder of Frank Harris.

Most of the others weren't even charged with a crime.

Detective Margaret Utley pleaded with her superiors, but at the end of the day the Hennepin County prosecutor decided he didn't have enough evidence to proceed.

Yes, it was determined that a nine-millimeter Glock taken from Jonathan Szereto's study had been used to kill Jonny Szereto, and yes, the fingerprints on the gun matched Jack Mc-Kasy's, but that didn't prove he used it on Jonny, only that he was the last one to touch it, and that could have been anytime in the past two and a half years.

Yes, Jack did own a black Toyota Camry that he sold a week after the shooting, but there were over four million Camrys sold in the United States in the past decade, and a lot of them were black.

Yes, phone records indicated that Candace Groot placed a call to the Szereto estate the evening Jonny was killed that lasted less than thirty seconds, but she said it was made to Evelyn about company business. She said the same thing about several considerably longer calls made to the estate in the days preceding the shooting as well, although it was so long ago she couldn't recall exactly what business.

Handwriting experts confirmed that the codicil discovered by Evelyn Szereto was a fraud—too many closed loops, not enough pressure applied to the paper, rising instead of falling line slopes—yet no one could identify the true author. Vanessa did not pursue the matter, happy enough that she now controlled a full two-thirds of the Szereto Corporation stock, which she used to vote Pamela Randall off the board of directors according to the firm's unfit-to-serve protocols.

Pamela was hiding out in Barcelona at the time. She kept drifting from one country to another until her army of attorneys was able to squash any attempt to link her to the killing of Frank Harris or the kidnapping and assault of Diane Dauria and myself. She did plead guilty to a single count of conspiracy to commit corporate fraud—in a Minnesota court, not a federal one—and received a sentence of one year probation, two months community service, and a $10,000 fine. I have often wondered how much all that had cost her.

Evelyn married Jack and moved out of state. To this day I don't know for sure if she was in on it. *Do you think it's possible for a mother to murder her only child?* She asked me that once. My answer was based on time and experience—*Yes.*

Candace Groot moved to the Florida Keys. I have no idea what happened to her after that.

I was content to let Katie Meyer go unpunished, but the cop in me couldn't leave Clark Downing hanging. After a while, I told him to match the contents of Katie's rape kit against the DNA collected on Raymond Bosh—and then destroy both.

"What will that tell me?" he asked.

"Nothing you can take to court," I said.

Detective Downing called me a couple of weeks later.

"Damnedest thing," he said. "Katie Meyer's rape kit, the evidence gathered on the Raymond Bosh homicide, somehow it's all gone missing."

"Butterfingers."

"I ever thank you for the Frank Harris thing?"

"I think you just did."

I haven't heard from the detective since, but I noticed that the New Brighton Police Division deleted Bosh from its cold case Web site a month later.

The third week of March, Katie Meyer contacted me and insisted that we meet at the Bru House. I didn't want to go; didn't want to face her. Yet I did.

She looked me in the eye and said, "You know, don't you? That's why you've been avoiding me. Diane told us all about Frank Harris and Szereto and how you were both taken prisoner, and McKenzie, oh my God, that woman who was going to shoot you and Diane, and you shot her first, and the man, the boxer who was shot by the woman by accident, it was an accident, wasn't it? And him confessing to everything, what a terrible thing. It's all so, so terrible, and I know that you know what I did; I can see it in your eyes just looking at you, and I don't know what to do about it. Should I tell you what happened? You know, after I was raped, my whole life changed. Even now I have issues. Remember that story I told about the college boys trying to pick me up in the bike shop? I was flattered, I told you that, but what I didn't tell you, oh my God, I was also terrified. When I went back to my car, my hands were shaking so much I couldn't drive. I sat there in the parking lot for I think it was an hour, could have been longer, and my heart was beating so hard it was like I was going through it all over again."

"I'm sorry, Katie."

"I don't need your comfort, McKenzie. That's what husbands

are for. And children. And my friends. Diane was my rock when it first happened, kept me strong; that's why I love her so much, and last week at the Hotdish she actually told a joke, oh my God. I have the best friends in the world. They all took care of me. They're still taking care of me. But you know what I did and they don't, and if they did know . . ."

"They would love you just as much as they do now," I said, although I wondered briefly if they *did* know; maybe from Critter or Malcolm quietly blabbing to someone who told someone else. It would explain why Diane Dauria wanted me off the Frank Harris investigation and why Annette Geddings followed me that night: the Hotdishers looking out for one of their own.

"McKenzie, when I saw him walking in the park—"

"I don't need to know."

"I need to tell you. When I saw him . . . All my life I've been a certain person, then for five minutes I became someone else. That's all the time it took. I walked up to him; he was pouring chalk into one of those things that they use to line the baseball field, and he looked at me and he smiled, actually smiled, no, not smiled, something else that was like a smile but wasn't, and he said, 'Back for more, honey?' I didn't even realize that I had Critter's bat in my hand until I hit him with it. I'm not making that up. Afterward, I looked at the bat and I thought, Where did this come from? I walked back to the field where the boys were going to play and I propped the bat against the backstop because that's what the boys liked; they always got upset when you dropped the bats in the dirt. I didn't even think to look for blood. And I'm sitting there and Philly, Jalen Phillips, he's one of the boys who played baseball, a very good player, and he appeared and I was like, oh my God, Philly, why do you look so sad, and I gave him a hug and I forgot all about what happened. Well, I didn't forget, but it was like something that happened in a dream, not real at all, but I knew, McKenzie, I knew it wasn't a dream. It was something I wished was a dream and oh my God, now what?"

"What do you mean?"

"It was only five minutes, but that doesn't matter. What I did, I deserve whatever happens to me, I know that, only, tell me, would it be better if I go to the police? What will they do? I've been wondering. For weeks now I've been wondering."

"They'll think that you're a crazy person and ask why you're trying to complicate their lives by confessing to a crime that there's no evidence was ever committed."

"No evidence?"

"Nope."

"I don't understand."

"Go home. Have a good life."

"What did you do?"

Katie was sitting in a chair opposite me. I rose from my own chair, circled the table, leaned down, took her face in both of my hands, and kissed her on the mouth. She didn't resist.

Afterward I said, "Be happy," and left the Bru House and never spoke to her again.

I returned to the condominium. Erica was standing in front of the small washer and dryer that were built into the wall off the kitchen next to the guest restroom. Her huge suitcase was open, and she was sorting soiled clothes into piles.

"Seriously," I said. "You flew your dirty laundry here all the way from New Orleans?"

"I ran out of quarters for the machine in the dorm."

"I'm surprised that you're actually spending spring break at home for a change. I expected you to go off somewhere with that kid from Notre Dame—Robin."

"Did you know that Evanston, Illinois, is only two hours' driving time from South Bend?"

"What's in Evanston, Illinois?"

"An English major attending Northwestern University. On the other hand, Tulane is fourteen hours away. Do the math. That's what Robin told me."

"I'm sorry."

"You learn as you go. Isn't that one of things you like to say?"

"I'm sorry," I repeated.

"I'm okay. Really."

"What about Malcolm Harris?"

"We don't see much of each other anymore. Apparently I'm a bad memory. Or I remind him of bad memories. Whatever."

"I don't know what to say."

"McKenzie, it's all good. I mean, look how long it took Mom to find the right guy."

"I'm sorry," I said again. I didn't know what else to say. But this time I wrapped Erica in my arms and held her tight.

She giggled.

"What?" I asked.

"You're hugging me."

I loosened my grip, but Erica said, "Don't you dare," so I hung on.

"I love you, McKenzie," she said.

"I love you, too."